speechless

a novel

lindsey lanza

Cover Design: Sam Valencia at Ink and Laurel

Editing: Caroline Acebo

Editing: Britt Tayler

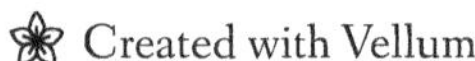

For anyone who's ever felt like they weren't enough.
You are.
You are so incredibly lovable.

And for Erik, who always reminds me that I am, even on the bad days.

a note to the bookstagram community

Thank you for making 2020 & 2021 bearable, and for encouraging all the reading (let's be real—book hoarding) that led me to spontaneously write a fucking *novel*. This book would never be real without all of you. Without your inspiration and your bookish love and yes, even your rage reviews. I hope Henry is a more than satisfactory book boyfriend. I hope you fall in love with Lucy's found family as much as she does. I hope the steam is on point. And most of all, I hope this cover inspires some great photography.

I love you all.

@READWITHLI

Music plays a crucial role in this story. This playlist is made up of many songs that directly inspired Lucy and Henry's journey, but it's also designed to be a soundtrack for the book. I hope it makes you feel something.

Something Just Like This - Alex Goot, Madilyn Bailey
Cornfield Chase - Hans Zimmer
Maestro - Hans Zimmer
High Hope - Patrick Droney
California - The Lagoons
Sunny - Bobby Hebb
I Believe - Jonas Brothers
Could You Love Me - Kygo
All I See Is You - UTAH
White Horse (Taylor's Version) - Taylor Swift
Lips On You - Maroon 5
Favorite Place - John Legend
Good Friend - JP Cooper
Young and Beautiful - Lana Del Rey
Slow Hands - Niall Horan
Over the Rainbow – Israel Kamakawiwo'ole
Wildest Dreams (Taylor's Version) - Taylor Swift
Bloodsport - Raleigh Ritchie
Conversations in the Dark - John Legend
Precious Love - James Morrison

Scan to view full list on Spotify:

prelude

Someday you will be old enough to start reading fairy tales again.

-C.S. Lewis

I'VE ALWAYS loved fairy tales. The fancy castles, handsome princes, snowy-haired horses. I love the magic, even the sinister kind. But most of all, I love the endings, the happily ever afters. There's something so comforting about knowing everything works out in the end.

But we don't actually know what happens *after* happily ever after, do we? What if Cinderella's perfect prince discovers he has a severe annoyance of singing birds and sewing rodents? What if Aladdin develops a tiger allergy? What if Snow White's Ferdinand is too insecure to share her with seven other men, no matter how platonic the relationships may be? And the question that has plagued me for years: What if Ariel realizes she wasn't actually meant to leave the ocean and she'll never be truly happy unless she goes back to live under the sea?

Fairy tales are so enchanting because they end as soon as everything becomes perfect. They never show the struggle of an orphan trying to adjust to life in the palace, or the inevitable arguments every couple will have one day. But *that's* the magic. That's why everyone loves a fairy tale—because we can pretend those parts don't exist, that everything just works out.

Forever.

But what's the point of a happy ending when it's not *truly* an ending? What's the point of it when the thing you've wanted all your life is snatched away? What do you do when the story ended, but actually didn't, and now you're just a wanna-be princess stuck in limbo waiting for something good to happen again?

In my case, you move across the country with nothing but two suitcases and a very fluffy dog.

1st movement

One good thing about music, when it hits you,
you feel no pain.

-Bob Marley

1

. . .

Lucy

"FLIGHT *727 to LAX is now delayed until 8:35. We have found a pilot and crew that will be arriving in Boston at 7:50. We're sorry for the inconvenience.*"

DELAYED? Again?

I've been sitting at Logan airport for over three hours and poor Rowan's already chewed through his only bully stick. I knew I should have brought two. My dog may look like a snuggly ball of fluff, but the dude can seriously chew. I give him a nice long scratch behind his ears and promise to get him lots of peanut butter as soon as we arrive in Los Angeles.

I dial Sarah one more time. It's ridiculous that she hasn't called me back yet. I'm supposed to be moving in with her in two hours—well, make that eight hours after the most recent flight delay—and she hasn't responded to a single call or text in three days. She's never been the most reliable, but she *is* my best friend. This is pretty bad, even for her.

I never thought I'd be living with my college roommate

again. I never thought I'd have another roommate, period. Once you get married and turn thirty, roommates aren't really on the radar. Jack was supposed to be my forever roommate, the only person I'd ever have to fight over the shower with. The person I'd snuggle up to every night, wake up to every morning. The person who was supposed to be my constant. Now he's just someone else who abandoned me.

Living with Sarah will be great though, considering how much fun we had together in college. She's the one who convinced me to join a sorority, taught me how to make the best Jell-O shots, taste-tested all of my experimental baked goods; she even introduced me to Jack. I guess it's time to take that off the list of reasons I love her.

Maybe this will be good for me. I need a distraction right now and Sarah is sort of a mess if I'm being honest. Always dating the wrong guys, the wrong girls, getting into trouble; she's never really grown up. Taking care of her will absolutely keep me busy; I love feeling needed.

My eyes wander around the gate to see all the equally frustrated passengers while I turn over my necklace a few times and give it a quick rub. Why do people always have to blame someone for things that are out of our control? It's like this inability to ever just accept our fate—someone always must be at fault.

There's a big family next to me; four beautifully blonde kids all elementary school-aged, and two parents who haven't once lifted their faces from their phones. The littlest girl looks like a miniature sci-fi princess in space buns, a pink tutu and light-up sneakers. My kind of outfit. She keeps tugging on her mom's shirt to get her attention, but never succeeds. I'm tempted to ask if she wants to pet Rowan even though I know it's inappropriate. Instead, I whisper to him conspiratorially.

"Row, what do you think? Doesn't she look like the perfect

modern-day princess for me to write about? What about a *Little Mermaid*-inspired Space Opera?"

The wheels are already spinning, which isn't surprising since I've never gone this long without writing before. Reimagined fairy tales aren't only my day job. They live in my brain rent free. But, I should probably stop staring at the potential space mermaid; maybe if I keep watching this crowd closely enough, I'll find myself a perfect villain.

I'm doing another quick scan when I notice the man directly across from me. Is he eyeing me or my dog? It's usually Rowan who gets the attention, but I could swear even with his eyes lowered he's looking right at me. It's when he briskly turns away that I suddenly notice how gorgeous he is. The dark wavy hair, the piercing sapphire eyes, that jaw. He looks like a Ben Barnes, Ian Somerhalder hybrid—that's jacked—and my inner teenager is starting to gawk. He's wearing what looks like a very expensive suit, no tie and the shirt is open at the top revealing the tiniest dusting of chest hair. He catches my eye just before I make an audible shriek when my phone starts buzzing in my lap.

"Sarah! Finally! I've been trying to reach you for days! My flight's been delayed more times than I can count at this point, but I'll be there tonight, just late. I'll get my own ride from the airport, no need for you to stay up."

"Luce! So sorry for being MIA, it's just been *crazy*."

Crazy. That's the Sarah I know. Every time she goes dark for a few days, a week, a month, it's always because things are *crazy*. Have I ever felt that way? Been able to make that excuse? I mean, in the last five years I've had four surgeries, lost my mom, gotten divorced...but have I ever felt like things were just *too* crazy to call my best friend back?

"That's okay, I know you're busy. I'm just glad you called

before I got on the plane. I'll let you know if anything else cha—"

"So, I have some really great news. Emmett and I got back together!"

"What? You're joking, right?" Emmett is Sarah's on-again, off-again boyfriend who recently moved out when he decided monogamy wasn't his "path." It really seemed like this was the breakup that would finally stick, especially considering he left her with a lease she could barely afford alone. He's also the only reason I'm even moving to LA. I wanted a fresh start, but my friend said she needed me, and LA became the destination. Thirty years old and divorced, moving across the country didn't sound half bad. The thought of running into Jack or our friends on a regular basis was much less appealing than moving to a city where I knew exactly one person.

"Joking? Of course not! You know how much I love him, Lu! I'm sorry, I know we were both so excited to be roomies again, but I really want to make this work, you know?"

"Okay, well, I'm happy for you if this is what you want." I'm not sure if that's the truth. "I guess I can start looking for my own place soon. I'll try to be out of your hair after a few weeks, okay?"

"Oh, Luce, I'm sorry but I don't think that's gonna work. I told Emmett about how much you helped me through the breakup and how amazing you are—obviously!—and he said he's really not comfortable with you being here or us hanging out. He thinks you might try to turn me against him or something, and honestly, we both know you're not his biggest fan, so I get where he's coming from . . ."

"He doesn't want us seeing each other at all? Sar—"

"I know. It seems drastic but I'm sure once things have settled it'll all be forgotten, just give him some time."

"Sarah, I'm about to get on a plane to come live with you. Rowan and I don't have anywhere else to stay."

"You know like every hotel in LA is dog friendly, right? You'll be fine! You said you wanted to try something new. You'll love LA."

I can't believe she's doing this to me. Or maybe I can, but it hurts the same either way.

"Sar, you're really telling me that you're not going to see me at all when I'm moving to LA for *you*?"

"Just not yet, okay? I'm sure Emmett will forget all about it eventually and then we can hang all the time! Oh, Luce, I gotta run. We're driving down to the beach to go watch the sunset together. Isn't that romantic?! Love you!"

I hear the click when she hangs up and I feel absolutely dumbstruck. "ARE YOU FUCKING KIDDING ME!?"

No, no, no, no, no.

I said that out loud. Everyone is looking at me.

Fuck.

How could she do this? I'm moving to LA because *she* asked me to.

Well, among other reasons. Okay, one *big* reason.

But now I'll be all alone. I have no home, no friends, no family, *no one* there. I guess I don't have much left here in Boston either.

Is it possible to die of loneliness?

I close my eyes, search for my mantra, the one I've been repeating for months now: *Control the controllable. Look on the bright side. Find the silver lining.*

Six months of therapy taught me not to dwell on all the things I can't fix, no matter how upsetting they are. There are some things that we're just completely powerless to change. And I guess my list of things I can't control just got longer. I can now add *lodging* to it.

I smile apologetically at no one in particular and put my massive noise-canceling headphones back on. I may look like an air traffic controller but at least the music will calm me down. I hear the piano first, and then the strings, and my heart starts to pound a little less. I've been listening to Henry Turner for years, but after the last surgery, the divorce, when I started feeling like I was having panic attacks every day, his scores became a lifeline for me.

Most people prefer what you see in movies, but the music is what I've always enjoyed the most. The music makes the film; it's what decides how the scene makes you *feel*. It can create tension or fear, can make a romantic moment magical, can transport you to a completely different time or place.

Well, to me at least.

Jack and our friends always thought I was looney talking about this stuff. At least I don't have to worry about that anymore.

So now my Spotify is full of all the scores by Henry Turner, and no one can judge me. I don't know why his music is so special to me; he must be some musical prodigy that's been playing piano for sixty years or something. I always imagine him looking like Beethoven: wild hair, angry eyes, heavily punctuating every note with force, but I love him deeply. His music cures my anxiety, and it always helps to ease my pain when my meds aren't enough. Henry Turner scores are like my own personal wonder drug. So I close my eyes and let the music do its magic.

2

• • •

Henry

THIS IS why I fly private. I'll never stop feeling like an arse, but airport delays due to no viable flight crew do not happen when I call the pilot myself to book the trip. Unfortunately, twenty-four hours' notice wasn't enough this time. The meeting in Boston was a very unexpected surprise and though my flight home is turning into a train wreck, I can't wait to start writing for this new project.

I pop another Xanax and hope no one needs me for the next twenty minutes. Once it kicks in, I'll be marginally better at handling conversations, or at least hand gestures. I hate how much of this crap I've needed today, but I just have to remind myself that as soon as I'm back in LA I can get back to work, drug-free, and enjoy my Malibu bubble.

I notice the woman sitting across from me again. She's been humming softly, and I could swear I recognize the melody. She looks a bit sad but also, hopeful maybe? She keeps talking to her dog which I can't help but find endearing. I realize I'm staring when she looks at me and I quickly divert my eyes.

Why do I have to be so bloody awkward?

I can't help but turn back for another peek and our eyes meet once more before she picks up her phone. She seems distracted now, so I use the opportunity to take her in.

She's quite lovely. Beautiful, really. But not like the women I usually meet. There's a sweetness emanating from her, like I can actually sense her compassion. She's dressed casually in black leggings and trainers, though they are bedazzled in glittery stars. Her lilac jumper is a few sizes too big—she's currently tucking her knees into it. My gaze travels to her face and I see eyes that are big and round and a deep shade of emerald green. Her golden hair is long and glossy, it looks so soft I want to reach out and run my fingers through it.

Songs have been written about much less. Suddenly she is a song, something in E with lots of trills. Maybe I'd call it Esme. I hear it so clearly, a melody heavy with melancholy but ending with a high note, maybe a—

"ARE YOU FUCKING KIDDING ME!?"

I snap out of my musical fog and see her breathing hard, face turning beet red, looking around the gate, wide-eyed and on the verge of tears. What happened on that phone call? I have a strange urge to go help her, comfort her in some way, but quickly think better of myself. It's hard to pull my gaze but I can't keep staring at her, so I drag my eyes to her dog instead.

He's quite cute, mostly white with gray ears, very shaggy fur. He looks a bit like the Old English I grew up with back in Bedford but seems much too small to be the same breed.

Now she's humming again, and I can clearly hear the tune. Is that really what she's listening to? I look around for a screen of some sort. Maybe she's watching the film on a tablet? I realize then that her eyes are actually closed and look back to the dog for answers.

A feeling comes over me, one that I'm entirely

inexperienced with: a compulsion to meet this woman, to speak to her, somehow.

But, *how?*

I'm always armed with medication when traveling alone—even though I hate the lingering effects it has on my writing—so I might be able to say *something.*

But I have no idea how to approach a woman. My social life consists of the mates I live with and the endless dates my agent forces on me that never end well. In reality my mum is my best friend, and I can't exactly call her right now to ask for advice.

I feel my nerves settle as the Xanax takes control.

This is it, now or never. Any moment now they could tell us the flight is canceled and I'll never see her again.

We're only a few feet away from each other. Should I stand? Move toward her? Close the distance between us? I don't want to invade her space, nor do I want to tower over her.

God, I think I'm sweating.

She should definitely be able to hear me alright from here, well, depending on how loud the volume is on those headphones she's wearing.

"Hello, erm, hi."

I did it.

I spoke to her. I didn't freeze. This is marvelous!

Shit. She can't hear me. I wave my hand around like some lunatic to get her attention.

Brilliant.

"Sorry?" She lowers her headphones onto her shoulders and looks up at me apologetically. Uncertainty knits her brows as she waits for me to dole out my complaint to her. And of course, I haven't any clue what to say.

"Your dog." That's it? Come on Henry, your English is better than *this.*

"Is he bothering you? I can move if you need me to, but I promise he's very friendly."

"No, of course he's not bothering me." I really do sound like an arse. Go on, say something else, anything else. "I was wondering what breed he was. He reminds me of my Old English but so much smaller."

"Oh!" Her face immediately lights up. "Yeah, he's a Sheepie, just a tiny one. Rowan was the runt of the litter but he's perfect for me. I don't know how I'd manage a dog over forty pounds."

"Rowan? Isn't that a name for redheads?"

"Yeah, I know. He's actually named after one of my favorite book characters. If you ever read *Throne of Glass*, and make it to book three in the series, his name will make perfect sense for his white fur." She smiles knowingly then, like I've just been invited into some secret club.

Mental note to read whatever *Throne of Glass* is.

There's a beat of silence that seems to stretch too long and I see her pick up her headphones again. Sweat starts pooling at the back of my neck but the tightness I'm so used to feeling around new people is absent.

"You were humming earlier."

"Ah, that's embarrassing. Sorry to bother you, I promise to keep it down." Her sheepish grin is absolutely adorable.

"No bother at all, I was just curious what the song was. It sounded a bit familiar."

"Oh. No, you probably heard wrong. It's not really a song even. It's a movie score. I'm kind of obsessed with this composer and I listen to his scores every day. This one is from a pretty bad movie actually, one of those teen vampire dramas, but the music is just magical. It's a full hour if you listen straight through so I figured it was perfect for waiting in the airport, but after all these delays I'm about to start round three..." She notices my face go slack and her eyes squint in what looks like embarrassment. "Sorry. I'm rambling. I have a habit of talking too much."

I've been at a loss for words millions of times in my life, but this is different.

She's a . . . fan?

I've had numerous women pretend to love my music, especially once they realize what I'm paid. I can't remember the last time a compliment was this genuine. Even in my meeting earlier today, when I was literally being wooed, it was all about the money. The number of films, their respective earnings, the producers who raved about my efficiency.

But *this* girl, she chose my music to keep her company while stuck in the airport.

Her eyes were closed. She was humming along to the melody . . .

And now she's looking at me like she's ready to call an ambulance. How long have I been staring with my mouth hanging ajar?

"Hey. Are you okay? They just called the first boarding group, so I need to go up there." She seems genuinely concerned and I just want to laugh it off but I'm still a bit shell-shocked.

"So sorry, please go ahead. Nice to meet you."

3

. . .

Lucy

OKAY LUCE, just board the plane and please forget about rambling on to the hot stranger. Did I really bore him into shock? I've seen many eye rolls in my day but that was a strange reaction to my blabbering.

Note to self: *Try* to think before you speak.

Moments after I get settled, the flight attendant offers some water and ice cubes for Rowan. I never know how the crew will react to having a dog in the front of the plane, so this is a good sign. Maybe things are turning around for me.

And . . . maybe not. An older man, mid-sixties by my guess, takes the seat next to me and looks anything but friendly. I offer a smile, but he ignores me and pulls out a newspaper. Well, at least I have Rowan to keep me company for the next six and a half hours.

"Okay Row, how are you doin' pal? I'm sorry I couldn't get us the aisle, but the front of the plane isn't bad, right? And first class! Look at all that leg room!"

The man seated next to me sniffs loudly as he turns away from me, clearly unhappy to have a dog sitting next to him. I start to apologize but realize that's all I've been doing lately. *Enough.*

I reach down to grab my headphones, ready to get lost in another world of Henry Turner's when my new neighbor starts yelling a string of profanities.

And then he smacks Rowan across the nose.

"What the hell are you doing!" I pull Rowan onto my lap and cuddle him fiercely, tears springing from my eyes.

"Excuse me, is there a problem, folks?" The flight attendant stares at us both intently.

"Her animal was licking my knee for fuck's sake. Get that thing in a cage down in cargo where it belongs."

I start to defend Rowan—he's incredibly well-trained and was only being friendly—but the flight attendant interrupts me.

"Sir, she has a service dog, and has the right to keep him at the seat with her. If you'd like to change your seat, I'd be happy to see if someone will switch with you."

"You want *me* to move? Oh sure, I bet half the plane would love to take my first-class seat that *I* paid for." His voice continues to rise, and I notice all the other passengers staring at us. I spot the hot stranger a few rows back and now I'm even more embarrassed by the scene we're causing.

But this man will not shut up.

"You expect me to believe that's a service dog?" He starts waving his hand in front of my face. "You can see just fine, sweetheart. Nice try."

I know I should let the staff on the plane handle this, but I can't hold my tongue anymore.

"Not all service dogs are to help the seeing impaired, you know—"

"Oh, right. What's that thing help you with? Does he steer you, so you don't get lost?" His tone gets more patronizing by the second. "Calm you down when you're too *emotional*?"

He's standing now, blocking the aisle completely, while Rowan and I are crouched in my window seat shaking together like a pair of tambourines. *No, asshole. Rowan is so intelligent, so much more than* you, *that he can actually sense when I'm in pain and when I'm in danger of passing out. Dick.*

"Sir." The voice comes from behind us, as firm and strong as a cold brew. "I'll switch seats with you." The British accent makes my stomach flip and I look up to see it's the hot stranger from before.

For all of his bravado, Dog-Hater doesn't move. But the hot stranger does. He pushes himself around Dog-Hater to the front row, plops his bag in the seat next to me, and then not-so-gently pushes my old seatmate back to row four.

Dog-Hater seems stunned into silence as he gets shoved down into his new seat. The rest of the first-class cabin claps enthusiastically.

"Thank you." The hot stranger sits down and I look over at him with as much gratitude as I can muster. His face seems strained with frustration. "You didn't have to do that."

"Someone did. That guy was a dick." He blows out a long breath. "Sorry it took me so long to say something. Are you all right?"

I chuckle softly as I try to slyly wipe the rest of the tears from my face. "Yeah, I'll be fine. It's so rare I get that reaction to Rowan. Most people love him."

"And why wouldn't they?" He reaches over to scratch Rowan's chin. Row immediately starts licking my new seatmate's hand. I never want to apologize for him being friendly again.

I'm able to compose myself while the rest of the plane boards and while I hold on to Rowan tightly during takeoff. I reach for my headphones again once we're airborne but get a light tap on the shoulder from my new seatmate.

"I'm actually quite glad I got to switch seats. I wanted to, erm, apologize for earlier, in the airport. Sometimes I have trouble finding my words and, well, you caught me off guard." He smiles shyly and brushes a fallen curl from his brow.

He looks . . . apprehensive?

"So, I thought maybe we could start over, with actual introductions. What do you think?"

"Sure, why not." I offer my hand to shake, wildly confused by the formality of this. "I'm Lucy Gold. Nice to meet you, airport stranger." I offer a grin.

He takes my hand in his. "Henry Turner."

What?

What?

No.

Now it's my turn to be tongue-tied. Henry Turner isn't that unique of a name, it's probably just a coincidence.

But it's not, I know it's not.

He's frowning at me like I didn't make the connection.

"How old are you?" Ok, not my best opening line but it just sort of popped out.

"Well, based on how old you seem to think I should be, I guess the correct term would be . . . three and thirty?"

But my Henry Turner is . . . old! At least in my head he is. Is it really possible I never googled the composer I've been obsessed with for years? He looks nothing like Beethoven. Even his eyebrows are perfectly groomed.

"I'm so sorry. I don't know why I thought you were older. And I really don't know why I just asked for your age. You're really *the* Henry Turner?" I show him my playlist with over fourteen hours of his scores. "This is all yours?"

"I'd prefer if you just called me Henry, although *The* Henry does have a nice ring to it. I'll have to discuss with my team when I get home."

I'm still gawking at him, and he offers a kind smile. He has really nice teeth. Aren't British people supposed to be lacking in that department?

"And I'm sorry I didn't say anything earlier in the airport. It was surprising to hear you talk about my music so . . . genuinely. Thank you, by the way, for that. It was quite nice to hear, actually."

"I—you're welcome." I shake my head, maybe a bit too vigorously. "But no, I should be thanking you. I've been—well, the last few months have been kind of tough for me, brutal really. Music can be so therapeutic, you know? It's always what I turn to when I'm stressed or struggling with pain."

How could I possibly convey how important his music is to me? How I can't even leave the house without arming myself with my headphones and his playlist. I'm sure everyone living with a chronic illness finds their own therapy, but for me, when I'm constantly deciding between pain and life-altering changes to my body, his music is the only thing that grounds me.

"Yours has really helped me." My voice breaks and I quickly turn away to pet Rowan.

Don't cry Luce, not now, not here, not *again*. You're sitting next to Henry Turner. Don't ruin the best thing that's happened to you in months!

He covers my hand with his over the armrest and I feel a bolt of electricity course through my body. His hand is so warm, I soak up every bit of comfort it provides. My eyes flutter closed as I breathe in, then out.

I can't remember the last time I was touched like this.

His fingers gently squeeze mine and I turn toward him but keep my eyes down, hoping the early signs of tears have vanished.

"I'm sad to hear you needed it, but I couldn't be happier that it helped you. Are you all right now? Want me to hum a tune for you?"

"I'm okay. Sorry, this is so embarrassing. I don't usually get choked up talking to strangers on airplanes."

"Well, I'm not a stranger anymore, am I?" He whispers loudly, "*Henry*, remember?"

I laugh and it comes out awkward and partially through my nose. He's charming and I'm *me*, unfortunately. "Yeah, I don't think I'm going to have any trouble remembering your name. I see it everyday on my phone."

"I don't actually think I've ever met someone who listens to my scores for fun. Some of the producers I work with don't even want to hear a bar unless it's already scoped for a scene. I'll have to write something special for you when I get home."

My gaze travels from our hands to his eyes, but I don't see a single hint of mockery.

"Do you live in LA?" he asks. "Maybe you could come see the studio sometime, meet the rest of my team. I really don't deserve all the credit."

"I . . . no . . . I . . . well . . . fuck." Do I live in LA? How do I casually mention that Rowan and I are currently homeless? I don't even know if I'll want to stay there. Maybe I should just roam the airport and book a flight somewhere new, try the whole starting over thing again someplace else. I have money. My last book is still selling well, probably because it was a Reese's YA book club pick. I could go anywhere, I suppose. I could go to Europe, try the whole *Eat, Pray, Love* thing. No, falling in love sounds miserable. I don't think I'm quite ready to deal with that kind of disappointment again. I'm not sure I'll ever be ready.

Shit, he's looking at me like I'm losing it again.

"Sorry. Honestly, I have no idea how to answer that question. I *was* moving to LA today. My friend begged me to come live with her after I, well, after I became single again." I offer a tight smile that hopefully sends the message: Please don't inquire further. "But she just called to let me know her plans have changed, so, I guess I need to decide what's next for me. I don't even know anyone else in LA." I laugh but it comes across more pathetic than aloof.

"You know me."

Every time he speaks it feels important, like he chooses each word with care. It must seem like the complete opposite listening to me, the girl who never stops talking. Even when he stutters, his words seem meaningful.

"What's your dog's name?" I ask.

"Pardon?"

"You said you have a sheep dog too?"

"Oh, right. His name was Mo—Motown, technically. He passed away several years ago. My parents got him right after they got...well, I was quite young." His voice sounds wistful.

He's still looking at me and I'm suddenly very aware that he's still holding my hand. It hurts to sever the connection, but I do it anyway. I miss the warmth instantly and desperately want it back. I decide to give Rowan a long pet instead.

"Mo and Row—I bet they would have been friends."

4

• • •

Henry

THIS IS the longest conversation I've had with a stranger in maybe my entire life. It feels *incredible.*

I don't know what it is about this girl, but I haven't frozen once since we got on the plane. I wonder what happened to her. She said she'd had a tough time recently but didn't share any details. She also mentioned she's single, but it definitely didn't feel like an invitation. More like the opposite.

After she let go of my hand, I could sense she needed a moment to herself. She closed her eyes and has been in and out of sleep for the last few hours, so I've been keeping Rowan company. I must have spoiled him with attention considering his head is now permanently stuck to my lap. I look over to her and see something twinkling in her hair.

"Lucy?" I know I should leave her alone, but I can't help myself. It feels too good talking with her.

"Mmm?" She turns her head toward me while still leaning back in her seat. Her eyes open drowsily, and I imagine this is what she looks like first thing in the morning. The image of her lustrous hair splayed across the pillow and her body tangled in sheets creeps into my head.

"I'm sorry to wake you." I'm not, but it seems like the right thing to say. "It looks like your necklace may have gotten tangled in your hair; can I help?"

She looks down and nods, sleep still visible in her eyes.

I gently untangle the pendant from her hair. It's even softer than I imagined earlier. The necklace is an interesting shape, curved like a rising sun and studded with tiny shimmering stones. I feel something engraved on the back but let go before I invade her privacy any further.

"It's quite pretty. What's the symbol?"

"It's a rainbow, an abstract one I guess. My mom got it for me right after, umm, after she got sick. It's supposed to represent our favorite song. See?"

She turns it over and I see the word *somewhere* stamped in cursive on the back. How lovely. My mum adores that song as well. It was one of the first pieces she taught me to play.

"She told me as long as I wore this, I would always have hope." I see her eyes turn glassy but she's smiling. A good memory, I take it.

"Your favorite song. Are you sure? I don't believe I wrote that one."

She gives me a slight chuckle. "I have a feeling you could write a version of it I'd love. I've never heard it performed by a whole symphony orchestra."

My God, this girl is flattering. I'm tempted to write the music for it now, have it ready to record and play for her before she disappears.

"I just have to ask. You said your moving plans have fallen through. When we arrive in LA, what will you do?" I'm trying to be delicate, but I see in her face that I just reminded her of something she did not want to think about.

"Oh, I don't know." Her tone is all nonchalance, but I know I've struck a chord. "I guess we'll grab a cab, find a hotel nearby . . ." She pinches her eyes closed. "And I guess tomorrow I'll go car shopping, because I'm not in Boston anymore, so I'll need some way to get around. Any models you recommend? I haven't needed a car in years, but I should probably just pick something quickly. Ubering from one dealership to the next all day with Rowan sounds like a dream."

Now she's slowly banging her head back against the seat, pinching her eyes shut. I watch her entire body grow tense, the anxiety taking over, something I'm all too familiar with.

She seems lost. Lonely, maybe. I can see it in her eyes, like she's given up, like maybe she used up every last bit of optimism she had left.

"Lucy, can I ask you something?"

She doesn't open her eyes but gives me a muted "sure."

"What is it about my music? I'm not fishing for praise or anything, but I'd like to know what it is that you feel connected to. Why was it able to have such an effect on you? If you don't mind my asking."

"Umm." She still hasn't opened her eyes, and her head is tilted back in her seat. "So that sci-fi movie you did, like forever ago."

Huh, one of my first major films. I must have recorded that over six years ago. It was just after I'd won my first awards, when real producers were courting me and James fucking Cameron asked for a meeting.

She continues, "I went to see it with my ex, and I thought the movie was good, kind of confusing, but I liked it. But I could barely keep my eyes open. I just wanted to listen to the music. I felt like when I closed my eyes and just listened, I was truly floating through space, traveling through time. It was—ethereal. I couldn't get it out of my head. I downloaded the soundtrack as soon as I got home, and I listened to it constantly, especially when I was in pain or when I was stressed, and it just helped everything else melt away, like there was nothing in the world but me and the music."

I exhale a bit too audibly, realizing I've been holding my breath. How is this possible? How am I randomly meeting this woman who can somehow see into my brain? I'll never forget that project. It was some of the most inspired work I've done, even to this day.

I clear my throat, swallowing my emotions. "So, is that your favorite score then?"

"No. My favorite is from your holiday movie, *The Christmas Swap*, I love that one. I don't usually like those kinds of movies to be honest. I always prefer books, especially when it comes to romance. But the music is just *so good*." She smiles and tilts her head back even further when she says *so*. "I have to watch it every year. I don't know what it is. I think your music made the actors seem more in love somehow. I've written books to that score. It's like the most perfect soundtrack for a happily ever after."

I don't tell her this is my favorite as well. In actuality, it is. But I doubt she'd believe me.

It feels like we met today for a reason, like I'm somehow meant to help her through whatever it is she's dealing with. Or maybe nothing's meant to be and I just *want* to help her.

I clear my throat and hope for courage. "Hey, look at me."

She turns and when I look into her eyes I have trouble finding my words again. My gaze travels and snags briefly on her lips, bright pink, full and smooth with a perfectly pronounced Cupid's bow. I have a strange urge to drag my finger across them, to feel how soft they are.

"Lucy, I think . . ." Fucking hell, am I really going to do this? "What if—come live with me for a while."

Her eyes go wide and then immediately squint at me incredulously. I might as well have just asked her for a shag.

"Sorry. I feel as though I might have frightened you?" She's still staring at me, but her face has softened ever so slightly. "I just thought you could use a mate right now, and I'd be happy to be that person. You did say my music helped you through a tough time, but it looks as though the tough time isn't over. I thought maybe I could help directly this go around?"

"That's really nice of you, but you don't even know me. And I don't know you either."

Is that true? It feels like I know her.

"Well, you do know my life's work. Quite intimately, from what I can tell. There's not much more to know about. I'm what you might call a workaholic." I throw up quotation fingers thinking I'll get a laugh, but her mouth doesn't even twitch. "If anyone would be taking a risk, it's definitely me. For all I know you're just some brilliant stalker who's weaseled her way into my life, with impressive ease I must say. I must be more careful about talking to strangers. My mum raised me better than that."

I finally get a smile out of her. Toothless, but I'll take it. She's warming up to me, I'm just not sure what else to say. Why is writing music so much easier than conversation?

I realize Rowan still has his head draped over my knee. She seems rather attached to the animal but hasn't minded his absence on the plane. I comb my fingers through his shaggy fur. It's almost as soft as her hair.

"Rowan seems to like me. Maybe you should talk it over with him before making a decision? I bet he'd love Malibu." I pull the dog into my lap and start rubbing his belly while I whisper to him about how much fun he'll have at the beach. "Wouldn't you Rowan? You could dig in the sand, and swim, and chase after hummingbirds."

He starts to lick my face aggressively, and I give Lucy a look that says, "See? Told you so."

"Cute, but, and I am sorry to do this to you, he loves everyone. Literally *everyone*."

"You wound me!" I set Rowan down and feign being stabbed in the chest. She giggles but I can tell I haven't won her over yet.

"Listen, I have a large house right by the beach. Very serene. Lots of space. It feels wasteful having empty rooms. You'd be doing me a favor. My writing team is there most of the time. We live together so it's not just me, you'll have several witnesses around if needed." I pause to gauge her reaction but she's just listening intently. "Let's see, what else? There are two guest rooms you can choose from, the largest is on the opposite side of the house from my room. Lots of space in between them. You may never even see me. Does that sound better?" Her mouth is sealed shut but her eyes are smiling. "I have a car, an SUV, actually. Lots of space in the back for your pup. You're welcome to use it any time. I hardly leave the house when I'm working. What else, what else? There's a pool! I rarely use it, more of an ocean swimmer myself, so you wouldn't be bothered if you care to go for a swim—"

"Okay." She leans back in her seat, not quite smiling, but not looking nearly as sad as she was earlier. She squeezes her eyes shut for a moment in a motion that is almost a grimace, then scoffs quietly. She turns to me but I can't wholly read her expression. "Why not."

5

. . .

Lucy

WHAT THE HELL am I doing? Did I actually agree to go *live* at his house?

I must have because we're currently in his Range Rover, on our way to Malibu. No turning back now, I guess.

I can't say I'm not grateful. It's almost four in the morning back in Boston. To say I'm sleep-deprived and cranky would be a significant understatement. Finding a hotel right now sounds like a genuine nightmare, and while I feel like I can take just about anything life throws at me these days, Rowan deserves better. When we got in the car Henry told me to go ahead and rest my eyes since it was a long drive and he'd wake me when we arrived. Unfortunately, my nerves have kept sleep from finding me, but I've stayed silent with my eyes shut, afraid of any further conversation.

"Siri, call HAAAM."

Ham? What the hell? Who is he calling right now? I hear a man answer with an Australian accent. Actually, maybe two men because now one sounds American. They're asking when he's getting home and how the meeting went. He tells them they'll discuss the project later but that they're "doing it" and they seem downright exuberant. It sounds like he's about to hang up, but I hear him quickly say he's bringing home a guest, which is then followed by a long beat of silence.

"Guest? Is your mum in town Henry?"

"No, Graham. I met someone on the plane and she's going to stay with us for a bit. Her living arrangements recently fell through."

"You met someone. You *met* someone!? How? Please explain this to me, because nothing makes sense anymore."

"Graham, enough. I'll fill you in later. She's sleeping in the car now and I'm sure she just wants to be left alone. It's been a long day for all of us. Please just make yourselves scarce when we get in, all right?"

"Fine, mate, whatever you say."

WE PULL into a long drive that becomes a semi-circle in front of the . . . well, house is not a sufficient word.

He said "large house on the beach" right? That was severely misleading.

This is an estate, a chateau, a Tuscan villa, replete with perfect symmetry and immaculately manicured hedges. It reminds me of all those fancy wineries I went to in Napa for my honeymoon. What am I *doing* here?

When I step inside there are four very attractive men lined up in the foyer, each holding an instrument. Three of them begin to play while the one in front holding a violin leans forward and, in a whisper, asks for my name. He's the largest of the group, almost as tall as Henry, and his Australian accent makes me think he's also the one from the phone call.

Suddenly, they're all belting out "*Lucy*, welcome home" in perfect harmony.

Henry walks in with our luggage, and I can tell he's angry. He did tell at least one of them on the phone to "make themselves scarce."

"Leave the girl alone, you twats! Lucy, I'm so sorry. My housemates have no manners. I'm planning to trade them all in for Englishmen as soon as I can. Also, this is HAAAM. HAAAM, say hello to Lucy, and then leave her be."

"Ham?"

The Australian one answers. "I'm Graham. This is Preston, Jayce and Craig." He points respectively. "Henry was too busy to learn all our names properly at first. He started calling us HAAAM so he wouldn't have to worry about messing us up. Kind of rude to be honest, but it stuck."

"I'm sorry, I still don't get it. Why ham?"

"It stands for Henry's Australian and American Musicians."

"No—it stands for Henry's American and Australian Musicians." The shortest one holding a saxophone speaks up this time.

"And this is why I just stick to HAAAM. All right Lucy, let's go pick out your room so you can get some sleep."

I DIDN'T REALLY FEEL comfortable evaluating the rooms in his house. I ended up just asking which was closest to a door to make early walks with Rowan easiest. But I'm sure this is the room I would have chosen. Everything is shades of white and blue, from cerulean to periwinkle. Huge gossamer curtains cover two of the walls and sway gently in the breeze. It has a beachy, dream-like quality. My mom would have adored this room and I feel a pinprick of sadness that I can't bring her here.

She always loved the ocean. Every vacation I went on growing up was somewhere coastal. It hurts to think about how long she was stuck in the midwest, unable to travel to her favorite places.

There's a sliding glass door on the wall opposite the bed that leads out to a small patio. It's almost two in the morning but I take Rowan outside quickly to get him acclimated to his new surroundings. I can hear the crashing waves of the ocean and I'm pleasantly surprised to notice the absence of mosquitos.

I decide to leave the door cracked open so the sounds of the ocean can lull me to sleep, and so Rowan can do his business in the morning without waking me. But once I'm lying in bed, my brain starts working overtime and sleep completely evades me as I start spiraling once again.

What am I doing? Did I really just agree to stay at a complete stranger's house? I'm living in Malibu with *five* men. Is this going to be like an *Entourage* situation? Parties every night, half-naked women floating around the house, trays of cocaine and tequila shots always available? Oh God, are Rowan and I just going to spend every minute hiding in this room avoiding debauchery? Henry hasn't exactly given off that vibe, but I don't really know him, only his music.

At first glance, my new life looks like the start of a romance novel. *Girl starting over after a devastating breakup suddenly winds up living in a mansion with five gorgeous men. One who happens to be the celebrity crush she never knew she's had for years!*

Sounds like something I'd read, even though I've never been a fan of writing anything based in reality.

And I know my life is not rom-com worthy. My love story ended a while ago. And in a shocking twist—no happy ending for this girl. Maybe this is just my really weird epilogue. *Well, Lucy didn't get the happily ever after she was hoping for, but hey, she's still having adventures and her new roommates are hot!* God, it sounds more like fanfiction. Maybe that's the best I can hope for at this point.

Rowan hops up on the bed and curls into me, warming me up and calming my nerves immediately. The image of Henry holding my hand on the plane enters my mind. Such a simple gesture. So much warmth emerged from that single touch. It gave me the same sense of calm that I get from listening to his music. It's the last image I see before I finally fall asleep.

6

. . .

Henry

"HAAAM, KITCHEN. *NOW*!" I yell as soon as Lucy's out of earshot.

I can't believe Graham orchestrated that entrance in the last twenty minutes. Actually, I can, but I'm pissed at myself for not expecting it.

"She's cute Henry. How on earth did you get her here? This isn't a kidnapping situation, is it?" Graham raises his eyebrows at me while he brushes a hand through his shaggy blonde hair. He is really on a roll tonight.

The rest of the team filters in and I'm hoping I can get this over with quickly so I can manage a couple hours of sleep before getting to work.

"*The Dragon Wars* is officially ours. This is the next *Game of Thrones*, lads. It's what we've been waiting for." I pause to let the news sink in. We've been hoping for something like this for a few years now.

They start to ask questions but I'm honestly too exhausted. I silence the group with a stern look.

"They want us on everything. I'm going to start work on the theme and opening credits. Once they have more footage to send over, we'll get going on the rest. Expect to be very busy for the next few months, hopefully longer."

"This is all very exciting Henry, but what we really want to know about is Lucy." Graham doesn't seem to know when to shut up.

"Seriously, though. Who is she?" Jayce looks mystified, offering one of his signature grins.

Unfortunately, the rest of them start nodding in agreement. I guess this is what happens when you're thirty-three and have never brought home a girl. I thought I'd made the boundaries clear in this house. We have a working arrangement, nothing more. Graham may refuse to accept it, but the others have never bothered me about my social life, or lack thereof.

I fill them in on our chance encounter and the conversation from the plane but stick to facts only. They don't need to know everything, especially not how good it felt to hold her hand. They have a million questions, but the most pressing one seems to be if I'm planning to date her.

"No, of course not. I'm just helping her out. I'm sure I'll barely even see her; I'll be busy working."

"What's so special about her anyway? You can get much hotter girls."

"Craig—what the fuck?" Graham jumps in to defend me, or maybe he's defending Lucy.

"What? It's true. Remember that time he went out with that Victoria's Secret Angel? She was an absolute smoke show. What happened with her anyway? Did you ever actually speak to her?"

Graham smacks Craig over the head at the same time I tell him to watch his fucking mouth.

"God, *sorry*. Forgot we're not supposed to talk about it." His tone is anything but sincere. "I'm out, see you guys tomorrow."

Jayce and Preston follow Craig upstairs while yawning dramatically, but of course, Graham stays behind. He knows me too well.

"So, you really just went up to her? Had a whole conversation?"

"Yeah, I know, I'm surprised too. It's not that big of a deal. Just let it go."

"It is a big deal. It's a really big fucking deal, mate." I give him a look that says "we're done" and head downstairs to the studio.

I'M SITTING on the piano bench, thinking I don't actually need to be working right now. But I've had these notes in my head ever since I saw Lucy and I can't seem to get them out. The urge to play is overwhelming, even though I know it will become an obsession and I'll be stuck in here until it's complete. Maybe my brain is doing this intentionally, giving me an excuse not to see her again so soon. The chance of her enjoying my company more than once is not something I feel good about. It hasn't happened with a woman before. Not that I've ever tried.

I'm picturing her face while my fingers start to dance over the keys.

Not her face, her eyes.

I saw an entire symphony in those eyes. There was so much sadness, maybe even despair, swimming through her irises. But there was also her smile. The way her entire face lit up while talking about Rowan. I hear the notes instantly change. The song was sounding quite Russian, a bit tragic even for my taste, and now it's transformed into something worthy of a harp, twinkling and effervescent.

I get up and move to the futon, grab some pages to write down a few bars. I stay up all night working on her song.

2nd movement

Why get up in the morning unless you're going to have an adventure?

-Hans Zimmer

7

• • •

Lucy

I WAKE to the scent of jasmine and a warm glow seeping through the window. The sound of seabirds is familiar and yet somehow foreign, a melody I can't place. My eyes are still closed when I feel Rowan's tongue on my cheek, before he rolls over to lie next to me, pressing into my side.

And then, I remember where I am.

Everything happened so fast last night, and all under the fog of desperation and exhaustion. Henry may have offered me the room, but surely I can't just act like this is my house now. I don't even have his phone number.

It feels like leaving this room might be as painful as my divorce.

Although, I guess it would have been worse had Jack's parents not insisted on that prenup. I may have spent the last six months living in a black hole of despair, but the paperwork was done with the speed of a Ferrari. Best to rip off the Band-Aid.

And more importantly, there's one need I have that eclipses

my pride: caffeine. After throwing on a tank top and leggings, I brave the world outside.

I pad through the living room and into the kitchen, but not before marveling at the gorgeous piano next to the window. The entire back of the house is glass, with stunning views of the pacific. I hope I can sneak around to see the rest later while avoiding my new housemates.

"Good morning, Lucy!"

Shit, I forgot this one's name. I can't actually call them HAAAM, can I? He's tall with deep caramel skin, short, buzzed hair on his head and face. Nothing shy of gorgeous if I'm being honest. He's got that Tyson Beckford thing going on and I wonder if he's a model too.

"Jayce." He points to himself and smiles, and *wow*, what a fucking smile. I haven't been single in over a decade, but I remember guys that looked like him in college: heartbreakers. "Sorry we didn't get to really meet last night. Coffee? You look hella tired."

Jeez, is it that obvious? If I'm going to be surrounded by beautiful men I better at least try to look well-rested.

"Yeah, late flight." I shrug just as my stomach rumbles so loudly I see him snicker. God, when's the last time I ate something? "Got anything I can make for breakfast? Happy to cook for you too."

I head toward the fridge hoping there's eggs when I spot two other members of HAAAM walk in. I'm pretty sure the blonde one told me his name was Graham but I'm drawing a blank for the shorter one.

"Hello, Lucy. Hope you had a nice rest. Yeah, nothing of use in there." Graham sees me opening the fridge and shakes his head. "No one really cooks in this house."

The shorter one speaks up, "What does everyone want? I'll get DoorDash."

"Seriously? You guys don't have any food in this house? You have a full chef's kitchen, basically my dream to cook in. You don't even have eggs?"

They all peer at me timidly, like I caught them doing something naughty. I could swear they're all around my age. What grown man can't cook an egg for breakfast?

"Are you offering to make us breakfast, Luce?" Graham sure is friendly, shortening my name after just meeting me. Given how temporary this situation is I might as well go with it. It's not like I have any real friends to talk to right now.

"Sure, I'd be happy to. Can someone point me to a grocery store?"

"Come on love," Graham says, "I'll drive."

"So, tell me what you guys like to eat."

The ride to Whole Foods was somehow not awkward at all. Graham is incredibly friendly, and I just love listening to him. His Australian accent is thick enough to spread on toast and he says the funniest things. He immediately asked for my "John Dory" which apparently means he wanted to know my story. Well, that was a loaded question. I gave him a very condensed version of what brought me to LA and quickly changed the subject. Now we're perusing the aisles and I'm not really sure what to get for them.

"Everything. You make it, we'll eat it."

"Are you sure? No dietary restrictions? Foods someone doesn't like?" I ask.

"Nah, we're easy. Oh, can you make french toast?" I silently cheer, my favorite.

"Graham, I'm gonna blow your mind."

After confirming that everyone in the house has a relative sweet tooth, I grab all the ingredients I need for chocolate and strawberry stuffed french toast. Jack told me once that he decided to marry me after I'd made it for him the first time. I figure it can't hurt to win over my new roommates. I get some thick-cut bacon too, just to cover all my bases.

Getting to work in their kitchen is honestly a dream. My mom ran a catering business for twenty years, so growing up I spent a lot of time in the kitchen with her. There's something so rewarding about making a meal for others; maybe it's just something I learned from her, but it always makes me feel warm and fuzzy.

I've barely used my kitchen back in Boston these past few months. At first, after Jack left, I started making homemade food for Rowan. It's not like I had anyone else to cook for. He was seriously eating like a king: sous vide salmon, bacon and sweet potato hash, homemade ice cream. I was surviving mainly on snickerdoodles and Rowan was the best fed dog east of the Mississippi.

Then eventually, when I was deepest into my depression, I got into a routine of nothing but takeout for both of us. He got addicted to breakfast burritos.

"Damn, girl. You can cook!" Jayce is literally licking his plate clean as the rest of us watch in a mix of awe and horror.

"Okay, I'm not gonna do that." Preston (I finally figured out the shorter one's name) points to Jayce's lizard tongue. "But Lucy, if you can teach my girlfriend to make this, I'll be happy to do dishes every single day."

I already told them I'd be happy to cook any time while I stay here. Henry seemed almost offended when I offered to pay rent, so I'm glad I can contribute something to the house.

"Are we already out of bacon?"

"Graham," I exclaim. "You've had at least eight pieces. Preston and I only shared one."

Graham looks at me with a thoroughly confused expression. "So there's no more?"

"I'll go make another batch."

I was so nervous when I was getting out of bed this morning, but so far, things are really good. These guys are hilarious and so welcoming. The only thing is, Henry isn't here. I haven't asked about him. No one else seems to notice his absence and I don't want to come across as needy—I'm already staying in their home. But I do wonder where he is, when I'll see him again.

While everyone's stomachs are settling, Jayce offers to give me the grand tour. I'd be lying if I said I wasn't hoping for this. I don't want to feel like I'm snooping but I'm dying to see the rest of this place. The kitchen alone is swoon worthy.

"Come on, let's start outside." I follow Jayce down the three steps from the kitchen to the living room and toward the beautiful piano. There's also a U-shaped sectional that might be the biggest couch I've ever seen. It's a deep gray leather and nice and cushiony, perfect for lounging around and binge-watching TV. But it faces the glass wall. When I ask if they don't watch TV, he shows me the projector that comes down from the ceiling. I'm drooling and praying someone in this house likes British period pieces because I'm two seasons behind on *Peaky Blinders*.

There's a large coffee table in front of the sofa, and two square poufs on the opposite side to complete the shape. When I look more closely, I see that they each have a sepia-toned design of the Union Jack.

Jayce notices my observation, "Yeah, Henry's mom tries to decorate every time she visits. She sort of went all out on your room—that's where she stays when she's here."

I think back to the feeling I got when I first saw my room, how it reminded me of my own mom. And then I wonder how often she visits. I probably shouldn't get too comfortable.

Apparently, what I had assumed were windows are actually sliding doors and the entire living room opens up to the patio. There's an eight-person dining table next to a large shiny grill that's built into a full bar and buffet area. There's a small refrigerator attached as well. This place would be perfect for parties.

"We should have eaten out here." I'm in awe of how beautiful this is. We're right above the beach, waves crashing just below us. The warm breeze rolls by with a light kiss of salt. "This view is incredible."

"Yeah, high tide is pretty sick too. The entire beach disappears so the water hits the rocks right there." He points directly below us. The house is basically built into the rock formations. I've spent a lot of time by the ocean, mostly in Cape Cod and the islands, but the houses there are nothing like this. "We really should use this patio more—it's such a waste. Come on, you wanna see the pool?"

Yes, yes I do.

We turn left to curve around the house, and I see a large rectangular pool with a smaller rectangular hot tub right at the back where a pink flamingo float bobs around. There's also a huge raft shaped like a pirate ship, and I imagine the rowdy soirees it's typically used for.

Looking back at the house I try to see what room we're in front of, but all the blinds are closed.

"That's Henry's room. I know it's his house and all, but it pisses me off that the only way to get into the outdoor shower is from his bathroom." He points to the teakwood structure that is in fact connected to a hallway from the inside. Henry must have a pretty nice bathroom . . .

"You sound a little bitter Jayce. What's wrong? Your room's not nice enough?" I flash him a teasing smile.

"Yeah, my room's fine. I really can't complain. Please don't tell him I said anything."

"How would I tell him anything? I haven't even seen him."

"That's Hermit Henry, always working. Fuck, don't tell him I said that either. He gets so pissed when we call him that. Just erase it from your brain, okay?"

Huh, Hermit Henry? I wonder why. "You can trust me; my lips are sealed."

Looking around, my only thought is, *this place is extravagant*. I don't know a better word to describe it. I already knew Henry was successful, but I had no idea musicians like him lived like this.

"Can I ask you something about the house?"

"Sure, whatever you want." Jayce looks intrigued and crosses his arms in front of him, ready for my interrogation.

"I hope this doesn't come across the wrong way. I'm just wondering, I mean, how do you guys...okay, I guess maybe I didn't realize musicians like you made this much money?" I should really shut up now, but I'm so damn curious I just can't stop. "I'm sorry. I know this is rude, I'm just . . . curious? This house seems crazy expensive. I've watched Million Dollar Listing LA, and I know the show's fake, but I'm assuming the prices are realistic . . ." Shit, I'm rambling again and Jayce is grinning at me wickedly.

"You don't understand how we can afford this." He looks at me pointedly and I give him a slight nod as I bare my teeth in embarrassment. "What are you trying to say, Luce? You think we're criminals or something?" He stares me down as a shake my head, because I obviously don't think that. But then his voice drops lower. "Are you a cop? FBI? Tell me now and I'll make sure this doesn't end badly."

What the ... I'm just staring back at him, completely frozen. What have I gotten myself into? He places a hand on my shoulder and squeezes not-so-gently. I stop breathing. His eyes bore into mine like he's sure he'll find all my secrets hidden behind them.

"Jayce, I—"

A laugh bursts through his mouth as he releases me from his grip. His entire body is shaking with glee.

"Jayce!" I punch him lightly in the shoulder. "Not cool."

"Your face is white as a sheet." He's pointing at me as he continues laughing. Luckily no one else is out here to witness my embarrassment. "*Whew.*" He blows out the lingering laughter, hands braced on his knees until he's finally done. "Sorry Luce, you kinda set me up for that one though. Also, you're right. I could never afford this place. None of us could, just Henry. He bought it and we all live here as part of our comp."

"Oh, so is he . . ."

"Super rich?" I grimace, realizing that was exactly what I was thinking but didn't want to say aloud. "Yeah, I mean he works so much. Some of the jobs pay a ton, like a shit ton. Most of them don't, but they add up. We just work with him on movie scores. He does everything else himself."

"What does he do besides movie scores?" I didn't realize there was more.

"Fucking *everything*. When we were still in school, he played piano in the pit for a couple different Broadway shows, then he started writing for them. Got real connected with theater people that I think he still writes for sometimes. Graham is such a hustler, he used to go out and get Henry jobs left and right. When he was still a nobody, when all we worked on were indie films that paid absolute crap. He's written some

TV themes. I think he even did a jingle for a commercial a while back. And then there's all the pop stuff."

Pop stuff? It takes effort not to ask for more information. There's so much to unpack, especially about Henry. It's funny how I used to think about him before we met, picturing him with his Beethoven intensity, wild hair and much older face. I'm still trying to fuse these two Henrys together in my mind and it's no easy feat. Luckily, Jayce interrupts my inner hamster wheel before I ask any more inappropriate questions.

"Wanna go inside and see the rest?"

Jayce takes me up one of the two curved staircases in the foyer and shows me all the guys' bedrooms. He's right, he shouldn't complain. They each basically have their own suite. I notice there's not much decor upstairs, but what they do have is all music related. There are a few vintage guitars hanging on the walls and a decent amount of frosted glass pieces that look like they're made from distorted musical photography. Many are of notes or bars, some of instruments and one that's just a quote from Stevie Wonder that I absolutely adore: *Music is a world within itself, with a language we all understand.*

Once we're back in the foyer I notice another staircase, but this one leads down. "What about the basement?"

"Sorry, you can't go down there."

"Come on, Jayce. Let me see the restricted section!"

"Nope. Off limits. Under no circumstances can you go down there, okay?" He looks serious but he has to be messing with me again, right? I give him a questioning look, but he doesn't crack.

"Okay. Is it haunted or something?"

"Yes." Nothing, no smile, no hint of laughter, what the hell?

"Jayce, what's down there? Seriously? You're freaking me out."

"Just do yourself a favor and stay away from the basement. It's not safe for you down there. Promise me, okay?"

Suddenly, I wonder if there's some sort of torture chamber down below us, or some Dexter-esque wet room.

They all seem so normal but what if . . .

I finally see the slightest movement of his nostrils flaring.

He's good.

"Damnit Jayce, stop screwing with me!" This time I shove him with both hands and finally the laughter escapes from him.

"Okay, okay I'm sorry. But honestly, don't go down there. Henry's in the studio, working. I'll show you some other time if he ever comes up for air."

Hermit Henry.

I'm learning so much today.

Jayce and I head back outside to enjoy the sunshine. Rowan napped through breakfast but now he's back at my heels, following us to the pool.

"Umm, does your dog always walk like this?"

"What do you mean?"

"I can feel his nose on the back of my leg. It's like he wants me to kick him or something."

I can't help laughing. He looks so bewildered.

"He's a sheep dog, Jayce—he's herding you!"

"Herding me?"

"Yeah. It's just his instinct to herd, to keep everyone together. You're part of the pack now. He must like you."

Jayce gives a show of pride at this. Then he starts weaving from side to side to see if Rowan follows suit. He never leaves his heels.

"Huh. I guess I never thought about how different breeds acted. I grew up with cats." He frowns at this and his shoulders slump a little.

"I take it you're not a cat person?" We take a seat by the

pool and I dip my toes in the water. I'm tempted to hop on the pirate raft but figure I should wait until I have a suit on.

"Nah, they're annoying. They don't really do anything but hide, and hiss. What's the point? But my parents would never let us get a dog."

"Why not?"

"My dad and stepmom are both surgeons and have crazy schedules. And they said my sisters and I weren't responsible enough, which was probably true."

"Well, you're welcome to hang out with Rowan as much as you like while we're here."

"Thanks Luce—he's really cute."

"I know. And so does he." I give a little ruffle to Rowan's head. "Do you visit your family a lot? You said you're from Northern California, right?"

"Yeah, Oakland. And no, I almost never see them. They kind of disowned me when I decided to be a musician instead of a doctor. I was cut off the minute I moved to New York."

"Really? It's not like you're playing in some garage band. Don't they know how successful you guys are?"

"Henry's the successful one, remember? And it wouldn't matter anyway. They'll never approve."

"I'm sorry. That really sucks. I hope they come around one day."

"Yeah, I won't hold my breath. Anyway, what brought you to LA? All Henry told us was that you were moving here with no place to live."

I'd already filled Graham in on the bullet points of what brought me here while we grocery shopped: the divorce, Sarah, my wonderful luck in life. I don't really feel like going over it again. And since Jayce seems to love messing with my head, I decide to have a little fun with him.

"Well, my church is based here and if I ever want to reach

the higher levels I need to be here where I can learn from the Captains."

"The *what?*"

"The leaders. By being here in LA I think I'll finally be able to find true spiritual enlightenment."

He deadpans, waiting for me to get to the punchline, but I just stare back at him with a glazed smile on my face.

"Hell no. You are not bringing any of that voodoo Scientology shit into our house."

He actually looks scared of me and I'm beyond elated to finally get him back for earlier. Part of me wants to keep this going but I slowly remove the entranced look on my face.

"Chill out. I'm Jewish. The only thing we push on other people is food."

"Luce, get your swimmers on—let's go."

During breakfast Graham insisted Rowan and I accompany him to the beach today. Apparently, he wants to teach me to surf.

Never going to happen.

He interrupts my peaceful chat with Jayce carrying two surfboards above his head and his eyes are filled with determination. I agree to walk down there because it's beautiful outside and I love lying on the beach, but I have no plans for doing more than dipping my toes in.

Once we make it down to the shore, he hands off one of the surfboards to me.

"Come on shark biscuit, I'm a terrific teacher, I'll have you standing in no time. I promise you there's no better feeling than surfing, it's fucking magic."

I'm . . . tempted. I've avoided the ocean for years, but Graham makes it seem so easy, natural, like it's not an incredibly dangerous sport that could have me drowning or eaten by a shark in a matter of seconds. His encouragement is making me feel braver than I have in a long time.

He *looks* like such a surfer too: sandy-blonde hair, vibrant turquoise eyes, the perfect golden tan that I'm sure is rampant in Australia. His body is well-defined with large muscles and smooth skin, like the perfect specimen of a rugged man. He reminds me of the guys Sarah and I saw in Vegas when we went to Thunder from Down Under for my bachelorette trip.

"Luce, you coming?" He smirks at me before raising his brows. Oh God, I've been openly ogling him. A hot guy in a wetsuit should not have this effect on me.

"I'll try. But no promises. I'm kind of scared of the ocean to be honest." I wade into the water behind him, awkwardly holding my board while his looks effortlessly balanced under his arm. My nerves start to surface but I'm determined to get knee deep.

As soon as the waves reach my chest, I start to feel the undertow. Feel my footing lose control, feel my body fight to stay upright.

No, I definitely cannot do this.

"I'm so sorry Graham, I can't. The current's too strong. I just . . . I'm sorry."

I run back to the beach as quickly as I can, grabbing Rowan and trying not to cry. This was silly. I should have known not to tempt fate. I haven't been in the ocean in almost a decade—we do not get along.

Graham is surprisingly understanding and offers to hang at the beach with me after he catches a few waves. He admits they're bigger today than usual so it's not the best day for a newbie, but makes me promise to try again another time.

"I'm going to get you on a board soon enough, you'll see." Doubtful. "Ah, that one's perfect!" Graham starts running down the beach and I see him grab a stick and jog back with it. "Can we play fetch?"

"Sure. Row, come here. Do you wanna play F-E-T-C-H?" Rowan stands up straight with a powerful wag going. Then he starts to hop up on his hind legs in excitement. Graham chucks the stick and I'm in mild shock at how far it goes. His arms are . . . whoa. He looked *very* good in the wetsuit, but now that it's folded down around his waist, I can't seem to drag my eyes away.

"Thanks Luce, I've wanted to get a dog since we moved here. I grew up with two labs back in Brisbane. Henry and I talked about getting . . ." Apparently, I'm still staring at him because he starts to snap his fingers at me. Oops.

"Sorry, I umm . . . you're like, really strong. Are you a bodybuilder or something?"

He chuckles. "God no, I mainly surf. Though Henry and I can be pretty competitive at the gym. Lucy, stop staring at me, I'm a person you know—not just some magnificent, beautiful object for you to drool over."

He's clearly being sarcastic, and *flexing*, but I'm not *not* staring. I'm also most definitely *not* imagining what Henry would look like in a wetsuit—or without one. Can't Graham just realize I've only seen one naked man since college? I'm living out the dreams of my slutty twenties that I never got to have.

Let me live.

Rowan prances back to us proudly with the stick in his mouth and Graham swoops him off of the sand before moving to face me.

"All right, Luce. Who's more beautiful? You have to choose —which one of us would you rather pet?" He has a mischievous, sultry look on his face, and no matter how much I know he's joking around, I can't help it when my cheeks bloom crimson.

I punch him in the shoulder—which is as hard as a rock—and take Row out of his arms. "Rowan. It'll always be Rowan."

GRAHAM and I are sprawled out on Squishy—yes, I've named their sectional—and I guess dreams do come true because he is also a *Peaky Blinders* addict. He's a season ahead of me but agrees to do a full re-watch so we start from the beginning.

"Are you sure this show isn't too violent for you, Little Lu?"

"Please. I love violence. On TV, obviously."

"Well, you look scared shitless. What's going on?" He nods toward my arms wrapped around my center. It's then I notice my knee has been bouncing up and down at a fast clip.

"Sorry, nothing to do with the show. I just umm, well I haven't been apart from Rowan in a really long time. I guess I'm a little stressed about it." Jayce begged me to let him take Row to the pet store to buy him some toys and treats. He said it was just down the road so I figured the time apart would be short enough not to bother me. I figured wrong.

Graham pauses the show and scoots closer to me. "What do you need?"

"I'm okay, really. I'll be fine."

Graham must think I'm a complete wimp. First the surfing, and now I'm scared to be without my dog? What a fabulous first impression. This isn't who I am, at least I don't want it to be. I know that I don't need Rowan around all the time, but he's turned into a security blanket. I think I'm just terrified of being left behind. An orphan at twenty-five, divorced at twenty-nine, is it that irrational for me to have some abandonment issues?

I'm a fucking mess.

"Thanks, Luce!" Jayce wanders back in just as I'm about to

tell Graham to re-start the show. Rowan jumps up in my lap and all my nerves start to dissolve.

"Well, did you finally do it?" Graham says, eyeing Jayce haughtily.

"Obviously." Jayce shows us his receipt that includes a handwritten phone number right under the name Crystal.

"I'm so confused. Can someone fill me in, please?

Jace quickly explains about the cute pet store cashier he's noticed in his travels, but for whatever reason, needed an excuse to approach. Insert Rowan.

"Seriously? You don't really come across as shy, Jayce. You couldn't just go up and ask her out?"

"I'm definitely not shy. I just prefer to play a winning hand. My chocolate skin and bone structure plus Rowan's fluffy face —she was never gonna say no to that." He smiles smugly at me and I'm not sure if I should feel bad for the pet store girl because he's right.

"She never had a chance." I say it under my breath, but he catches every word. He winks at me, proud, and plops down on the couch beside me. He leans over to get face-to-face with Rowan and starts thanking him for being the best wingman he's ever had.

"Excuse me? I know I've gotten you laid at least twice," Graham mutters. "All the pup got you was a number."

"But he's just so much cuter than you."

Graham scoffs at Jayce's insult but we're all laughing. I sink deeper into the couch, feeling relaxed and weirdly at home. How do I already feel so close to these guys? I just met them, but it feels like we're real friends somehow.

"Can I ask you guys something?"

"No, I don't have a girlfriend. Yes, I'm interested." Jayce wraps an arm around me. "But only when you move out. I don't do morning afters."

I wiggle out of Jayce's embrace as Graham starts cracking up.

"What?" That smile. He is dangerous.

"No, thank you."

"Thatta girl!" Graham pats me on the shoulder, impressed I was able to resist Jayce's charm. "Ignore him, love. What's your question?"

"Well . . . I was going to ask why you guys are being so nice to me." They both squint at me. "Don't get me wrong, I'm not complaining. I just—well, it's been a really fun day. You guys were all so welcoming this morning, but I'm just some random stranger that showed up at your house."

Jayce looks pensive for a moment and I'm sure I'm about to get a snarky, typical-Jayce response, but he surprises me. "I guess, well, Henry doesn't really bring home girls, so I figured you must be important."

"Oh, I'm not a girl." *Jesus Lucy, do you ever think before you speak?* "I mean, I'm a girl, obviously. But not to Henry. Well, okay, I'm sure he knows I'm a girl, but not like that. Please tell me you understand what I'm saying so I can stop embarrassing myself?" I can see him struggling to hold in the laughter.

"You're definitely a girl, love," Graham says. "Plus, we work all the time and see way too much of each other. It's nice to have some fresh blood."

8

. . .

Lucy

AFTER A DINNER of delicious (delivered) pizza with Graham and my new favorite sectional, I head to my room for an early night. My first day here was strangely awesome. For the first time in a long time, I'm looking forward to tomorrow. It feels kind of amazing.

I'm finally motivated to start writing again.

Where to begin? My take on *Sleeping Beauty* has been my most popular book so far. I think because it was quite a bit darker than my previous ones. Everyone seems to like murder and espionage these days, even tweens. For years I've been planning to do my take on *The Little Mermaid*. It was by far my favorite story as a girl—hell, I've wanted to get a sheepdog ever since I saw Prince Eric and Max. I picture the little girl from the airport. Am I really brave enough to attempt a space odyssey?

There are so many different directions I could go in, but I've been trying to write for the last year, and I've been completely blocked. It's hard to be inspired by perfect princes and magical love at first sight when you're in my current position. My editor is expecting a full draft three months from now and I don't have a single word.

Maybe it's time I write something without a happy ending.

I think back to my house tour earlier with Jayce, how he pretended the basement was a secret lair I must avoid at all costs. It reminds me of *Beauty and the Beast*. I pull up the Disney app to see if it's available to watch. Maybe this is the inspiration I need. And if not, I do love seeing Belle flit around the library.

My slumber ceases abruptly at four in the morning when Rowan starts pressing down on me, licking my nose and tapping my shoulder with his paw.

Then I feel it.

"Ahhh." I bend at the waist, trying to displace the sharpness in my lower back. I scoot backward, trying to prop myself up on the pillows. "Thanks Row. You know the drill."

He hops off the bed to go snatch one of my Warmies and returns with my favorite one tucked in his mouth: the otter, one of many that Sarah gifted me.

In college, it wasn't always easy finding an outlet in convenient spots, so Sarah introduced me to Warmies. A cute stuffed animal next to the bed or thrown in my backpack was much less conspicuous than a heating pad, and I can take them just about anywhere.

"Thank you, my love. Let's go heat this bad boy up."

Rowan snatches my pill bottle and follows me closely to the kitchen. It's early enough that I'm not worried about bumping into anyone, so I don't bother changing out of my PJs. I toss the cute little otter in the microwave and heat him up for a couple of minutes. Then we head back to bed and form a nice and toasty cuddle party.

There's a bit of a ritual to this. First the Warmies, then my pills, then I turn on my "Take a Breath" playlist and let Henry's music do its thing while we build the snuggle pile under every available blanket. I keep the volume low this morning, not wanting anyone in the house to hear.

I don't take Rowan with me everywhere. His training helps him sense my pain a bit before I do, especially if I'm at risk of fainting. But as long as I'm not alone, it's more than safe to go places without him.

The thing is, lately, I've been alone *a lot*. Pretty much every day until I got to LA. It's bonded us together, made us closer than we ever were before the divorce. It's nice to know I can depend on him, that I don't need anyone else around.

It also scares me a little, how easily I've adjusted to this isolated existence.

A FEW HOURS later I'm feeling back to normal. I'm also starving, so I throw on some clothes and head to the kitchen to make breakfast. HAAAM—still no Henry in sight—seem to be waiting for me. They're all toasting bagels—the ones I convinced Graham we should get at the store so there was *something* to eat in the house—and Jayce casually asks which one I want. To him it's nothing, but to me . . . day two of my new life and I'm not feeling so alone. Maybe it won't just be me and Rowan forever.

While we indulge in my favorite carbs, a singular thought bounces back and forth in my head: Where the *hell* is Henry?

I'm not sure what I expected when he invited me here. I definitely didn't think we'd be spending every day together. And he did mention being a workaholic. But he doesn't even eat breakfast with his housemates? Maybe he has a girlfriend and he's been staying somewhere else. That doesn't feel right, but who knows.

I have to constantly remind myself that no matter how well I know his music, the man is still a stranger to me. More like a mystery I'm itching to solve.

I decide not to dwell on the Henry conundrum and focus on Graham while he convinces me to try surfing again today. We head down to the water with Rowan close on my heels.

It's hot this morning but it doesn't bother me. There's something special about the air here. It's always simmering with jasmine and salty citrus. Every time I walk outside, I feel like twirling around, letting my long hair get blown into the wind like that girl from *Mamma Mia* everyone says I look like.

Once we've walked down to the beach and checked the surf, Graham looks at me with a serious expression, none of the typical mirth in his eyes.

"I'm getting you on a board today. All you have to do is lie on it. It's unseasonably warm too. I won't even make you wear a wetsuit." He notices me chewing on my lip. "There are literally no waves, there's nothing to be afraid of. Come on, we'll just be floating. Rowan can come too."

Yesterday I may have chickened out pretty early on. But today, I'm going for it. I feel like I'm safe with Graham, like he'll protect me.

Rowan's a great swimmer but I still put on the life jacket that I got him last summer. It says *This Dog Digs Nantucket* across the back which always makes me laugh. Graham looks like he means business today, so I do as I'm told and grab onto the board for dear life.

Paddling out to sea is actually relaxing. He was right about the swell; it's so calm today I don't feel scared at all. The water glitters all around me like fairy dust and I wonder why it's taken me this long to get back in the ocean. Once we make it past all the breaks, Graham stops paddling and sits up straddling his board. He motions for me to follow suit before grabbing Rowan and plopping him on his board as well. Then he does that "hot man hair shake" thing and I get a salt spray to the face.

"Let's float for a minute, see if the tide changes a bit."

"Sounds good to me. This is a part of surfing I can definitely get behind."

"I still can't believe you've never done this, Luce. I got on my first board when I was just a wee thing, maybe five or six."

"Well, I'm sure in Australia everyone goes surfing as kids. The only water we had in Cleveland was Lake Erie and trust me, you would not be impressed."

"Cleveland, hey. Sounds like a magical place. Is that where your family is then?"

"No, no family there." I try my best to sound casual.

"Right. Boston! That's where you came from. Never been myself, maybe I'll tag along with you some time. When do you think you'll go back for a visit?"

"I don't, umm, I don't have anyone to visit there. I don't have any family." He looks at me questioning, wanting me to go on. There's so much sincerity in his eyes, I feel like maybe I can get through this.

"Well, my dad died when I was ten—heart attack." *Breathe, Luce, you can do this.* "And my mom, she was sick for a pretty long time, but she passed away three years ago, from Leukemia." I turn my head swiftly, knowing the tears are coming. I miss her so much. She was like the brightest star in my sky. Without her in the world everything seems slightly faded. Nothing glows anymore. The last time I saw her was the day after Jack proposed.

She was so happy, ooh-ing and aah-ing over my 2-carat oval-cut, perfect diamond. But every time she took my hand all

I could feel was how cold and frail she was. I'd told her Jack wanted to get married right away, do whatever we needed to make sure she could be there, but she shook her head at me.

"Lucy, I'm sorry I won't be there to see you in your dress, but you deserve to have the wedding you've always dreamed of. We've been planning this since you were a little girl. My life may be ending but yours is just beginning. What kind of mother would I be to take that away from you? I'm just so sorry I'll never get to meet my grandchildren. You and Jack will have such beautiful babies. Will you promise to spoil them every once in a while, for me?"

She passed away that night, still holding my hand, but I'd already called Jack to tell him that we couldn't get married for at least a year. If she wouldn't let me have a quickie wedding to include her, I was going to have the most extravagant event I could in her honor.

"LUCE, I'm so sorry. I shouldn't have pried. Go ahead, ask me anything you like. All my deepest, darkest secrets are yours."

I scoff, but I'm grateful for his smooth segue. Graham has this easy way of disarming me, freeing me from the constant cloud of negativity I seem to be stuck under.

I'm trying to think of a good question when a wave comes out of nowhere and knocks me off my board. I go under and try not to panic. I know where I am, Graham is here, there's no undertow, I just need to swim. I think *up* might be a good direction. My hair whips around my face and I try not to imagine a tangle of seaweed holding me down. Then something sharp scratches at my back and I kick my legs harder.

I quickly surface, gasping for air and grab on to the board. Graham reaches out a large hand to help me up but I shove him away. While I was never in any serious danger, sweet Rowan dove in to save me and God love him, only managed to loosen my bikini top with his paws. Now it's floating out to sea and I'm half naked with nothing but a wet dog to help cover me up.

Of course this would happen to me, especially since all I have at the beach is a pair of cutoff shorts. Why did it have to be so hot today? Things have been going a little too well since I got here; I should have known it couldn't be that easy.

Graham is laughing at me. No, he's *heckling* me.

"Quite a predicament, Little Lu. What will the topless lady do? Ooooh, I think there's a song there. Got a pen, missy? I don't want to forget this."

"Fuck off, Graham. This is your fault. You brought me here against my will and now I have to do a literal walk of shame back to the house. Just stay here while I swim back, okay? At least I don't know anyone on the beach."

"Luce, calm down. Get up on your board and let's go. I left my jumper by the rocks over there, see?" He points toward the far end of the beach. Luckily there isn't a soul in sight down there, but there's still no way I'm getting *up* on anything until I'm far enough away from Graham that I look like a tiny speck. I glare at him and shake my head.

"No offense love, I'm sure that body's a hit with men far and wide, but I'm more of a boomer guy myself, all right? Now give me your hand and I'll help you up."

"Umm, what?"

"Oh, sweet little Lucy, I couldn't care less about your tits, ok? That bloke over there?" He points to a man north of us, also straddling his board. "If you have any ideas on how to get *his* clothes off, let me know." He pauses, winks at me. "You're gorgeous, love, but nothing under the water is doing anything for me, so just use this as an opportunity to get rid of those tan lines."

Graham's gay?

I'm dumbstruck for a moment, wondering if I should have known this already, but I guess it just hasn't really come up. I suddenly love him even more, or maybe I'm just slightly less embarrassed about my current boob crisis. His hand is still stretched toward me and he's chuckling at my bewilderment. I take his hand and let him haul me up, then I start laughing with him until I'm completely out of breath and lying flat on my back. I let him tow me back to shore as I work on my tan.

I DECIDE to make shrimp on the barbie for dinner tonight in Graham's honor. Maybe if I suck up to him a bit, he won't tell the rest of HAAAM about the surfing incident. I honestly have no idea what else is considered Australian food, so I grill some coconut-rum-soaked pineapple and veggie kebabs and make a big pitcher of mezcal margaritas.

I'd be lying if I said I wasn't hoping to see Henry tonight. It just feels weird being here without him when he's the one who invited me. But I guess he just saw someone who needed a place to stay and figured he has extra bedrooms.

"This pineapple is like crack," Craig declares. "I'm gonna need you to make this every day." I haven't gotten to spend much time with him, but he seems to be the least friendly member of HAAAM. Even the way he looks, tall and lanky, beady brown eyes devoid of much warmth; he just gives me a "don't come too close" vibe.

I flash him a smile and choose not to respond to his request slash demand of me.

"He's right. This pineapple is killer, Lucy. What did you do to make this so delicious? I want to bathe in it." Jayce seductively takes another bite.

I roll my eyes. "I'll tell you my secrets, when you tell me yours, Jayce."

He opens his arms wide. "I'm an open book. Ask away Little Lu."

"Hmm." What do I want to know? Jayce is fun, but his social life really doesn't concern me that much. I'm more interested in the group as a whole. It's wild how different these guys are. They don't make any sense together.

"How do you all know each other? I mean, I know because you work together, obviously, but how did you meet? How did HAAAM come to be?"

Graham shakes his head at me like a disappointed parent.

"Lucy, *Lucy*, how could you deny us an actual dirty secret? I can answer that for you!"

"Well, that was her question, so I shall oblige." Jayce winks at me. "We all met in New York at school, at Juilliard. We weren't friends exactly, well not at all actually. Especially not Henry. He knew he was better than all of us, kind of antisocial too."

"He was not antisocial Jayce, what the fuck?" Graham jumps in, clearly offended on Henry's behalf. This is already interesting . . .

"Okay, maybe antisocial isn't the right word, but he was, well, how the hell would you describe it, G?"

"He was . . . focused. He didn't spend every second banging ballerinas like you mate."

"Don't judge me. We were severely lacking in the ballerina department where I grew up. I was just learning to enjoy the finer things in life." Jayce has a wistful look in his eye and I wonder if there is a particular ballerina he's remembering or if they all blur together in his mind. "I guess you're right though. Henry didn't have the same distractions I did—he got me to prioritize."

"What do you mean? What'd he do?" I've been trying not to interject but I can't help myself. Every time Henry's name comes up in conversation I find myself overeager to learn more about him.

"Well, I was pretty close to losing my scholarship," Jayce says. "They run a tight ship at Juilliard, and I wasn't ready for that course load. Way too much pressure. I just wanted to play, ya know? I was playing drums like five nights a week at clubs in the city, had a couple house bands that were trying to recruit me, but they paid practically nothing. Thought about dropping out actually, moving back home, even if it meant I'd face the wrath of my father for not going to *real* college."

He pauses for a moment, and I remember what he said the other day about his family not supporting his musical endeavors. "Then Graham came at me one day. Said Henry wanted to work with me, said he knew I could do more than just play drums. I didn't even realize Henry knew me. Everyone thought he was a fuckin' genius, so I was intrigued. Graham filled me in on their side project, some indie film. Said Henry could even help me with orchestration."

He looks over at Graham and I can see deep gratitude in his eyes.

"So yeah, Henry was right. I didn't just wanna play in a band. Percussion is so much bigger than a drum set. You ever heard a marimba? That shit is so sick!" He must note my brows raised in confusion. "Don't worry, Luce. I'll play for you later—you'll love it. You know I got to write a whole score for bongo drums for our last movie? We have the best fucking job. And yeah, I owe it all to Henry, antisocial or not."

"Percussion? Try playing the french horn—that's a real instrument. You know, the kind that takes actual skills?" Craig smiles smugly, and I honestly can't tell if he's joking or not.

Jayce gives him a quick "screw you" expression and follows it with a hand gesture.

Craig ignores him and continues, "Henry collected all of us. We weren't *all* in trouble for banging ballerinas, but I don't think any of us knew what we were doing, long-term at least. I couldn't seem to focus on an instrument, and he pushed me towards orchestration. Made my degree so much easier." Craig speaks with a more serious tone this time.

They all tell me more about how they got together. Apparently, Craig was in the marching band at Ohio State for a year before transferring to Juilliard. This definitely helps me warm up to him and it's hard not to discuss Script Ohio for the rest of dinner. Buckeye pride runs strong when you're born in the state, even if you never went to school there. He promises to play their anthem, *Hang on Sloopy*, for me one day soon.

But my favorite story is Preston's. He grew up in Chicago and was really into jazz—it sounds like a lot of influence from his parents and older siblings. He says he was the awkward kid in school, a self-proclaimed math geek, but was madly in love with a very popular girl. He wasn't sure she even knew he existed. It's hard not to audibly "awww" at him. He decided if he could become an expert musician, she'd notice him so he chose to master the saxophone. He made it all the way to Juilliard so I guess he succeeded. I ask if he ever got the girl and I see his eyes glitter conspiratorially.

"What do you think?" He says it right as he slips his arm around the woman who's been quietly taking in our conversation since she sat down for dinner. Adamma came in right as we started eating, so I haven't had much of a chance to talk to her yet. She tells me her and Preston got together right after high school, but she moved out to LA for college, knowing she wanted to work in the movie business. They got back together as soon as he came out here and say they owe it all to Henry.

They're quite the odd couple if I'm being honest. Preston can't be over five foot eight and it's not just his stature that's small. He exudes *old soul* in every way, even down to his attempt at a James Dean style: slicked-back hair, white T-shirt, jeans and a leather jacket even though it's eighty degrees outside.

Adamma is basically a goddess. She's tall, perfectly toned, has an impeccable sense of style—*modern* style. She showed up tonight looking absolutely effortless in a white jumpsuit that would surely make me look like a mini marshmallow. Her ebony skin is undeniably flawless, and her tightly coiled Afro somehow looks like she spent hours at the salon but is also perfectly natural. I learn even her name means beautiful girl—like her parents just knew from the beginning.

They're so different, but it's easy to tell how in love they are. I adore their story; it sounds so much like a modern-day fairy tale that I'm tempted to write it.

If I wanted to write another love story, that is.

And I can't miss the fact that they both keep mentioning Henry's part in bringing them back together.

Henry. These guys make him seem like some sort of deity. Maybe he's just incredibly charitable? He offered to help me in a time of need just like all of HAAAM. Part of me wishes his motives were different, but I'm not sure why.

Adamma looks toward me. Her deep brown eyes have a golden glow as warm as melted honey.

"Lucy, what is it you do?"

"Oh, Lucy here writes fairy tales. Fancies herself a princess, I think."

"Graham, I don't write fairy tales. I write novels that are

inspired by fairy tales." I turn back toward Adamma. "My last one was a modern take on *Sleeping Beauty*."

"That sounds so cool! What's it about?"

"Well, it's *loosely* based on the original. It's about an evil doctor who poisons young women and they all fall into a coma, a seemingly incurable coma. But one of them has a boyfriend determined to find the cure and, well, you know, save the kingdom." I throw up my hands in a gesture that means absolutely nothing but for some reason helps me articulate my point.

"Wild. I'll have to read it. What's it called?"

"*Sleeping Darlings*. I'll give you a copy though, if you actually want to read it. You really shouldn't feel obligated."

"No, I absolutely want to! Is it steamy?"

"Umm, no. It's Young Adult, so definitely romantic but nothing explicit."

"That's a shame." She winks at me even though her disappointment is more than apparent. "Are you working on anything now?"

"Yeah, just started though. Not sure exactly what it is yet. What about you, Adamma? I know you said you came out here to work in the movie industry, but what do you do? Are you an actress?"

"God, no. I'm a production designer. I've done everything from costume to set design and finally am starting to work on the big picture stuff. My goal has always been to be a producer, but this industry is fucking brutal."

Preston beams. "She's amazing. Just wait a few years and her name's gonna be on everything." It's so sweet how supportive he is. Jack never wanted to discuss anything related to my books. I even heard him refer to them as "teenage fairy porn" to his friends once.

Jayce stands up and clears his throat like he's ready to give a speech.

"I'd like to make a toast." Oh, he *is* making a speech. "To Lucy, our newest housemate, may she never leave. For I'm afraid we'll starve. Also, she makes a damn good margarita! Lucy, we're so glad you're here. Thank you for finally getting us to use this patio. But please, try to keep your clothes on. It's not that kind of house." He winks at me before throwing a quick glance at Graham.

I turn to look at him, and I'm sure there's steam coming out of my ears right now as I give him a glare that promises vengeance. I can't believe he already told all of them—this is so embarrassing. But they're all cracking up, and I feel like I've somehow already been welcomed into this family, and there's nothing I can do to stop the massive grin from spreading across my face.

9

• • •

Lucy

HE'S . . . here.

Two days after the bikini incident, HAAAM and I are about to take Rowan for a walk along the beach. We just polished off my blue crab enchiladas for dinner and everyone could use a walk after that much cheese. But when I return to the kitchen after grabbing Row's leash, I'm met with utter silence and skittish expressions.

"What's going on, guys?"

Graham throws me a subtle smirk before tilting his head just slightly in the direction of the foyer.

Henry.

Is *here*.

In my head, I think I wasn't sure I'd ever see him again. Like maybe he was just this mythical being I dreamt up on our flight in order to deal with the trauma of my life. But he sure looks real now. And as if he wants to make sure I don't forget again, his eyes bore into mine like laser beams of lust. My knees press together involuntarily as I try—and fail—to break his gaze.

I'd almost forgotten how gorgeous he is, how someone who

looks like him is the same man who wrote every note on my "Take a Breath" playlist. I definitely forgot how tall he is, how broad, how commanding. He hasn't said a single word and yet every set of eyes in the room is locked on him, like they're waiting for his royal decree. Even Rowan is sitting at attention.

How can one man look undeniably smoldering but still adorably shy? He's such an enigma. I take in his face. His eyes are vibrant, a deep azure that almost glows. His hair is a bit disheveled, like he's been combing his fingers through it over and over. The color is such a rich, chocolatey brown, I imagine it's exactly the shade women ask for at their salon. I'm openly gaping at him now, memorizing each of his features. I know I should say something, but the words just aren't coming.

"Sorry for—well, I've been a bit busy since you've been here." He's looking down at his shoes, biting the inside of his cheek and I can see his jaw popping with nervous energy. "Once I start working on something new, it can get a bit compulsive. I just can't stop."

"It's fine. Spending time together was never part of the arrangement." I hate how bitter I sound. Why should he have to apologize for working? Working on music that's like a drug for me.

"Would you like to see the studio? I think I did promise you that much."

I glance back at the guys and Graham speaks up. "I'll take Rowan out. Go get the tour, Luce."

"Thanks." I turn back to Henry and can't help but beam at him. "Okay."

I follow him down the stairs ready for my big tour. It's weird being with him again. The flight seems so much longer than four days ago, but I remember how easy it was talking to him. Henry wrote the soundtrack to my therapy. He cured my pain without ever knowing who I was. Of course it feels good to be near him.

"You're really spoiling HAAAM with all your cooking. It's delicious by the way." He's walking ahead of me and can't see my face, but he must take my silence as surprise since he follows up with: "They, umm . . . bring me the leftovers."

The room we enter has a glossy white grand piano, three floating shelves covered in plaques and statues and the largest futon I've ever seen. There's also a mini fridge, possibly the same model I had in my dorm at Emory, with a foot-high stack of sheet music and other papers on top.

I'm not sure what I expected from his studio, but this is not it.

He watches as I survey the room and chuckles at my confused expression. His gaze feels heavy on me and I try to remember the last time a man watched me this closely.

"This is just my solo writing space, for when I need to work alone. It's also kind of my sanctuary. There's more to see, I promise."

"I was just surprised is all, but it's beautiful. Especially the piano." I walk over to the wall to sneak a peek at his trophy shelf. He has four Oscars, two Emmys, a Tony, a . . . "You won a Grammy?"

"Ouch. And here I thought you were my biggest fan. Not worthy of a Grammy, eh?"

"No, no of course you are. I just didn't know they had a category for you."

"It was for album of the year actually. Remember Adam Levi's first solo album? I happened to write the music and lyrics." He says it like it's nothing. Like there weren't at least seven singles from that album that I can remember. Like those aren't still the most played songs on every radio station in the country. I walked down the aisle to *Better than Waffles*. Our first dance was to *City of Starlight*.

I *love* that album. Sure, Adam Levi can sing, but the music, the lyrics . . . the lyrics.

Henry wrote those lyrics? Some girl is *very* lucky. I can't tell if he's in a relationship now; he's made no hints at one. Maybe there are several girls. He doesn't really seem like the type, but he's gorgeous, rich, has a mansion in Malibu. It would be easy for him to have a different model or actress on his arm every night.

"Lucy?"

"Sorry, I was just thinking—I was thinking about how much I love that album. I'm sad I never knew it was you. Actually, why didn't I? And come to think of it, why didn't I know what you looked like when you've won all these awards? I know I've watched at least a few of them on TV over the years."

"Well—I've never actually gone to one of them. These were all sent to me. You know I'm not the best with words. I really prefer to stay out of the spotlight."

Our eyes meet and I can see a hint of shame in them, like he thinks he's let me down, like he's failed. A feeling I'm only too familiar with myself. I step closer to him and offer a supportive smile. "I think your words are perfect. Can I see the rest now?"

He shows me five more rooms and I notice how much more comfortable he gets the deeper we go into the studio. He's fully in his element now, never stumbling over his words or showing nervous energy.

Me, on the other hand; I'm fan-girling hard. For me, this is basically the exact opposite of what people think of when they say "how the sausage gets made."

The main studio looks exactly like the ones I've seen in TV

documentaries: a massive sound board with thousands of buttons that do who knows what, separated from a large recording room by a single glass wall. There's a full keyboard and numerous computer monitors. It's kind of a mess to be honest. What's unique is the flat screen TV mounted above. He explains how producers will send him clips to watch as he writes and then records. Sometimes he even sends *them* clips to time out scenes for filming.

The whole process sounds fascinating. He breaks down how composers typically work with orchestrators once the writing is done. Orchestrators will then turn the original songs into sheet music for individual instruments. Apparently, this is why Henry and his writing team live together and work so closely. They do all the composing and orchestration together: Graham on strings, Preston on woodwinds, Craig on brass and Jayce on percussion.

Henry says piano is the entire orchestra in itself, so he keeps his focus there even though it's obvious he can play and write for pretty much anything. He doesn't like working with new people on each project like most composers do which is why he created HAAAM. They only work with musicians outside of their circle once they're ready to record with a full symphony orchestra.

He tells me about spotting, syncing and other terms I don't fully understand. But it's the way he talks so passionately about what he does that keeps me enthralled by every word. I can tell how much he loves every aspect of it, down to the tiniest details like working with the director to sync one simple drum beat to the flap of a dragon's wings.

I'm tempted to ask him about every score he's written. I want to know his favorite part of each one, why he chose all strings for one or to go fully electronic for another. His attention to detail reminds me of my own writing. How I'll put together a ninety-thousand-word manuscript, but will always have that singular sentence I'm particularly proud of.

I feel overwhelmed with questions but try my best to relax. This doesn't have to be my only chance. Maybe Henry and I can become friends, or at least stay in touch after I move out. That is if he doesn't *always* disappear for days at a time.

There are a few other connected rooms with shiny instruments and other recording gear, a state-of-the-art gym that I plan on using daily now that I've been allowed downstairs. But we breeze through them to end up back in the white piano room. I've been thinking about the futon since we first came down here—its' just so *big*—so I decide to take a seat.

"Wow. This is the most comfortable thing I've ever sat on—it feels like my bed. What is this sorcery!?"

He's clearly amused and just stands there watching me sprawl out as much as I can.

"It's like your bed. I had it made by the same mattress company. I like having a futon down here. Sometimes I just want to sit and write somewhere comfortable but still be close to the piano if I need it. And I also end up sleeping here quite a bit. As you may have noticed, my working hours aren't exactly normal." He smiles solemnly. "I never found a futon that was big enough for me to fit on comfortably so I had this made." He looks embarrassed, but I'm not sure why. Henry's huge, but in a superhero way. Of course he needs a custom futon. "Here, let me show you how it works. This is my favorite part."

He offers his hand to help me stand and then grabs a remote from on top of the mini fridge. When he presses it, the futon flattens out into what I assume is at least a king-size bed. He said this room is his sanctuary, but I can imagine it would feel lonely here too. Just a piano, a bed and his awards to look at. I wonder how much time he spends here all by himself. It seems like most of it from what I can tell.

"Henry, this place is incredible. Thank you again for offering to let me stay here. It's been really nice, not being alone. I'm meeting with an agent tomorrow to go look for a place. I promise I won't overstay my welcome."

He looks at me quizzically. "But you just got here."

"Well, yeah. I just don't want to be in the way, you know. You already have a pretty full house."

He's still looking at me like I'm speaking a different language.

"You're welcome here as long as you'd like. And I think the guys would be sad to see you go. Especially Graham."

This makes me smile. It's only been a few days but I already feel like Graham is a close friend. He's part of the reason I decided I want to stay in LA, at least for the time being.

"Stay a little longer, what's the rush?"

I do love living here; this house is amazing. I doubt I can afford anything overlooking the ocean in Malibu, nothing decent anyway. And honestly, I love having people around. There's always someone here. The thought of living alone again, just me and Rowan, sounds so . . . lonely.

"Okay, well, if you promise I'm not taking advantage of you."

He cocks his head slightly and smiles. "I don't think that's possible. Stay. You're welcome here as long as you like."

I grin, just as I try to stifle a quick yawn. Unfortunately, he's too observant. "Sorry, I'm not bored, I promise, just exhausted from falling off a surfboard all day." It's true. My body feels like it's taken a serious beating. After flopping into the water my second day here, my fears have subsided a bit and I'm actually letting Graham give me surf lessons. I'll never be without a wetsuit again though.

"Ahh, well I'd blame the instructor. I bet I could get you

standing in no time." Every so often he speaks with this innate confidence. It's such an interesting side of him, and I wonder why he's so hard to read. "I wanted to play you something, if you don't mind staying up a bit? I promise I'll have you off to bed soon, but I'd like you to hear this."

He tells me to lay down and rest my sea legs while he settles in at the piano.

This is surreal.

Henry Turner is playing a song for *me* in the same place he calls his sanctuary. For the last year, I've felt nothing but shame, disappointment, grief—just overall gloom. But not right now.

Right now, I feel honored.

The music is beautiful, but it has a sad quality to it. It sounds like longing. Like the notes are reaching out for something that's unattainable. It reminds me of my own life, of everything I want and can never have. It reminds me of my mom, of all the times I wish she were here, of how much I miss her. I feel the tears start to slip down my cheek, but I let them fall. His back is to me and it's like I'm completely alone with the music. I close my eyes and let it surround me, let my heart ache freely.

I PEEL off the hospital gown and slowly get dressed. Jack and I have discussed this before, but his look of utter shock tells me he was never fully paying attention. We spend the car ride home in silence and he drops me off, telling me he needs to go blow off some steam. I draw myself a bath and cry.

My mom is here. In Boston. When's the last time she was here? She and Jack are sitting across from me on our couch, but they won't look at me.

"Hello—can you guys hear me?" I wave my hands at them but get no reaction.

"It's okay Jack, you made the right decision. She's disappointed us both. You'll choose better next time, don't worry." My mom is stroking his back like he's her kid. I feel sick.

"Mom! Mom, why are you doing this?"

I'm drowning in the ocean, seaweed tangled around my legs, saltwater burning in my lungs . . .

I WAKE ABRUPTLY, and I try to shake off the nightmare.

I feel something warm and hard moving up and down underneath my arm and my eyes flash open.

Henry.

Why is Henry lying here? And why am I wrapped around him like a koala?

I shut my eyes and try to remember. I must have dozed off while he was still playing, so why is he here and not in his bed? Or I guess this is his bed, and I'm the one out of place. I haven't moved a muscle, and if I'm being honest, I want to linger here as long as I can. His body feels so good against mine. What is it about a muscly man in a cotton T-shirt? His scent washes over me, masculine and sweet, maybe sandalwood?

I could lie like this for hours.

But I'm also *terrified* of him waking up to find me snuggled up to him. He's snoring lightly so I try to move my arm and leg off of him as quietly and slowly as possible. I cannot wake him up. I'm inching backward, I'll just slide off the bed, crawl up the stairs, and he'll never know I just used him as a human body pillow.

"Owww!"

Fuck. Did I seriously just bang my head against his mini fridge? I reach for the back of my head, knowing a large bump will be forming soon.

"Hey. Are you okay?"

Dammit, he's definitely awake now. At least I was already detached from his torso.

"Sorry. I was trying to sneak out before I woke you up. And clearly misjudged how far away the fridge was."

"It's okay, I'm a light sleeper." He's sitting up and looking near me but his eyes are darting around. "I hope I didn't frighten you. You . . . erm, fell asleep while I was playing last night, and I decided to work for a while. I sleep here a lot. I, err, must have crashed without realizing you were still here."

I notice his hair is mussed from sleep and can't help but admire how sexy he looks. Wait, did he just say he didn't know I was there?

"I better go check on Row." I bolt upstairs as fast as my legs will take me.

I'm mortified.

Luckily, I find Rowan in the kitchen and quickly bring him to my room to snuggle with me in bed. My body is vibrating with so many emotions—mostly embarrassment, but something else I'm not sure I'm ready to admit. I try not to think about it. It was obviously a weird, cuddly mistake that we will not be making again.

I know waking up next to Henry didn't mean anything—he made that perfectly clear—but my body feels differently. I've always craved connection. I love being held, belonging to someone else in a physical way. That may have been the hardest part of the divorce. I always feel cold now, detached, like I'm missing a limb or something.

I close my eyes and hold on to Row, but I can't stop picturing Henry's chest rising and falling underneath me.

10

• • •

Henry

I DIDN'T MEAN to do it. Well, I don't think I meant to. At least, not at first. I just . . . couldn't seem to walk away.

I could hear Lucy crying while I was playing for her. It really shouldn't have surprised me considering she inspired the song. She wasn't exactly in high spirits the night we met. But when I finished and turned around, seeing her asleep, wet streaks still visible on her cheeks, it just felt wrong to leave her there alone. I meant to lie down for just a moment, then ease her awake and help her upstairs. But once I was lying next to her, once I could feel the heat of our bodies mingling together, I just kept telling myself *one more minute.*

She was clearly freaked out this morning when she woke, and I can't exactly blame her. I just hope I haven't lost the little bit of trust we forged on our flight together. I feel so desperate to talk to her again, to just have a conversation, get to know her better. It felt so easy on the plane; maybe because we were trapped together, no distractions. I want to be alone with her again, and yet, even thinking those words terrifies me.

I grab my phone to call Mum. It's still early enough in

England to speak with her. She's the only person on the planet who will understand my current predicament. Well, there's Graham, but I really don't want to hear what sort of advice he'd come up with right now.

"Henry! How's my star doing tonight?"

"Hi Mum. I'm good. I, well, I need some advice." There's a long pause. She's not used to this kind of call. "There's a erm . . . there's a girl."

A very long pause. I know I've got her attention now.

"A girl? A girl! Henry, tell me everything! Is it serious? How long have you been together? How did you meet her? Do you have a photo? Oh, I'm sure she's gorgeous. When can I—"

"Mum, calm down. There's a girl, that I met. We're not, we're not anything, really."

"Oh."

Her disappointment is palpable and I feel like an idiot for not being clearer straight away. I should have thought this through before picking up the phone. Getting her hopes up and letting her down breaks my heart. All my mum has ever wanted is for me to be happy, to find a perfect love like she had with my dad. I know she's proud of my success, but she never cared about fame or money, less than I do even.

"I'm sorry, Mum. I didn't mean to confuse you. I just, well, she seems special. We've had a few conversations. You'd be shocked to hear how easy it was when we first met, actually. I'd like to get to know her better. But now I'm not sure how to go about that, without scaring her away. You know I don't really have any experience with this part. I was hoping maybe you'd have some motherly advice?"

"Oh Henry, that's easy darling. I know it won't sound appealing to you, but just do as your mum says. Take the girl to dinner."

11

• • •

Lucy

"NO MORE SURFING. EVERYTHING HURTS."

I'm doing my best to convince Graham we need a day off as I'm flipping banana pancakes for breakfast.

"Come on Luce, don't abandon me! I finally have a surfing buddy. Everyone here works too much." He ruffles my hair a bit. "I'm gonna go grab a quick shower. Holler when the food's ready."

I'm already so sore and I've barely even done anything besides paddle and fall down. He agreed to give me a break, wave-dependent, so I pray to the moon for a full-on tempest. After the dramatic morning I had, waking up on the futon, I just want to lie around and eat my feelings.

Maybe I'll bake some brownies.

My chocolatey trance is interrupted by the other thing taking up too much space in my brain.

"Hi. Did you get some more rest?" Henry asks, walking into the kitchen.

It takes a moment to collect myself. Henry's body is only a few feet away from me and I'm using every bit of effort not to lean into him. I know it's only in my head, but I just felt so connected to him when I woke up today, like our bodies were destined to fit together. It's been so long since I've been with anyone other than Jack. Being near Henry, inhaling his scent; I feel like I'm nineteen again, with no idea how to coolly interact with him.

I'm still flustered about what happened earlier, but he seems perfectly normal. But what is his normal? I'm not sure I know yet. He keeps saying he has trouble with words and sometimes he does seem shy. Then other times he's perfectly confident and dare I say, eloquent. More than I am at least.

"Yeah, a bit. Want some pancakes?"

"Thanks, I'm okay. Just had a protein bar." Of course he did. And that's why everything about his body is hard. Jesus, now I'm thinking about all the *parts* of him that get hard.

"I wanted to ask you something. If that's all right."

His fingers start fidgeting while his muscles go taut, his eyes darting around the same way they did earlier this morning. Why does he look nervous? For a moment I wonder if he can read minds and knows where mine was a second ago.

"Of course. What's up?"

"Would you, erm—would you like to go out to dinner tonight?"

He must notice my eyes go wide in surprise. Is he asking me out?

I instinctively start eating one of the finished pancakes with my hands—like a damn heathen. After one massive bite I set it down and hope he missed this lovely moment of stress eating.

"I, erm, I'd like to treat you—you've been cooking so much for everyone. I thought you might like to go out? As a thank you."

Okay. Not a date.

But still intriguing.

"Sure. That sounds nice."

"How do you feel about sushi?"

"Good, really good. Great, actually." There's a subtle smirk he's trying his best to hide. "I just really love sushi. Haven't had it in a while."

"Same for me. Let's leave here at seven."

And just as quickly as he materialized, he disappears back down to the studio.

"So, everyone else told me their story the other night, but I just realized I still don't know how you met Henry, how you got into all this."

Once I tempted Graham with the offer of warm brownies, he agreed to skip surfing today. Instead, we're binging on chocolate and watching reality TV. He has a massive flat screen in his room so we're watching in bed for ultimate comfort, and to not bother anyone with our commentary. I'm particularly glad we're alone so no one else can see me stuffing the banana pancake-brownie-sandwich in my mouth. Yes, it's being dipped in whipped cream, and yes, it's delicious.

"Ahh, you noticed that, eh? Was hoping I could avoid it to be honest. No one really knows exactly how Henry and I met, just that I was the first member of HAAAM and therefore the most important." He smirks at me in his usual cocky-Graham fashion, but I'm definitely more interested now than before.

"Come on, you can tell me. I'm a great secret keeper." I really am. I've told exactly zero people why I'm thirty and divorced, even though I want to scream it from a mountaintop most of the time. I take another massive bite of the sugar bomb.

Maybe it would ease the pain to talk about it more, to not

feel so alone in my misery, but since being in Malibu, I've been too distracted to feel the doom and gloom that has surrounded me all year. Why would I want to give that up?

"You really have that innocent doe-eye thing going for you, you know. How do straight men ever deny you a thing?"

I want to appreciate the compliment, but Jack used to say something similar. I offer a tight smile but keep working the eyes because—it works.

"All right, short version," Graham finally says, turning over to balance his head in his hand. "Try to limit your questions, okay?"

I nod. What is he about to tell me?

"I moved to New York after my parents threw me out when I was seventeen. They were very . . . religious. And that is a subject I'd really prefer not to talk about." I give him another nod of understanding. "Once I got there, I realized playing in a band wasn't actually going to pay my way to school, not even close. I was so broke it was laughable. Did some things I'm not exactly proud of. Henry helped me out."

"Okay. But how did you meet him, you weren't at Juilliard?"

"Nope, I never actually attended. But I was a pretty good guitar player, violin too. My whole family are musicians. You could say it's in my blood. I snuck into a few classes when I was feeling ballsy, wanting to learn anything I could. And then I met Henry. He was halfway through his first master's, already getting some job inquiries, and needed some help with the . . . uh . . . business side of things. He let me move in with him, got me out of a pretty bad situation. Even helped teach me to write music."

I have a million questions swirling through my head.

"Lucy, stop looking at me like that."

"Like what? What do you mean?"

"Like I'm some abandoned puppy dog you found on the street. I don't need your pity. Things worked out quite well for me, don't you think?"

"I don't pity you. And I'm glad things worked out, but that doesn't mean I can't feel bad about the times that you struggled. No one should have to go through that."

"Eh, things were rough for a while, but I would never be here if it had gone differently. I mean honestly, if I'd never left Brisbane, you may have never had the chance to meet me—and that would be the real travesty, don't you think?" He smirks. "Life goes on, love. I never dwell on the past."

Graham's so tough. Seeing his inner strength match his outer muscles makes me smile. It also makes me feel small, like a child whining for their mom. I know I need to figure out how to get by on my own, but sometimes it feels impossible. Graham makes it seem so easy to put all the negative stuff behind him, to only focus on the good. I just don't know how to do that yet. But I hope one day I will.

He must see the emotions clearly on my face. "Shake it off, Little Lu. Look around us. I live in a mansion, get to surf every day *and* get paid to write music. Plus, Henry's like a brother to me. I love my life." He starts to tickle me until I'm smiling again. "All right, what's next? Switch to *Top Chef* or more housewives from hell?"

12

• • •

Lucy

"THIS IS NOT A DATE."

"Seriously, Row. If you cock your head at me one more time I'm throwing out all the peanut butter. It's not a date!"

This riveting, one-sided conversation has been going on for about an hour.

Poor Rowan. "I take it all back. You'll get *all* the peanut butter when I get home, okay?"

I'm not sure why this internal pep talk is needed, but sadly, it is.

I have no idea what to wear tonight, or how much effort I should put into this dinner. I'm a grown woman for fuck's sake. I shouldn't be freaking out over a simple dinner, no matter how handsome Henry is.

I strip off the shorts and tank top I have on. It's obviously too casual for dinner. Then I pull out my tiny makeup bag hoping I have at least one mascara that's not completely dried up, and a blush that's only partially cracked.

It's a crush. A silly little *nothing* crush. It'd be strange if I didn't have a crush. Henry is objectively gorgeous. And so tall.

I'm not blind.

And I can't forget about his music. The same music that I would consume through a vein if possible. The same music that I'm ironically listening to now, in the hopes that it will relax my nerves.

Most recently divorced women are clueless about how to act around men, right? I can't be the outlier here. And if I am, I'm pretty sure I blame Jack. Ugh. I toss a few more dresses on to the bed.

I wish Sarah were here. She may not be my favorite person at the moment—understatement of the century—but this sort of situation is where she shines. I know she'd pick out the perfect outfit that would be flattering and still look effortless. She'd cover my face in makeup that would make me look naturally beautiful. She'd immediately switch out my playlist for something we could dance to, and then tell me how hot I am while I'd jump around on the bed. I think about calling her again but considering she hasn't responded to anything since I left Boston, I decide against it.

I take a deep breath and try to settle my thoughts. I throw on a simple sundress and squeeze Rowan a bit too hard.

"You're right, pal. I'm freaking out over nothing. It's not like Henry is interested in me anyway. And even if he was, it'd be too short-lived to matter."

"What do you like to listen to?"

He's only being polite, making conversation on our drive to dinner, but Henry asking me this question has me in a breathless fit of giggles. I might be living at his house, but it still feels bizarre to be doing something as mundane as picking a radio station with *Henry Turner.*

"I think you know the answer to that. Car, airport, bedroom"—*why the hell did I say bedroom?*—"it's always you I'm listening to."

"Oh."

Luckily he seems about as nervous as I do. He doesn't say much during the short drive after that, mostly just asks what kind of sushi I like.

When we arrive at Nobu we're instantly seated on their impressive patio overlooking the Pacific Ocean. It's clear Henry planned this meticulously, because the sun is just starting to set. It's that perfect time of night when the clouds look like every flavor of cotton candy. Even the ocean is glimmering with shades of lilac and bubblegum. And it's all set ablaze in a stunning tangerine glow.

Henry and I are both gazing into the Pacific, when our waitress comes by and asks him if we'd like something to drink. She's tall with olive skin and dark shiny hair—very pretty; probably an aspiring actress or influencer. She's smiling at him in a seductive way that looks like an invitation. I wonder how often women behave like this for him, if it's always this easy. I wonder if I look like a child compared to women like her. I silently applaud myself for wearing a dress tonight, even if it fits more like a swim cover-up.

He stares up at her and I brace myself for some flirtatious conversation to begin, but instead his face suddenly goes slack. I see his eyes start to dart side to side, up and down. What is he doing? His lips part briefly but then they're sealed, no hint of movement. Moments pass but he never says a word. I'm not sure what's happening. She rolls her eyes and leans her head forward as if to say "hello in there" but he's frozen.

"Yeah, okay, I'll come back." She drops her voice but there's still a clearly audible "freak" as she walks away.

My eyes turn to Henry but his face has gone completely blank.

"Are you all right? Can I help?" I keep my voice as breezy as possible, but he just stares back at me.

Nothing.

I try holding my hand out for him to take but I'm not even sure he notices the gesture.

Is he having a panic attack? He seems calm, but also . . . not? I want to help him but I have no clue how.

Then I see the waitress coming back and start to panic a bit myself.

"So, anything you'd like to order *now*?" She's looking at him with open mockery and I want to smack her. I silently urge Henry to say something, just to get rid of her. I start to speak up but he holds up a hand toward me, wanting to handle this himself.

A few more beats pass. He's just staring at her, and of course, she starts to laugh. It comes out as a cackle and I instantly imagine her as some evil Disney villain. I'll definitely be using her as inspiration later, but she'll be much less pretty in my words.

"Okay, dude, this is getting kind of creepy." She turns to me and says, "What's wrong with him?"

I have always been a well-mannered, even-tempered, good little girl. I don't pick fights and rarely involve myself in even minor confrontations, but the rage building inside me at the moment is palpable.

How fucking dare she.

"Actually, we just overheard that table complaining about how disgusting their food is. He was trying to find a polite way to tell you we're leaving. I don't really care about being polite since you're a huge bitch." I raise my voice a bit at the end, not caring at all if I'm overheard. "Come on Henry, let's go. Just like you said, the wine list here is absolute rubbish."

Shit.

Henry follows me outside the restaurant in utter silence as I debate what to do. He's gone completely mute, eyes wide, mouth shut like a bear trap. Should we go back to the house? I hate to admit defeat, and he seemed so excited about going out. In the car he said it's been over a *year* since he had sushi—the horror!

Plus, he spends so much time alone in that studio, he deserves this.

Okay Luce, you're having a panic attack, your nice dinner just got ruined, what would you want to do? Think . . . think . . . think! Comfort food, definitely.

"Henry, what do you think about Italian?" He gives me a weak nod followed by a thumbs-up. I'll take that as a win. "Good. I never wanted sushi anyway."

We get to the car and I pull out my phone to type Fritto Misto into Google Maps. It's thirty minutes away but it's the only place in LA that I can vouch for. I remember Sarah took me there on my last visit and they had the most amazing homemade pasta. When I offer to drive, Henry just brushes me off and opens the passenger door for me. I assume if he feels comfortable driving I shouldn't be too worried, right?

During the ride to Santa Monica, Henry is so focused on the road, he never once turns his head toward me. I can see his anxiety like a physical, tangible thing, the muscle in his jaw popping, the quick blinks of his eyes, the tension throughout his entire body, every muscle taut and rigid. I wish I knew what was going on in his head. My instinct is always to fill the silence, but I'm not sure what the right words are. He seemed okay when I suggested a different restaurant, so I'm hoping we can just start over once we get there.

I know that miracles do exist when we get to Fritto Misto and there's a parking spot right outside. This is a sign; I made the right call not taking him straight home. I tell him how excited I am for some delicious pasta and he smiles. I've always said I could have a sparkling conversation with a brick wall.

Here's your time to shine, Luce!

This restaurant is much less *grand* than Nobu. The space is small with minimal artwork. There's no view but the aroma coming from the kitchen is heavenly. Once we're seated and perusing the menu, I see his face tighten up again.

"I'm starving, and would love to try a bunch of things," I say, realizing I need to take charge of ordering. "Would you mind sharing with me? I promise to pick the perfect assortment."

I see him exhale and the look he gives me makes me want to hug him ferociously. I want him to know this is fine, there's nothing to be ashamed of, but I can tell it's not that simple for him. Our waitress comes over and looks directly at Henry. Of course, he's gorgeous, she probably thinks he's some big movie star she can't place.

"Hi!" I force her to acknowledge me. "We're just going to share a bunch of stuff, so I'll order." I realize I have no idea what Henry likes, so I get a little of everything. And by a little, I mean I order more than half the menu. "Oh and wine. How about a bottle of pinot and also one of chardonnay."

The waitress gives me a puzzled look but writes everything down and walks away.

"Did any of that sound good to you?"

He smiles and gives me a nod. I watch him take a big gulp of water before staring back at me in a way I can only describe as lovingly.

"Thank you. You're . . . thank you."

"Oh my God, I've never been so stuffed in my life. Why did you let me order all that food?" I've barely made it inside the house before collapsing onto the couch.

"Let you? I definitely remember saying we do *not* need dessert, but you insisted that it's not a real Italian dinner if you don't end it with Tiramisu."

"I stand by that."

I really do. Dinner without dessert is like saying goodnight without a kiss.

It's after eleven and there's no sign of HAAAM hanging around so I ask Henry if he needs to go do some work or if he has time to watch a movie. Once the food came, he was back to his confident self, and we had so much fun together. I don't want this night to end.

"Work can wait." Henry grabs a piece of paper from the kitchen island. "Oh, Graham left a note here for you. It says, 'Took out Rowan since Mum forgot about him, sleeping in bed with me tonight, need a good cuddle,' Interesting. Well, I guess you're dog-free tonight. How does it feel?"

Honestly, not great. What if I need a cuddle? I know I'll be safe without him considering there's five other people in this house, but I hate sleeping alone. The only thing that made Jack's disappearance bearable at first was having Rowan in bed every night. Not cool, Graham.

"You look upset. Want me to go and wrangle the dog thief?"

"No, it's fine. I'm just not used to having a bed to myself. It'll be weird but I'm sure Rowan appreciates some new smells."

Henry cocks his head and looks at me like he sees through everything I'm saying, like he knows exactly how much I'm dreading getting into bed alone tonight. I wish I could read him as easily. Maybe then I could have figured out what happened tonight that had him so frozen.

"Well, I can't remember how many times I've fallen asleep on this couch. Maybe your luck will really take a turn for the worse and you'll wake up next to me again."

His crooked grin is so endearing. If he only knew how I actually woke up this morning, not next to him, but wrapped around him as if he were a eucalyptus tree. My face heats and I push the thought away. He really just offered to sleep on the couch so I don't feel alone. It's refreshing to be around someone who can read me so well, who cares about how I'm feeling. I give him a silent thank you.

"I'm gonna go throw on some pajamas, just in case. Feel free to pick a movie." I scurry across the living room to go change and pick out a warm but flattering pair of PJs.

Once we're settled in, he turns on *The Vampire Chronicles*. I look over to see him trying, and failing, to stifle a grin.

"Really? This is what you want to watch?"

"Hey, I have a new appreciation for this one. If I hadn't heard you humming along to the music, I may never have met you." He's right, it still feels surreal that I met him at all, let alone that I'm now living in his house. I decide to be quiet and give the movie another shot. At least I know I love the score.

A little over halfway through he turns it off and looks at me apologetically.

"You're right, that film is absolute crap. Are we really expected to believe vampires glow like the bloody northern lights? Absolute idiocy."

I can't stop laughing. I love this side of Henry. His wit, sarcasm—it's infectious. At dinner, he wrote a song about a love triangle between the rigatoni, ravioli and gnocchi. It was hilarious, and somehow still more romantic than this movie.

When you're hollow inside, she'll take
you for a ride
If you're stuffed with cheese, she'll bring
you to your knees
Gnocchi is the bite you've been
dreaming of
So soft so smooth, you're falling in love
A bit of a slut, she wants them all
Pastas big, stuffed, or small

Now I can't get it out of my head . . .

"Lucy, you all right?"

"Yeah, just thinking about your upcoming album: *Love & Pasta.* Think you'll win another Grammy?"

"Only if I can get John Legend on vocals. Pasta's quite soulful, don't you think?"

We spend the rest of the night coming up with more lyrics and picking the right singer for each one. Hearing Henry rhyme "bucatini" to "string bikini" and "shells and cheese" to "oh baby please" has me giggling to the point of being completely breathless. I'm not sure when he goes to grab his guitar, but actual music is being made now, even if it's just for fun.

Fun.

I can't remember the last time I had this much fun. The last thing I recall before dozing off is the line "you make me want to be al dente," and feeling his feet lightly brush mine in the corner of the couch.

13

. . .

Henry

LAST NIGHT WAS the best night of my life.

Even now, sitting at the piano, I can't stop smiling. I'm worried my face may get stuck this way. I've completely lost track of time today. I'm not even sure if I've eaten, though after last night's feast I doubt I need any sustenance. I haven't left the studio once.

It's not uncommon for a melody to suddenly pour out of me. This one has been on repeat for hours now. Lyrics are usually another story—something I have to dig deep for—which is why I rarely write them. Today though, I'm not even sure where the words are coming from. It's like they've manifested directly from my lips, bypassing my thinking center entirely. Maybe all the pasta rhymes from last night jump started something inside me.

Maybe it's just Lucy.

The sun rises in the east
But Zephyr brought her west to me

A light I never knew I'd find
Shining so bright I have to shield
my eyes

Can I find my way out of the dark
This gilded star strumming at my heart
A life I thought was never real
A light I thought I'd never feel

What am I supposed to do
With something that feels so strange
and new
A life I thought was never real
A light I thought I'd never feel

I FINALLY THINK I've got the notes right, the perfect mix of ache and desire. Better write it down before I alter it any more.

"Hey, umm, Henry?" Jayce interrupts me.

"Yeah, what's up?" I grab the notebook anyway. I can multitask with whatever he needs. I look up to see Craig standing there as well. He has a grimace on his face and moves closer before he starts speaking.

"Can you like, do something about Lucy?" Jayce shoves him and mumbles something under his breath. "What? It's fucking annoying. Why is she even here?"

"Can someone explain what the problem is, please?"

"Sorry boss," Jayce chimes in, "I just thought you might want to know that Lucy's been kind of . . . sad? Crying, actually. She's been watching Disney movies all day."

"Yeah, and I've had enough of—"

"Craig, I've had enough of you." This one has been

seriously aggravating lately. "Why don't you go work on something and leave Lucy alone, okay? Jayce, thanks for letting me know."

I run upstairs to figure out what's going on. They're right, she's on the couch, I think *Aladdin* is playing on the big screen. But Lucy isn't watching the movie. She has a tablet propped up on her lap and she seems to be scrolling through pictures. I can't be sure, but I think they might be of her mum. I see a woman who looks a bit like Lucy and a young girl with Lucy's radiant smile and mossy green eyes. She's looking at pictures of them together from when she was younger.

I learned last night that her mum passed away a few years ago. It must have been around the same time I lost my dad. And while it's been tough for me, I can tell that Lucy and her mum had a unique bond, something that's made the loss especially painful for her. I wonder if this is what she'd been referring to on our flight. I know she's getting over her divorce, but she also mentioned pain. I'm not sure if it was physical or something else entirely.

"Hi there." She turns and looks a bit startled to see me. She's been in her own little world; I doubt if she ever noticed Craig's or Jayce's presence earlier. She wipes her eyes quickly with the back of her hand.

"Hey." She sets down the tablet abruptly and looks over at the screen. "Sorry if I commandeered the TV today. I think I may have lost track of time."

"No worries at all. Everyone else has work to do. Are you feeling okay? You look a bit—down?"

"I'm fine. Sorry, just dealing with some stuff."

I move around the couch to sit down next to her. I think about giving her a hug but it doesn't seem like the right response. I'm so bad at this and so frustrated with myself for not knowing what to say to her. I can write a soundtrack for every moment we spend together, yet I can never find the right words.

"Want me to go get you some Tiramisu?" I discovered she's a major fan of desserts last night. I bet she'd get along very well with my mum in that regard.

Lucy gives me a slight chuckle. "I'm okay, I ate enough last night for about a week. But I appreciate the gesture. Tiramisu can make almost anything better." She offers a cheerless smile that tugs at my heart. She's wearing the same hopeless look I saw on the plane. All the joy from last night seems to have dissipated. "I should probably go do some work. I have a lot of research to do before I start writing this new book."

I don't believe she's actually going to do any work today, and the thought of her alone in her room just staring at old photos makes me ache. I tentatively place my hand over her arm, hoping this is the right gesture.

"Tell me about her. Your mum. Would you?"

Her gaze travels up to meet my eyes. There's a hint of surprise but it softens quickly.

"Umm, okay." She readjusts herself on the couch and I can't help but grin. She already looks more comfortable. "Well, it might sound weird, or maybe even a little pathetic, but she was my best friend. I know most girls go through phases of hating their moms, but I never did. We were always close, ever since I can remember."

"It doesn't sound weird at all, Luce. And if anyone's pathetic, it's me. I'm a grown man and I will gladly tell you my mum is my best friend in the world. I've even tried to get her to move in with me." She chuckles at this, and I wonder if she thinks I'm joking. It doesn't matter, I just love hearing the ring of her laughter. "You told me she was a chef, right? That's where your cooking skills are from?"

"Not a chef; a caterer. She was completely self-taught, but

everything she made was incredible. I'll never be able to cook like she did."

"What was her favorite thing to make?" Lucy smiles wide at this, and I love that she doesn't have to think for a moment about her answer.

"Chocolate chip cookies. She was addicted."

"Ahh, and now I see where the sweet tooth comes from."

"You caught me. I have a major weakness for sugar." She readjusts herself again and sinks deeper into the sofa. At the same moment Rowan pops up—I had no idea he'd been hiding under the couch—and nestles into her lap. "He must have heard us. He loves sugar too. I never should have introduced him to ice cream."

I'm feeling a bit brave right now, so I move before I have time to think. I stand up and reach for Lucy's hand.

"Come on. No more wallowing. Let's go make some biscuits." Her eyes narrow and she opens her mouth to correct me but I cut her off. "My mum would have a stroke if I used the C word. Please don't make me do it."

She just laughs and follows me into the kitchen. And then, almost under her breath, she says, "I hope we have enough butter."

"You KNOW, you might actually be the first guy to bake with me. Is that crazy? Jack would never help out in the kitchen."

"I feel honored. How many cups of flour did you say?" I'm trying to act confident, but I'm afraid it's quite obvious I have no clue what I'm doing. It's also difficult to keep my eyes off Lucy. I like to consider myself a feminist but there's something undeniably sexy about watching her in the kitchen. Maybe it's just seeing how comfortable she is in my home, how well she fits here. The term 'domestic bliss' pops into my head, but I jiggle it out before I start wanting things I know I can't have.

"Here, I got it." Lucy takes the paper bag out of my hands and gets to work. "Can you preheat the oven? And use this to spray the cookie sheet?" She hands me a bottle of coconut oil.

"He really never baked with you? Not once?" She swiftly shakes her head as she continues mixing the rest of the ingredients. It already smells amazing somehow. "I just have to say it. He didn't deserve you. Truly. I hope you didn't let him lick the batter. My mum always said that was a treat reserved for the chef." Lucy giggles as she flits around the kitchen, completely in her element. I grab the bag of chocolate chips and nudge her gently with my hip. "My turn. Tell me when." I tip over the bag until almost the entire contents have fallen into the bowl. Our eyes meet as I give her a look that says "Did I mess up?"

"Don't worry. You can never have too much chocolate." The spatula whirls and swirls by her hand at a slow and purposeful pace. I'm hypnotized by the movement. "And no, by the way. He wasn't a bad guy, really. But licking batter off the spoon? That was always reserved for me and Rowan. Your mom is very wise."

"Tell me to stop if I'm being an arse, but what really happened with him? You told me he left but, he really just . . . asked for a divorce? So suddenly? It doesn't make sense."

She's rolling the dough into little balls with her head down, pensively watching herself work. It seems like she's not going to answer so I grab some dough from the bowl and follow her lead. I need to do something to fill the silence.

"I'm sorry, Lucy. You deserve your privacy. Forget I said anything."

"It's okay. The way you say privacy is just precious. I can't be upset with you." She grins as our eyes meet. "And yeah, he —well, he had future plans that I couldn't be a part of anymore."

Well that's fucking cryptic. What kind of future plans couldn't include Lucy?

"Sorry, it's still tough for me to talk about. He kind of abandoned me, or at least that's how it felt."

"I'm really sorry to hear that, Luce. I know exactly how that feels." I pause, unsure if I should or even could explain but immediately decide to move on. "Well, like I said, he didn't deserve you."

She expels a small huff. I don't know what comes over me, but I ask, "Do you still love him?"

"Not even a little."

Relief floods my bloodstream enough to catch me off guard. It's ridiculous how much I care for this woman, how happy it makes me that she isn't still pining after her ex. Almost as ridiculous as how much I'm enjoying rolling balls of biscuit dough.

"Oh my God, your balls are *way* too big!"

A strangled, choking sound spews out of me and Lucy doubles over with laughter.

"Sorry, sorry. I didn't mean . . . I'm sure your balls are great. Small. The perfect size. Fuck. Please just—don't look at me." Lucy's laughter has converted to plump tears streaming down her face while she tries to hide behind her hands.

"It's fine, really. How would you erm, like me to make them smaller?" The smirk I'm attempting to hide is clearly visible and she swats me with a dish towel.

"Eh, screw it. They'll all just meld together and we can have one huge cookie. Then there's no way to count how many we actually eat!" She beams as she takes a little celebratory hop and it knocks the wind out of me. But then she truly takes my breath away when she raises the spatula with extra batter up toward my lips. "You've earned it."

Our eyes lock for just a moment. Her smile is so genuine, her eyes bright and clear. I'm utterly transfixed as I take a small bite. Lucy is feeding me and this small act feels momentous somehow. There's a level of intimacy here I've never felt before and I can sense my heartbeat quicken. I can't look away from her face.

But the spell is suddenly broken when Rowan jumps up to steal my prize.

"He can't eat this right?"

"No, but I saved some sans chocolate for him. Come here Row—get your Treat-O!"

Lucy insists I tell all the guys that there's freshly baked biscuits for them. After hearing Craig complain about her crying I don't believe he deserves to partake, but I wouldn't want to embarrass her by sharing what he said. Luckily Graham devours most of the massive biscuit before anyone else can get a second bite. There's a reason we call him the human garbage disposal. I only wish he wouldn't talk so much with his mouth full.

"Luce, come here love—let me kiss the chef!" He smothers her with a big hug and a sloppy kiss just centimeters away from her lips. The familiarity between them takes me by surprise. I knew when I met Lucy she needed a friend. Maybe it was silly to think I could fill that role. Graham's the obvious choice with his infectious positivity and keen social prowess—It's still unclear how I landed him as a mate when I'd truly never had one. I'm glad she has him though, even if their closeness sparks a bit of envy from me.

Graham finally finishes the last of the crumbles. "These

were delicious. But I think I need a chaser. Anyone up for some margaritas at Moonshadow?"

"Margs sound amazing right now. I need to take Row out before I go though. Does anyone know where he went?"

Jayce gets up and moves toward the patio, his face twisted into a grin. "I could tell you where he is, but I'd rather you see for yourself."

Lucy gives him a strange look but we all follow him outside. When we turn toward the pool it becomes clear what he meant. Rowan is in the middle of the pool, laying in the center of our pirate ship raft. Honestly, I have no idea how he got out there since we usually keep it out of the water. Everyone's cameras come out to snap a photo of the scene before us. Not only has Rowan made his way onto the raft, and into the water, but he's lying flat on his back, spread eagle with his front legs held straight up in the air. It honestly looks like he's trying to block the sun from his eyes.

"He looks like a movie star!" Preston chuckles.

"Can someone get the pup some sunnies?" Graham reaches to grab a pair off Jayce's head.

Lucy's face is gleaming with pride. "Nice job, Row! You're such a good pirate!"

Watching Lucy and the guys get ready to go out gives me a sharp pang of jealousy. The joy I felt from last night still lingers but I know better than to expect that sort of luck two days in a row. Lucy hasn't made a single remark about my freak-out at Nobu. She probably thinks it was a fluke, and I'd prefer to keep it that way.

I tell them all I have too much to work on so I'll be staying behind, and offer to walk Rowan so they don't have to rush home. The guys never expected me to join them. Actually, they'd be shocked if I said I was coming. We may not discuss my anxiety or anything to do with where it stems from, and they have no idea what I went through as a child, but they've all seen me go mute, freeze completely around new people. They've seen the worst of it, when it's happened during important meetings, all the times Graham's had to save the day.

No. They're not wondering why I'm staying behind. They'd prefer it this way.

But Lucy doesn't understand why I'm not coming. I can see it in the confused tilt of her chin. I wish I could explain it to her, but more so I wish I didn't have to. I wish I could just push everything in my past down so deep, that I could toss every fear aside and jump in the car with them. Suddenly I feel like that little boy again, terrified and alone. I need to get back to the piano.

I catch Lucy's gaze right before she closes the door, her disappointment on display. And then they're gone.

14

• • •

Lucy

AFTER SPENDING ALMOST four hundred dollars at various stores around LA today, I am officially ready to start preparing our sushi dinner. I've been determined to do this ever since our botched night at Nobu last week. No one should ever go a year without this Japanese delight.

Have I ever even attempted to make sushi before? Absolutely not. I never thought I'd try surfing either, so I guess this is the new Lucy, the one who's already accustomed to failure, the one who says "why the fuck not?"

"Need any help in here?" Adamma pops her head into the kitchen. I'm so happy she's here. Having another woman in the house is great on its own, but I also just really enjoy her company. She's fucking hilarious.

"I think I'm almost done. I'm having some issues cutting though. I guess that guy had a point when he said I'd need a special knife . . ." I show her what I'm struggling with. "Maybe handrolls will work?"

She chokes out a laugh—obviously, my presentation looks

fairly pathetic. But she helps me grab some more plates to put everything on before bringing it out to the table on the patio.

I will never get sick of this view. The beautiful rock formations right below us, the waves crashing so close I can hear every splash, the smell of salt and citrus and jasmine permeating the air all around us. The food might be a failure but the atmosphere is better than any five star restaurant.

"Lucy, my dinner feels a bit . . . flaccid." Craig is waving his sushi around in a motion I find distasteful.

"Tastes good to me!" Graham shoves a huge piece in his mouth and continues talking even though no one can understand him. It sounds like it's complimentary, and I'm tempted to get up and give him a hug.

"Sorry it's not really staying together. It's my first time and I think I must have messed up the rice, and the seaweed just kept breaking and the knives weren't sharp enough and—"

"Lucy, it's delicious. Stop apologizing. What's the sauce on this one?" Henry points to the mango, serrano and salmon roll.

"Thanks. It's a yuzu vinaigrette—citrus basically, I'm obsessed with the flavor. If you want more I made a huge batch in the fridge. Oh, and I made yuzu hot sauce as well if anyone wants some."

"Yuzu, eh? Is that why our fridge is always full of those sparkling yuzu coconut waters?" Henry asks.

I shrug, because yes, I'm obsessed with all things yuzu.

I look around to see everyone struggling with the chopsticks. "Maybe it's just easier to eat it like a poke bowl? Does anyone want me to make a plate like that?"

"Eat woman, stop obsessing." Graham is still talking with food in his mouth, clearly enjoying himself. "It might not look like sushi but it tastes amazing. Craig, if the flaccid roll is making you insecure, I'll be happy to eat yours."

I'll admit that even though the presentation isn't up to my standard, it does taste good.

Adamma gets up from the table and strides over to me.

"Luce, will you come into the kitchen with me for a sec?"

I follow her toward the house in silence and she turns to me the second we shut the door.

"I have an idea, just roll with it okay?" Adamma's eyes are so full of mischief I start feeling energized even though I'm completely in the dark. She tells me to start making one more roll as she heads up the stairs.

Adamma comes back with something shiny in her hands and I throw her a very confused expression.

"Step aside Luce, I have a sushi roll to . . . roll." She gives a quick shrug and gets to work, adding her mystery ingredient to a perfect layer of rice. She even adds a drizzle of yuzu and I raise a brow at her. "What? I don't want it to be bland."

It takes a while to get our faces zipped up, but as soon as we're able to control the laughter, we bring the plate outside and Adamma hands it to Craig.

"Here, I showed Luce a trick to get the hand roll nice and tight. We made this just for you." She winks back at me and it takes every ounce of control to keep a straight face.

Craig seems pleased and lifts it to take a bite. You can clearly see the stages of his facial expression change with each chew. It starts out slightly pompous, pleased that we tried to appease him, then the confusion settles, wondering what the hell he's eating, and when he finally drops the roll and pulls out a condom from in between the rice, his face is one hundred percent fury.

"Now *that* looks pretty flaccid." Adamma delivers the punchline and everyone at the table starts to roar.

Craig clearly does not appreciate the joke. "You're disgusting! What the fuck is wrong with you!?" Craig stands up and moves toward Adamma, but Preston and Graham both rise swiftly to block him from getting any further.

"Take a fucking joke, mate. It's just a rubber." Graham gives him a light but meaningful shove to the chest.

"You fucking bitch!" He turns toward me now. "Both of you can suck my dick."

Henry doesn't speak but he moves like lightning. In a matter of seconds he's out of his chair, grabbing Craig by the back of his shirt and dragging him around the corner to the other side of the house. We're all silent, hoping to hear what's going on with them but none of us can make out the words until Craig starts yelling.

We all run over to see what happened and find Henry leaning over Craig with a knee pressed to his chest, pinning him down.

Henry's panting, his eyes filled with rage. Suddenly he looks larger, taller, almost feral. His muscles are taut and his eyes are dark as night as he stares down at Craig, no hint of remorse in his face.

I am . . . so turned on right now. Oh my God, what is wrong with me!? I try to look away but he's like the damn sun and the gravitational pull has me helpless.

He finally looks up and sees me staring. His face changes immediately and now all I see is shame. He steps away from Craig before looking back down at him.

"You're done. Go pack your shit and get out of my house. *Now.*"

"Well, that was dramatic." Adamma raises her brows at me. "I guess pranks are officially off limits in this house."

HAAAM are helping Craig pack while Adamma and I sit by the pool to avoid any further man-drama. I think I heard Henry say he'd take care of cleaning up dinner. I wanted to talk to him, figure out what happened, but I could tell he wanted to be alone.

I'm feeling embarrassed about the thoughts in my head seeing Henry so . . . wild. I didn't even know that was something I liked. God knows Jack wasn't the bar fight kind of guy. But I can't get Henry's predatory eyes out of my mind. I feel my heartbeat speed up just thinking about it.

Luckily, Adamma brings me back to reality.

"So, why were you being so hard on yourself about dinner? That was ambitious, and you said you've never even tried to make sushi before, right?" She looks at me incredulously.

"Well, Henry and I went to Nobu the other night, and he told me how much he loves sushi, and then the dinner kind of . . . didn't happen, so I was just trying to make it up to him, I guess?"

What I don't mention is that it's also a thank you for him baking cookies with me the other day. For how he wanted to do something nice for me. For how he looked at me when I let him lick the spatula . . .

"What do you mean, the dinner didn't happen?"

"Well, I don't know, actually. I haven't really talked to him about it either, he just kind of froze up? So we left." It feels like a betrayal telling her this and I immediately feel the guilt rising in my belly. I should change the subject.

"Oh, well that's not surprising. He doesn't exactly get out much."

"What do you mean? Because of work?" The quick pang of guilt has now changed into curiosity as I remember him passing on our margarita outing a few days ago. Maybe Adamma knows more than I thought.

"Hey, erm, mind if I interrupt for a moment?" Henry appears beside me and I say a silent prayer that he didn't hear us talking about him.

"Hi." I smile up at him and there's a brief moment of silence. He looks so handsome in the moonlight.

"Thank you for a lovely dinner, yet again. Sorry about the, erm . . . after-meal entertainment." He winces at his own joke—adorable. "It really was delicious; I hope Craig didn't ruin the night for you."

"Are you kidding?" Adamma cuts in. "That was the most exciting meal I've ever had in this house. What the hell did he say to you?"

Henry looks pensive but doesn't respond.

"I just hope you're okay," I jump in, trying to ease the tension. "You looked pretty upset."

"I'm fine, really, just embarrassed. He should never have spoken to either of you like that. And I refuse to work with someone who treats people that way."

He pauses, looks like he's deciding if he wants to say more. "Luce, your meal tonight was wonderful, truly, but I was, erm, hoping we could try getting sushi out again, a different place of course."

"Sure. Of course, any time. I don't think I want to try making it again. Honestly, once was enough."

"Great, let's plan on Friday. We'll go at six." Another pause. I wonder how often he plans what he wants to say like this. "Looking forward to it—Luzu." He winks and disappears as quickly as he materialized before.

Adamma looks mystified. "Umm . . . *Luzu*? Did he just ask you on a date? *And* give you a nickname? Are you guys *dating*?"

"No! Of course not. We're just friends grabbing dinner."

She clearly thinks I'm delusional from the look she gives me.

I know the wide smile I'm sporting betrays me but I tell her, "Seriously, just friends, I swear."

15

• • •

Henry

I HAVEN'T LEFT the studio since I got home from surfing with Graham this morning. I know it's been hours from the stiff muscles in my neck and the numbness in my toes. I really need to get outside.

Graham is usually the one person I don't avoid, but today, I needed space. He wouldn't shut up about what happened last night, and while I typically can tell him anything, I don't want him or anyone else to know what Craig said to me.

As soon as I had him away from the group, he started in. "There's too many damn women in this house."

"Watch it, Craig."

"Why the hell is she still here? She's never gonna fuck you, you socially awkward bitch."

I was fuming. I could actually feel the rush of blood, feel my face heat up. My fists clenched, nails digging so hard into my palms I may have drawn blood. I wanted to hit him. I wanted to knock him unconscious and barrel into him until he was unrecognizable.

I tried to compose myself. I hadn't had a physical altercation in years. When I was young it was more difficult to control my anger. When words were rarely available to me, my fists always were. I'm not proud of the times I hurt people, no matter how much I felt they deserved it.

My dad thought channeling my anger was the key. He started me on boxing lessons and before long I was training with a personal coach. Being Chief Constable meant he had unlimited resources for that sort of thing. His friends loved coming by the house to test my skills.

His plan backfired though. Learning to fight just made me stronger, better. It didn't stop arseholes from provoking me. Fucking bullies.

But I wasn't a kid anymore. It didn't matter what Craig deserved. So I kept repeating the same words in my head: I'm not going to hit him. I'm not going to hit him. I'm not going to *fucking* hit him.

"That damaged bitch isn't worth it anyway."

The vision came into focus, of how easy it would be to knock him out, how good it would feel to make contact, to see him go down from one hit. But then I remembered how valuable my hands were these days.

His eyes tracked the tight fists at my side and his scowl looked ready for a fight as he stalked closer.

"Don't," *I warned.*

He snickered before throwing a punch that I dodged easily. Pitiful. He brought up both hands to shove me instead.

As soon as he made contact I saw the flash of fear in his eyes. He knows I'm twice as strong as he is. Maybe he thought I'm as feeble as I sound, but I learned to fight a long time ago.

Before he could throw anything else at me I charged forward with just enough effort to flip him on his back. He hit the ground with an angry grunt and I held him down with my knee before he could get back up.

"You're a feckless moron, Craig. You really want to fight me?"

"And you're fucking pathetic. You're not better than all of us, you fucking pussy. Get the hell off of me!"

I was thinking how good it would feel to let him up, let him try and fight, make him bleed. Then I saw Lucy staring at me and immediately stepped away.

I HEAD to my room to change into some trunks. The weather has been especially warm lately and a night swim sounds like the perfect activity to get last night's drama out of my head.

When I make my way outside I find the pool is already occupied.

Lucy and Rowan are lying on the pirate raft together. Cuddling. From what I can see, both of their eyes look closed. His head is tucked into her chest as he sprawls out on his back while she's curled around him. Are they *sleeping* out here? I check my watch and see it's only just after nine.

I should say something; I feel like a voyeur just standing here watching them. But my brain is distracted by Lucy's skin glowing in the pool lights. She has on a pale-yellow bikini that reminds me of butter. It makes her skin look even smoother, her hair extra golden.

"Henry?" Shit, how long has she seen me staring? I must look like a creep.

"So sorry, didn't realize anyone was out here." I turn back toward the house but she calls after me.

"Wait. Did you want to swim? I think the pool's big enough

for us to share." She's mocking me. "Or if not, Row and I can go . . ."

"Of course, of course. Sorry, just thought you may want some privacy." I make my way back to the pool before sitting down on the edge.

"I will never get tired of hearing you say privacy. You're so proper Henry, it's adorable." Adorable. Do I want her to think I'm adorable? "Aren't you gonna get in?"

I lower myself into the pool and go all the way under. Beneath the water I see Lucy's fingers swaying back and forth. There's a rhythm to the movement and I wonder what tune is playing in her head.

Could it be one of mine?

I swim toward the raft ready to pop up beside her but . . . proper? Too proper? *Don't overthink it.*

I dive under the pirate ship before propelling up to flip the raft, throwing Lucy and Rowan overboard.

"Ahhhh, Henry!" *Splash.* "No, no, no, Row I'm fine—I'm *fine*! Get away from my bikini strings. You will not get me this time!"

Lucy's hands and Rowan's paws seem to be caught in a battle of wills. I haven't a clue what I'm witnessing right now. She quickly wrestles him into submission and plops him onto the flamingo raft. And then we're treated to a massive spritz of water as he shakes himself dry.

My arms are covering my face as I attempt to block the spray so I don't see Lucy charging until she's right in front of me, shoving me into the water.

Her hands press down on my shoulders as she attempts to drown me. It's cute that she thinks she can overpower me when I'm more than twice her size. I easily resist going under as I wrap my arms around her middle to hold her in place. She fits perfectly here. It takes more effort than I care to admit not to slide my hands lower.

"Hey, not fair." She swats at me but my hold keeps her body still, and flush against my chest. My temperature rises steadily with each second we're connected. I'm struck with her scent, sweet like a sugary concoction with a touch of citrus. I wonder if she always smells like dessert. "How am I supposed to get you back when I can't even move?"

Now she's kicking her feet, well, trying. She's splashing herself more than her intended target.

"Lucy, stop resisting!"

"Stop squeezing me so hard!"

"You're kicking me!"

"I'll stop when you let me go!"

I loosen my grip on her and she immediately shoves me down again, this time kicking up her legs for more leverage. I let her push me under just once, feeling the need to reward her efforts, but I get her back right away, easily dunking her below the surface.

"Henry!" She's giggling as she simultaneously curses at me and spits out water. Distracted by her laughter, I miss her charging again, trying to submerge me once more.

This time I wrap one arm around her legs and the other around her back, cradling her against me like a baby. She's locked in place, going nowhere. I expect her to resist some more but she just leans into me, her head against my chest.

"This feels kind of nice actually. It's like I'm weightless." She dips her head back so her hair floats around her in the water like a fluid crown. Her grin has me awestruck. She looks drunk on life.

"You feel kind of nice." I definitely did not mean to say that aloud. *Shit.* She picks up her head and turns toward me, our noses almost touching. I should release her but I feel frozen in place. I don't want to let her go.

"Ahhh!"

"*Oh my God*, Row!" Lucy's dog just leapt from the raft, directly onto her lap. I'm certain his claws made permanent grooves on my chest. She moves out of my arms and grabs him forcefully, dragging him out of the pool. "Bad boy! Henry is our friend. I was fine!"

I'm in mild shock. Just seconds ago I had Lucy wrapped in my arms. "Erm, what just happened?"

"I'm sorry, Henry. He's not used to seeing me that close to anyone." She looks down at her feet like she's ashamed. "He must have thought I was in danger. I'm so sorry. I should go dry him off before your whole house smells like wet-dog."

"It's no problem. Thanks for the, erm, swim."

16

. . .

Lucy

"GRAHAM! *Graa-haam*! Can you come down here? I need help with this zipper. I don't know how but my boobs have somehow grown or something."

I'm not sure exactly why I chose to wear a real dress for the first time in months. Maybe it's all the beautiful women in LA, maybe it's Adamma's comment about this being a date, but I felt the need to up the ante just a bit with my wardrobe tonight. And now I remember why I always wear things that are loose and stretchy and easy. I got the zipper halfway up my back and now it's stuck with both of my arms twisted in knots trying to work it up.

I don't remember this dress being so tight, though it has been over a year since I've worn it. The soft yellow color is not something everyone can pull off, but I love the way it plays off my honeyed hair and peachy complexion. Plus the material's just thick enough to hug every curve and not be remotely see-through, which is especially good since I can't wear a bra with it.

"Graham! Where *are* you?" I yell up the stairs one more time.

"Hi. Do you need something?" Henry strolls into the living room as I'm waddling around trying to keep my dress from falling down.

And he looks *good.*

He's in dark jeans, a crisp blue shirt that brings out his eyes. My eyes, unfortunately, are drawn to the gleaming H on his Hermes belt.

Shake it off, Luce.

"Hey. Yeah, I'm just having a little trouble zipping up my dress. Do you mind? I don't know where Graham is."

"Well, you're definitely yelling in the wrong direction. He's been downstairs working for a few hours now. But I'm happy to be of service."

He reaches his hand out as if to say "turn around now" so I follow suit. This really shouldn't be a big deal but whenever I get this close to Henry my whole body warms up. Ever since I woke up wrapped around him I can't get these thoughts out of my head. I feel his knuckles against my bare back as he reaches for the zipper. He stands so close I can feel the warmth coming off of his body, and it takes effort not to sigh. His skin feels rough against my own, and I can't stop the image of both of his hands splayed against my bare back from entering my mind. He places a hand at the nape of my neck to scoop my hair over a shoulder and I shiver at the touch. My mind has now gone from his hands on my back to him tugging on my hair—I can hear my breath catch. The vision is blinding.

Henry clears his throat as he removes his hands from me. "All set, then. How'd I do?"

I think pretty well, considering I've dreamed up an entire fantasy in the last twenty seconds. I banish the image and turn toward him, smoothing down the sides of my dress. "Great, I think. I just hope this thing still fits me, I don't remember it being this difficult to put on."

"Wow." He doesn't say anything else, just holds his gaze toward me. I guess it's still a good dress.

"Shall we?" He extends his hand toward the door and for a second, I wonder if this *is* a date.

Once we're seated at Sugarfish all I can think about is what's going to happen when we order. Was Nobu just a fluke? Does he always get like that at restaurants? Should I just assume I'm going to order for both of us? We haven't talked about what happened the other night, and I don't really want to bring it up. He's made enough comments about his way with words that I know he has some anxiety about public situations. But why make him revisit something he finds embarrassing? It doesn't bother me and he shouldn't have to feel bad about himself, ever.

The waiter approaches and pours us each a glass of water. I'm trying to catch Henry's eye so we can gameplan but he just smiles at me.

"We'll both have the Nozawa, and a bottle of Sauv Blanc. Thank you." The waiter gives a slight bow and walks away with our menus.

Huh, it's almost like he rehearsed that. I didn't miss that he never moved his eyes from me when he spoke, but the look on his face screams *proud* so I'm happy for him.

"It's a prix fixe menu. Don't worry, you'll love it. It's one of the few places I've actually been before." He pauses but has a strained look on his face. "I erm, I just have to say—your dress is —yellow looks great on you."

The way he stumbles over his words makes me smile. "Thanks, it's my favorite color."

"Sunny." The word sounds melodic as it escapes his lips. And then he starts singing something else under this breath.

"What was that, Henry?"

"Ah, sorry. I can get lost in my head sometimes. You just reminded me of a song, *Sunny*. Do you know it?" He hums quietly but I don't recognize the tune. I can make out some lines though, specifically: *my life was filled with rain*, and then *now the dark days are gone, and the bright days are here*. It sounds like something I'd like to listen to.

As I shake my head he promises to play it for me later. "You'll love it. It's the perfect song for you."

"Oh really? Why's that?"

"Because you remind me of sunshine."

We talk about Henry's current project, *The Dragon Wars*, over edamame, and transition to some of his older stuff that I'm eager to learn about when the tuna sashimi arrives. But once the sushi courses start coming, he says he wants to talk about me.

"Really, my life is not very interesting. You already know anything of significance. Wow, the rice is warm. This is incredible." I make a note to never attempt sushi at home again, I just want to become a regular at Sugarfish.

"I think yours was just as delicious." He takes a small sip of wine. I've been noticing he's not a big drinker compared to the rest of the house. "Tell me about your new book. You said you've been writing a bit these last few days."

"Okay. Still very early stages. I barely have an outline to be honest. It's kind of a *Beauty and the Beast* retelling, except backward, I think?"

"So, the female's the beast? How feminist of you."

"No, no I'm thinking she goes to the mansion on purpose,

maybe agrees to an engagement or something, maybe it's arranged by her parents? Like the end of a typical fairy tale but it's the beginning of the story instead."

"A reverse fairy tale. Sounds interesting. Can you tell me more? I need details if I'm to write a song for it."

A song for *my* book? Henry is like my own personal brand of swoon.

"Okay, so it seems like the perfect fairy tale romance, but then once she gets there, she slowly realizes he's a 'beast' and there's this secret room in the house that she's not allowed in but when she sneaks in there she finds this whole group of men that he works with . . . I don't know . . . maybe psychopaths? Serial killers? A cult? Actually, maybe vampires. I haven't really gotten that far. I just know I want it to be dark, no happily ever after for this one. I'm trying something new."

Woah, Luce, way to sell it. I better not ramble like this to my agent.

"Lucy, have we really been that cruel to you?"

"What? No, what do you mean?"

"Well, I'm no fairy tale expert but it sounds like you're unhappy with the current living situation and are taking it out on me in your book. Am I the beast in this scenario? Are you planning to kill me in your pages?"

He looks upset.

Shit.

I guess I've been mildly inspired by the house, but not from anything bad. I'm just tired of writing sappy love stories. It was so much easier when I was living in one.

Was I? Living in one? Sometimes I wonder if it was all in my head.

"I swear it's not about you. I think I just got the idea when Jayce told me I couldn't go in the basement because it was haunted. Really, it's all fiction. Nothing to do with you or HAAAM. You've all been so great to me. I would never—"

He beams. He was screwing with me? For a second I thought this was going to be a very uncomfortable evening.

"You will let me know how the story progresses, right? If the villain turns out to be an incredibly talented musician, you're going to have some serious explaining to do."

After a few laughs I feel the conversation lull. Of course Henry looks perfectly content, but it's just not in my nature to allow for silence.

"So the guys all told me how you collected them. You're like some musical hero, huh?"

"Hero? Why on earth would you think that?"

"Well, Jayce told me how you helped him from getting suspended, and Preston said he may never have graduated if you didn't encourage him to switch majors. You're like the Santa Claus of Juilliard."

Henry clears his throat, visibly uncomfortable, though I don't know why. I've only been complimenting him, right?

"Lucy, they may have exaggerated. I just needed help and they happened to be the people who joined my team. Really, I'm no hero."

"Oh, come on, don't be so modest! They worship you for everything you've done for them. You shouldn't downplay it like that, you're amaz—"

"Lucy, I'm not some savior. I didn't 'collect them' to help anyone but myself, okay? Jayce was clearly flunking out, but he had heaps of talent, so I made him an offer he couldn't refuse. Preston and Craig were never going to play professionally. I gave them jobs because I knew they'd have to say yes. They all may enjoy their work and the house I bought for us, but it doesn't mean I didn't use them, that I'm not still using them every day to get what I want. Please don't think I'm any better than I am. They owe me nothing."

He looks down, his face twisted in shame.

I shouldn't have brought this up; I had no idea it would upset him.

But I also don't fully believe him.

"What about Graham? He wasn't even in school. You really don't think you helped him?"

He starts to laugh, but it's joyless, self-deprecating.

"What do you know about Graham?" His tone is laced with something bitter. He's not asking out of curiosity. He thinks I'm clueless.

"I know you got him out of a bad situation. I know he's grateful."

"A bad situation? Graham was my dealer, Lucy. He got me weed and Xanax when my prescriptions ran out, and anything else he could find to help with my anxiety. I needed it to go to class, to get through school." He huffs out a long breath. "I could tell his life was not on a good path and, well, I knew he had a sharp tongue so when I got my first meeting with a film producer I asked for his help. I offered Graham my couch in exchange for him pretending to be my business partner. It was all a fucking lie because I couldn't meet with anyone on my own. But then the partnership just sort of, became real."

I guess Graham never told me all the details. This is more than unexpected. Henry's face is turned down and he's rubbing the heel of his hand between his eyes. Maybe he doesn't see it the same way HAAAM does, but he did help them. It was just more of a symbiotic relationship than they made it out to be.

"Graham loves you, and he loves the life he has *because* of you. He said you're like a brother to him. Does it really matter if it went both ways? Just because you got something out of it doesn't take away the good you did. Maybe you just haven't let yourself realize how much you helped him."

Henry blinks a few times but his expression only softens a little.

"That's . . . nice to hear, really. I guess things worked out well for both of us. I could tell he was in a bad place when we met. Honestly, I had no idea he could even play an instrument until I caught him practicing with one of my violins. We got lucky, both of us."

His eyes are swimming with memories, good or bad I can't tell.

Why do I always have to say everything I'm thinking? Maybe I can turn this around, lighten things up a bit. "Well, it's a good thing you're a musical genius. You're really carrying the team, aren't you?" I offer the widest smile I can, hoping to bust him out of this mood, but nothing changes.

"Henry, listen to me. There's nothing wrong with how things happened for you and HAAAM. I can tell you're uncomfortable and I'm sorry for bringing this up, but honestly, that doesn't make me think any less of you. If anything, I like you more. I mean, I can't trust someone who's really *that* good of a person, it's just not natural."

He fidgets with his chopsticks, then his wine glass. He finally looks up and smiles at me. "I think you might be that good of a person."

For a moment I'm not sure what to say. This feels like we're heading into deep conversation territory and I don't think that's something I can handle right now. Technically, I know this isn't a date. But when he smiles at me this way, it feels like one. Or maybe I'm clueless. The last time I went on a first date I was twenty-one.

"Aww, that's sweet, but grossly untrue. You obviously don't know about the time I stalked my favorite celebrity, tricked my way into his house and convinced him to take me out for sushi while I hired professionals to rob him blind."

He looks up at me and his lips twitch. "I knew it!"

Before I get to respond, two leggy women gliding by stop directly in front of our table.

"*Henryyyy*. I thought that was you." She turns back toward her friend and her eyes dance as she drops her voice, "This is the guy."

He stares up at the woman but doesn't say anything. I can see him trying to form a smile but it doesn't fully appear. I'd think they didn't know each other from his reaction, but she *clearly* knows him. Her perfect smile drops for just a second, the moment she realizes he isn't going to say anything. She catches herself almost immediately and her pearly whites are shining again.

She actually looks familiar to me, maybe she's an actress? Model? She must be, the way she's towering over us makes me think she's at least five foot ten. I can't even imagine what the world looks like from up there. Her dark auburn hair falls down to her waist, the color being one of many things that doesn't look quite real on her. I want to hate her but she's freaking gorgeous.

"Rebecca, but you obviously remember, right Hen?" Hen? Who the hell calls him *Hen*? She turns back and whispers to her friend again. "I told you, strong silent type. I love when I can make a guy that nervous."

He looks up at her and nods, but still doesn't speak. He turns his head toward me, clearly not wanting to engage in further conversation, but she places a hand on his shoulder and bends slightly, offering a nice view of her cleavage.

"That was *such* a fun night. I never do that, really, but I just couldn't help myself. We should hang out again soon." She leans down further when she says this part, with a very fake giggle. Okay, they definitely slept together. I could not feel more uncomfortable.

He briefly looks at her and offers a tight, half smile before turning back to me. He's focusing on me the same way they tell dancers to focus on a single point when spinning, something to tether you to a spot so as not to get dizzy or off balance. He isn't moving at all but I can see the muscles on his forearms go taut, the only indicator that maybe he's feeling the same anxiety from the other night. *Does* she make him nervous?

"See you soon, Hen." The women finally walk away with a dramatic swish of their hips and Henry still hasn't taken his eyes off my face. I feel like an anchor, holding him in place, but I don't understand it. After a few more beats pass, he takes a long drink of water and speaks again.

"So, want anything else or should I get the check?"

"Henry, the car's this way, remember? We valeted."

"Sorry Luce, need to make a quick stop. Just wait here, I'll be right back."

This is weird. Neither of us have mentioned the run-in with Rebecca. He seems fine now, and I don't really feel comfortable badgering him about his love life. But now he's acting strange, speed walking down the street and telling me to just wait around for him.

I see him stop less than two blocks away and fist bump some guy standing on the sidewalk. Henry pulls out some cash from his pocket and hands it over while the mystery man passes him a large white paper bag.

Is this some sort of weird Beverly Hills drug deal? What the hell am I getting involved in?

I wait until we're in the car, several questions ready to slip out of my mouth. "Okay, are you going to explain any of that?"

"What?"

"What was that secret meeting about?"

He looks over at me and smirks. "Wouldn't you like to know."

"Henry, come on. Since when are you so secretive? Tell me."

"A man needs secrets." He raises an eyebrow at me, clearly amused with my impatience. But then he clears his throat softly, his levity falling a bit. "I'm sorry about earlier. That was rude of me. I should have introduced you or something. I just, I didn't remember her and—sometimes I have trouble."

"It's okay, you have nothing to apologize for. Although I think *she* was disappointed. Who knew *Hen* was such a ladies man." I keep my tone light, making sure to keep any hint of jealousy hidden well.

He scoffs, definitely not the reaction I was expecting, and doesn't say another word. How many times am I going to kill the vibe tonight?

"So, I was thinking," I say. "The sushi we had tonight, it's probably jealous." He lifts a brow, eyeing me suspiciously. "I mean, don't you think it's jealous of our pasta from last week? We made up a whole song for that meal. I think it's only fair..." I trail off, hoping he gets the hint and wants to help me liven the mood.

"By all means, Luce. Let's hear what you've got."

That might have backfired. I may be a writer for a living, but songs and rhymes aren't exactly in my wheelhouse. I guess there's no time like the present to completely embarrass myself. If it gets Henry smiling again, I'll be happy to take the bullet.

"Okay, Grammy, Tony, Emmy winner. Sure, *I'll* come up with the song."

"Don't forget the Oscars."

"Oh, I could never. What a coincidence that EGOT starts with ego . . ."

He smacks my leg, but he's grinning.

"I got this, feel free to harmonize or whatever." I let out a long breath.

"*Sushi, sushi, sushi*
You make me feel all mushy

Oh God, I think I'm singing the dreidel song. Help!" His laugh is lush and throaty, and damn sexy if I'm being honest. "Seriously Henry, stop laughing and give me a new melody. This is stuck in my head now."

He comes up with a tune quickly and I get my head back in the song game. His singing voice is deep and—annoyingly—beautiful. I would definitely listen to an album of him singing. Hell, I'd listen to him humming along to his movie scores.

"Okay, I think I got it!

Tuna, salmon, all the maki
Love that you are not too talky
Roll it up with rice so sticky
All the toppings, I'm not picky
I love sushi, yes I do—"

"*And don't forget the yuzu*!"

"*Henry*! That was perfect! It's like you're reading my mind." Even though I was actually going to go with the old standby: "How about you," his version is *way* better.

"Okay, now we need a chorus, or was that the chorus? No, let's not overthink this. How about, umm . . .

I love the way you roll
I'm losing all control
I love the way you roll
I feel it in my soul"

We're at a stop light and he looks over at me, examining every inch of my face. "You, Luzu, are a natural born songwriter. Seriously, I think you've chosen the wrong career. What can I do to get you on my team?"

"I'm on your team, Henry. Good luck trying to get rid of me."

As soon as we get home, Henry approaches me with a mischievous glint in his eye. His mood rebounded on the ride home, but now his smile is different, conspicuous. He tells me he has a surprise for me, but I have to go put on pajamas first. This could really go in a *lot* of different directions, but he seems excited, so I decide to roll with it and go slip into some joggers and my favorite *Blissfully Bookish* T-shirt.

When I get back to the living room he directs me to sit on the couch, covers me in a plush blanket that's extra toasty and just out of the dryer and presents me with the paper bag he picked up from his earlier rendezvous. Not a drug deal then, whew.

"Open it." I pull out a plastic container filled with something that resembles cake. I'm intrigued and give him a quick smile.

"Thanks."

"Why aren't you more excited? This is the dessert Preston was talking about the other day, the butter cake. It's famous."

"Thank you. I love it, just surprised, I guess."

"Excuse me, was it not just last week you said, and I quote,

'Dessert is the best part of every meal. But it's a million times better when you can eat it in your PJs, on the couch, wrapped in a warm fluffy blanket'?"

He remembered that? He had no recollection of a woman whom he's definitely hooked up with, but he remembers me rambling on about how much I like to eat cupcakes on the couch? He looks so defeated I can't help but laugh. He really put in some effort to plan this for me, and it's so sweet. I wonder if this is why we went to a restaurant over thirty minutes away. I take a *very* large bite of cake.

It might be the best thing I've ever put in my mouth.

"Okay, this *is* amazing." Now he looks satisfied, happy with the outcome of his little surprise. "Well, are you gonna join me? PJ up and grab a spoon, Maestro."

"I do love it when you call me that." He doesn't change out of his jeans and button down—he's always so perfectly polished—but he settles in next to me and grabs the spoon out of my hand. I guess if I have to share, I'm glad it's with him.

"Do you think we could give Rowan a bite?" Henry's sitting so close to me he barely moves when he nudges my shoulder questioning.

"Sure, he loves cake. Just a tiny piece though—he will definitely not appreciate the gooey perfection."

"Row Boat, come here mate!"

"I'm sorry, what did you just call him?" I've never referred to my dog as anything but Rowan, Row, pal, or good boy—because he is.

"Row Boat, he loves it. It's his favorite song." Rowan has appeared from wherever he was hiding and is perched on Henry's lap, happily licking every morsel he can from his fingers. Suddenly, I'm envisioning *myself* on Henry's knee, languidly lapping at his sugarcoated digits, those long dexterous fingers that create such beautiful sounds . . .

"Luce? You okay? I swear he loves the tune." I quickly snap myself back to reality. It's getting more and more difficult to focus around Henry.

"What do you mean he loves it? Are you singing to him now?"

"Singing? Don't be silly. That's reserved for the dinner table—or my car." He winks. "I play it for him on the piano. Never seen him so entranced."

"Okay, I have to see this."

Without a word, Henry moves over to the glossy black piano by the window, and to my shock and awe, he's right. I can't tell if it's the song itself or the sound of the piano, but I've never seen Rowan sit so perfectly still for this long, gazing at Henry like he's covered in peanut butter and string cheese.

Henry stays at the piano and plays some less childish music for me as I savor my scrumptious dessert. I'll never tire of hearing him. When he plays the *Moonlight Sonata* I go completely still by the third movement. And he somehow smoothly transitions from Beethoven to *Somewhere Over the Rainbow*, apparently remembering our conversation from the plane. His hands on those keys puts me in an actual trance.

I think I'll have to append my earlier statement. Dessert is best in PJs, on the couch, wrapped in a warm fluffy blanket, *while* listening to Henry at the piano.

"Lucy, there you are! I've been looking for you all night."

"Hey, Jayce—we just got back from dinner. What's up? You look a little unhinged."

"Crystal's coming over—like right now. Can you get a swimsuit on? And bring Rowan outside. Hurry."

"What the . . . can you slow down? What's going on, and who's Crystal?" Jayce is always the cool, calm and collected one of the house, the one with swagger. This nervous, frantic energy he's giving off is completely foreign to me.

"Crystal. From the pet store! I asked her out but she was all shy about it and said she wasn't sure because she doesn't know me at all. So I told her we were having a pool party. And that our dog would be there."

"I'm sorry—*our* dog?" I say as Henry starts to laugh, still sitting at the piano, evidently not getting involved in this conversation.

"I know, I know. Yell at me about it later though, okay? Please just, do this for me? I'll make it up to you I swear—anything you want. I need you. If it's all dudes she's gonna think I'm a creep."

I doubt I'll ever call in a favor, but I would love to have something hanging over him, and I'm not exactly tired—it's just after nine.

"Fine—but she better give me a discount."

Crystal is sweet, way too sweet for Jayce, and he knows it. It's kind of hilarious watching him change into a different person while he tries to impress her. She seems more interested in Rowan.

Our "pool party" consists of six people—not exactly a rager. Graham, Crystal and I are sharing the pirate ship. When I asked her if she wanted to share with me I could tell she was excited to create a little distance from Jayce, but then Graham jumped on us and snuggled up next to me and it was obvious she wasn't sure if she made the right decision. Now he has his arm wrapped around my shoulders, our bodies flush together from hip to heel, and she's as far to the other side as she can get.

Henry, Preston and Jayce are sitting along the pool's edge, Jayce holding on to Rowan as best he can, claiming him as his own, with his foot lightly balancing on our raft so he can control the direction we float in. I wish Adamma were here but

Preston said she has to get up at four am every day this week for work, so she hasn't been staying over.

"Let's play a game." Jayce is rubbing his hands together like he's about to share his bank robbery plan with us. "Crystal, you know you're at a house full of professional musicians, right?"

"I think you may have mentioned what you do once or twice." She flashes a coy smile. I know she's still a bit uncomfortable with our group, but she's clearly crushing on Jayce.

Graham leans even closer to me to whisper in my ear, "Get ready, he does this with every girl, and somehow it fucking *works*."

"So, if you could be any instrument, what would you be? Obviously something beautiful." Jayce bites at the corner of his lip as his eyes rake over her body. Could he be any more obvious right now? "And, how would I play you?"

Okay, yep, he can.

And Graham's right, it's working, because the blush on Crystal's face is visible in nothing but the pool lights and her smile is wider than the 405. Unbelievable.

"What's it gonna be, gorgeous?" Jayce almost purrs.

"Umm . . . maybe a piano?" The poor girl looks so embarrassed but Jayce has not taken his eyes off of her. He's smooth.

"Oh, so you like to be tickled, huh?"

"Maybe this is more of a private conversation for you two?" I hate to ruin the moment but it's getting a little weird for me. Graham pinches my thigh before telling me Jayce will get me back for that one.

"Actually, Lucy, why don't you answer the question too. You've been here a couple weeks, seen all the instruments in the house. Which one would you be?"

Graham was right, Jayce's tone makes this question feel accusatory somehow. I don't love it.

I glare right back at him. "I'm not sure, too many to choose from."

Graham leans in again so no one else can hear him. "You'd be a flute, darling. I'm sure you'd like to feel Henry's flutter tonguing." I elbow him in the ribs as my jaw drops open. What is flutter tonguing? I need to remind myself to google that later. "How about a trumpet? Would you prefer to be sucked or blown?"

"Graham! Oh my God!" I shove him with all my might but he barely moves off the raft. I try pushing harder and we start wrestling with our arms like children. I'm determined to get him off this raft but his body is like a brick wall.

"Lucy, stop flirting and give us an answer. Unless you want me to pick for you—"

"She'd be a harp." Henry cuts Jayce off, and it's one of the first things he's said since we came out here.

I stop pushing at Graham and look toward Henry, his eyes sparkling as he stares at me intensely. I try but I can't look away. My gaze moves down to his mouth. I cannot stop thinking about whatever flutter tonguing is.

Henry gets up and tells everyone he needs to do some work. He's always disappearing to the basement. I think about following him, thanking him again for the butter cake—I can still taste it on my lips. Why a harp? I can't think of any obvious pun.

"Graham, what's the sexual innuendo for a harp?"

He frowns as his brows pinch together. "I honestly have no idea."

. . .

I TRIED WAITING a reasonable amount of time before saying I was sleepy and following Henry. I'm not sure why, but I didn't want anyone to think I was going after him, which I am. As I head down the stairs part of me wonders if I'm imposing on his private space by coming down uninvited, though he never seems to mind when I do.

"Hey, Maestro, I hope I'm not intruding."

His hands stay on the piano but he turns toward me. "Luce, you are never intruding. I love having you down here with me." He smiles shyly like his own words surprised him.

"I just wanted to thank you again. For dinner, and really dessert. That was so sweet of you."

"I just hope it wasn't too sweet. I know you prefer your desserts to be well-balanced."

I laugh at the pun; he must be remembering my addition of smoked sea salt to our cookies the other day. I take a seat on the futon and he makes a full turn on the bench to face me.

"It was perfect. So gooey!" I make a lip smacking motion and immediately regret it. "So, you kind of left abruptly tonight. Not a fan of pool parties?"

"I'm not really great with new people. I just thought you'd all be more comfortable without me."

It's now that I realize he never said a word to Crystal. He sort of had a deer-in-headlights thing going on when we were all introduced. Not very different from the night we went to Nobu and the waitress tried talking to him. It isn't strange to be shy around new people, but I know he's not always like that.

"Why not with me?"

"Hmm?"

"I can tell you're shy, which is completely fine by the way. Sometimes I wish I was shy, just to get myself to shut up." *Like right now, this very moment.* "But when we met, you didn't seem shy at all, and you didn't know me."

His eyes find mine but they look different, warmer; they're starting to glisten. I can't tell if he's about to cry or come wrap me up in a bear hug. Neither happens.

"You're special."

I wait for the punchline but nothing comes. Then I notice his subtle nod, like he's doubling down on the statement, leaving no room for discussion. There's a booming "no, I'm not" crawling its way up my throat, begging my mouth for release, but I suppress it with the might of a lion.

Take the compliment. Don't argue. Don't ask why.

I'm not sure what to say after that. His simple words feel potent, heavy. *You're special.* Maybe I'm reading too much into what he says, but I don't think I am. I think Henry is the kind of man who only says exactly what he means.

I think he is the perfect amount of sweet.

"Can you play me something? Jayce interrupted your performance earlier."

"Sure. Why don't we finish up your little masterpiece from the ride home, the sushi sonata. Want to remind me of the lyrics?"

I can't stop myself from cracking up. Those lyrics were beyond pitiful.

"I'm not joking. Come here." He looks so serious.

"What?"

"Come over here." He taps the bench next to him. "I never start a song I don't intend to finish. Let's get this over with."

We stay up until four in the morning, but *I Love the Way You Roll* is indeed a masterpiece.

For the next three weeks, not a day goes by that I don't find myself in Henry's studio.

interlude

Love, love, love, that is the soul of genius.

-Mozart

17

• • •

Henry

"I THINK I'm falling in love with her."

I don't know what to make of the look on Graham's face. I'm bearing my soul to him and I could swear he's wincing. "Henry, are you sure? You just met the girl. Have you even *been* in love before?"

I follow him over to the squat rack. It's Sunday and everyone else is out of the house enjoying brunch, but it's leg day for us, a tradition we've had ever since he first moved in with me. I finally found the perfect time to bring this up to Graham and his response is less than desirable.

Lucy's been staying here for over a month now. It may seem fast to Graham, but it's already the longest relationship I've had with a woman, platonic or otherwise.

And who cares when we met, or what silly rules people expect us to follow. My world, my tiny, insignificant little world is unequivocally better with her in it. What else truly matters?

"You know I haven't been in love." He gives me a knowing glance. "Don't look at me like that. How on earth would I have been in love before?"

"Exactly. How do you know you love her?"

"I just do. I've never felt like this before. Everything in my life is better with her in it. She makes me feel like I'm not—like I'm not broken. Can't you see how different things are when I'm around her? I actually enjoy doing things. I enjoy . . . life."

"Henry, that's great for you. I'm happy you feel so comfortable with her, truly. I love seeing you going out to dinner; hell, I love seeing you talk to someone other than me! But have you thought about her? She *is* normal. If you're actually thinking about a relationship with her, she needs to know what that entails. Because it's not going to be normal for her."

I think back to the night at Nobu; damn was I foolish for taking her out. I knew my track record at restaurants was dismal, but she gave me this sense of confidence. And even when it did go to shit, she was never fazed. That night was incredible. I actually had fun with her, out in public, where there were strangers all around me. I started singing at the table for God's sake.

Graham passes me a towel now that my fourth set is finished. He adds another seventy pounds on the bar and leers at me before he gets started.

"Maybe she doesn't have to give anything up for me. Maybe I can be normal, if I'm with her. We spend time together every day, and when she's with me it just feels . . . right. Easy. Like I never have to think about what I'm supposed to do or say. She understands me."

It's true. I rarely stumble over my words with her anymore. And I swear sometimes it feels like there's this otherworldly connection between us. Almost daily, she brings her laptop down to the studio to work with me; she says my music inspires her. Even when I'm just tinkering or trying to find the right key, she always knows what's going on in my head, can easily describe the scene, the feeling I'm working to capture.

No one has ever understood me like that before.

"And we even went to Fish Grill the other day—it was packed. You know how much I avoid those places. But she wanted to go and . . ." And I cared more about making her happy than worrying about my own issues.

Graham grunts loudly before setting the bar down. "I'm impressed Henry, really. You've gone out to restaurants more in the last month than in the whole time I've known you. And I'm glad she makes you feel so at ease. But you've got to know there's more to dating than going out to eat. What if she wants you to meet her friends? To go . . . golfing?"

"Golfing? Does Lucy play golf?"

"I don't fucking know, Henry. But what if she wants to? What if she wants to do something that involves anyone but you two? You know how much you love surfing? Paddle Boarding? You love them because you can be alone. Other people actually enjoy group activities."

"So you believe Lucy wants to go play golf . . . in a group?"

"She might. Maybe not today, but yeah, she might. Have you considered just talking to her about . . . you know?"

I feel like I'm being crushed by a stack of weights. I was so excited to have this conversation with Graham. I know how much he loves Lucy—they're practically inseparable. For some reason, I thought he'd be happy for me, for us.

I told Lucy about my past, obviously not about my childhood, but I told her about Graham, about how I used him and the rest of HAAAM for selfish reasons, to further my career. And she didn't care. She told me it didn't matter. Maybe she won't care about any of it. She might not know my entire history, and I hope I never have to tell her, but she understands *me.*

She understands my music, the very essence of who I am. She said it helped her through a tough time. I wonder if she realizes what it's done for my own tough times. I can't even comprehend what my life would look like if I hadn't discovered the piano.

I think it was C.S. Lewis who said "ink is the great cure for all human ills." Storytelling and writing songs aren't so different, just like Lucy and me.

I'm sick of being Hermit Henry, of watching my housemates have lives outside of our work, lives that I lust after. I've spent all my life *knowing* I'd never be normal: friends, love, family; none of it was possible for me. But what if that's not the whole truth?

Being with Lucy has changed everything for me. Maybe I just wasn't motivated before, but now—now I know what it's like, to fall for someone, to want her around all the time in lieu of my solitude, to constantly think about how to make her smile.

I'm in it now; I can't just go back.

18

. . .

Lucy

I'M in love with Malibu.

The guys have been warning me about June gloom, that summer in California isn't like the East Coast. But I'm addicted. I love waking up to swirls of fog hugging the coastline, walking Rowan in the misty mornings that are cool enough to wear a sweatshirt. I love watching the fog burn off in the afternoon, suddenly broken up by the bright summer sun shining through. The evenings are sublime. Every night I go outside to the pool and watch the sky change from cerulean to violet and rosy pink, all streaked with flame from the setting sun.

The last few weeks have been . . . incredible.

Most mornings after breakfast I go to the beach with Graham. He refused to give up on his "shark biscuit" and I have to admit that I'm glad he didn't. Henry was right though, Graham's a horrible teacher. Luckily Henry has joined us enough times that he's been able to get me standing. Apparently, practicing on the beach is incredibly helpful before you try it in the water. Henry is the opposite of Graham when it comes to teaching styles. He's so patient with me, so encouraging no matter how many times I fall. And he never yells weird Australian obscenities that I can barely comprehend.

Nights are the most unpredictable for me. Sometimes we have big family dinners when Adamma's over. Sometimes they all go out and I have the house to myself (with Henry working of course) to write or get lost in a book. Sometimes I find Henry and Rowan cuddling on the rug next to the piano and my heart feels like it might burst out of my chest; and maybe I stay out of sight and just watch them for a while, listening to Henry sing softly to him, adding Rowan's name into every song.

And sometimes I spend hours in the studio listening to Henry on the piano. I've actually been getting a lot of writing done down there; it's the perfect creative atmosphere. One day last week we spent so long working together in the studio—by the time we came upstairs the entire house was asleep.

"WOULD you mind playing something in C minor? I'm working on a scene that needs to be really suspenseful but I'm not getting there. I could use some of that magical Henry Turner inspo right now."

The music stopped and Henry turned around to look at me lying on the futon. "Did I hear that correctly? Did you actually just mention a key*? You think your scene calls for* C minor*, eh?"*

"I honestly have no idea. I was hoping if I sounded confident enough you'd be overcome with pride at how much I've learned." I batted my eyelashes a little. "Is that a relatively suspenseful key to play in? Please say yes. I'd be so impressed with myself!"

He smirked at me but didn't respond. Then he turned back

to the piano and started playing something . . . very *suspenseful. It was perfect. My fingers started flying over the keyboard.*

We both worked silently—save for the music—for several hours. I wrote five full chapters and honestly loved them. And then I wondered if Henry was actually working at all. I can never tell if it's work, tinkering, as he likes to say, or something else entirely. I've spent so much time down here I wish I could tell the difference by now. But no matter what he's playing, his focus is unwavering. I create worlds through my writing and Henry does the same through sound.

I heard the notes change suddenly. It was beautiful. It sounded like shimmering starlight and midnight kisses. Like a ballerina floating through the air waiting to be effortlessly caught by strong hands.

"What is that? It's so pretty." Pretty? That word seemed so trivial compared to what I was listening to. It sounded like love.

He stopped playing, more abruptly than usual, but he didn't turn around. "Eh, nothing really, just fooling around."

I STILL CAN'T GET that melody out of my head.

For years I've listened to his scores while I work, but nothing really compares to the live experience. He told me once that music saved his life. I felt like I wasn't supposed to ask for details so I didn't, yet I can see it when he plays. Everything about him softens—all the hard edges, the taut muscles—it's kind of mesmerizing.

But the best part of being in Malibu? The pain.

It's gone.

Besides the minor flare-up my first week here, my endometriosis has been basically silent. I can't remember a time when I've gone this long without needing my pain medicine or my Warmies time with Rowan. I can't remember a time when I went more than one week.

I haven't told anyone here details about my chronic illness, partly because I love that they don't know that side of me, and partly because I haven't *had* to. So I just talk to Row.

I tell him all my wild theories. Like how the healing properties of the Pacific Ocean have somehow cured me, how being around Henry is like a more potent injection of his music (this is my current frontrunner), or how Row is officially a magic dog that takes my pain away before it reaches my brain receptors (I think he likes this one best).

I'm not sure if it's the surfing, or Henry's music, or my health, or this weird little family I've acquired, but I love the way I *feel* here. Like anything could happen, like doors are opening instead of closing on me, like my life isn't over.

Like the ending to my story is still waiting on the edits.

3rd movement

Give every day the chance to become the most beautiful of your life.

-Mark Twain

19

. . .

Lucy

ADAMMA HAS BEEN ASKING me for a while to go shopping together. Honestly, I'm a little embarrassed to go, considering how stylish she is. I'm, well, not. There are certain colors I like to wear and I usually go for dresses, but only because I find them comfortable. Chic is not a word that's ever been used to describe me. But today, I've finally agreed. I'm feeling really good. I've been making a ton of progress on my book and I'm in the best shape of my life thanks to all the attempted surfing. Plus, I'm living rent-free and have basically zero expenses. I deserve to go blow some cash.

Adamma picks me up in her red Audi convertible and the few nerves I had about shopping officially dissipate. Especially when she tells me we're starting the day with boba tea from Urth, my newest obsession.

"Okay, don't freak out but I have a surprise for you. Before we shop we're getting our makeup done, professionally."

Well, I *was* enjoying my delicious, blended Earl Grey with boba but now the tapioca pearls feel heavy in my mouth. I almost never wear makeup. The worst fight Sarah and I ever had was about my refusal to put on false eyelashes for my wedding. I wonder what she's doing now, when I'll see her again.

"Luce, don't look so scared. It'll be fun! I know you've been hesitant to go shopping and honestly, it's a million times better when you look your best. You'll appreciate it, I swear."

A beautiful man named Stefan paints my face while I stare at his lashes that are equal parts feathers and glitter. We make a lot of small talk, because apparently it takes over an hour to do makeup—I don't think I've ever spent more than ten minutes on myself—and when I tell him about the books I've written he squeals with glee. Stefan is a big fan of all things fairy tales and I promise to name a character after him in my next book. I leave out the fact that so far, all the characters are villains.

He spins my chair and I'm finally able to see my reflection in the mirror.

"Whoa." I look . . . well, I don't look like me anymore, that's for sure. My normally bright pink lips are nude and glossy, and my eyes are smoked out with different shades of chocolate and plum. I rarely wear more than mascara on them since they're already quite pronounced. I look like an alien, maybe a sexy alien, but this whole face looks foreign to me.

Something hits me, a small flood of memories with Sarah. She was my fashion guru, hair and makeup artist, style coach, you name it. No matter how hard she worked on me, I could never achieve the effortless beauty she possessed, but just remembering all the times she forced eyeliner on me has me feeling the loss of her deeply. I can't believe I still haven't heard from her since I got to LA. She knew I lost all my Boston friends when Jack and I split up. I never thought she'd truly abandon me like this.

"Right?" Stefan brings me out of my woeful reverie. "You look gorgeous. I'd kill for those big doe eyes of yours. You obviously didn't need much but I wanted to punch up the sex appeal. You just went from 'girl next door' to smoke show."

He blows on his finger guns to help articulate the point.

"Damn, girl—if Henry could see you now he'd have a coronary." Again, with the Henry talk. Adamma refuses to believe we're not hopelessly in love with each other. "Okay, let's go get the car. I know exactly where I want to take you next."

"THIS. Oh, definitely this one. Do you like ruching? Don't answer that. Just try it. Okay, this color is stunning. Here, hold this up. Yep, gorgeous."

We arrived at Rebecca Taylor a few minutes ago, Adamma swearing this is the perfect store for me, 'not too edgy but just enough glamour.' Now she's grabbing pieces of clothing left and right and piling them into my arms. Finally, she's done and we head to the dressing rooms.

"Try on the bubble dress first."

"Umm, which one is that?"

"The ivory one, spaghetti straps and a bubble hem? It's sort of stretchy."

"Okay, it's on." I come outside of the room to show Adamma. All the clothes she picked out are nice, but they seem fancy to me. I don't know if it's because I've always worked from home or it's just my personality but dressing up has never felt natural. Beach life definitely agrees with me.

"Hmm . . ." She looks me up and down, lips pinched together. "I love this color on you. Creamy white, not optic, it's perfect for your skin tone. But I hate the silhouette. You look like a little girl playing dress up." She points back to the room I was in. "Next."

I do feel like a little girl playing dress up. I'm trying to get dress number two off, but it's all twisted, so I ask her to come in and help me.

"Luce, tell me what you have coming up so I can help you plan outfits. Right now we're just flying blind. It's fun, but I need some direction."

"I don't have anything coming up. You know my life. I have no need for new clothes. This is just for fun."

"Come on. What about for a date? Don't you and Henry have plans again soon?" We finally got the dress off and now I'm feeling very exposed, in more ways than one.

"I told you that was never a date. And yeah we've gone out to eat a few times but it's usually just to grab something by the beach. We mostly just hang out at home—I mean at his house. I have no need for date attire."

"Are you really gonna keep saying nothing's going on with you two? I see the way he looks at you." She raises her voice to be overly dramatic. "Like he wants to slay dragons and whisk you out of the tower and into his bed." I give her the biggest eye roll I can manage. "*And* every time I mention his name you can't stop smiling!"

"I always smile! And he looks at me perfectly normally. You just think that because of his dimple. It makes him look flirtatious, but it's just his face."

"His dimple, huh? I don't think I've ever noticed he *has* a dimple. Sounds like you're paying close attention though." I roll my eyes at her. "Here, try this one on. This sandy color will look so good with your tan. And the pleats will make it lay really nicely."

"Dami, there's nothing going on, okay. Henry's a flirt! And he is obviously—objectively—hot, so is it crazy if I smile at him or notice he has one dimple? The women he dates look like, or are actually, models. There is nothing going on with us."

"I'm sorry, what women? I have never once in the last six

years heard about or seen a single girl. And he is *not* a flirt. He barely even speaks to anyone who doesn't live in that house."

"There are girls, trust me. We ran into one on our *date*." I hold up finger quotes to emphasize, once again, that it was not a date. "Seriously, maybe he's just really private about who he dates. But leave it alone, nothing's going to happen with us." She holds up her hands letting me know she'll drop it, for now.

I try on the dress and I honestly love it. The fabric is a shiny satin but has mini pleats throughout and a thin tie around the waist. It's comfortable too, not baggy but not fitted, just cinched right above my hips. It fits perfectly. I hate that the first thought I have is if Henry will like it. Adamma might be more intuitive than either of us realize. "I'm getting it."

Adamma cheers. Then she rips off the tag. "And you're wearing it the rest of the day."

We pick up pizzas to bring home to the boys. After a day of spoiling ourselves while they all work, it seems like the right thing to do. Considering we're both wearing brand new dresses and sporting full makeup, carrying a bunch of cardboard pizza boxes inside is only a little ironic. I desperately want to change into sweats before we eat but Adamma shoots daggers at me when I mention it. I stumble into the house—literally stumble, because she forced me to wear the wedges she picked out earlier—and I run right into Henry.

"Whoa." He grabs the pizza box from me with one of his hands and steadies me with the other. I see his gaze travel up my body as he takes me in, and when it lands on my face he gapes, just a tad.

"Hey Henry! I'll take that." Adamma grabs the pizza box from him to stack with the others on the kitchen island. "Isn't she *dazzling*? And three inches taller!" She winks at me and looks back at Henry, and then she smacks him on the shoulder. "Dude, stop gawking at her."

Henry clears his throat and I briefly meet his gaze. It's easy to get lost in his sapphire eyes. I also notice he has quite a bit of stubble on his chin when he's usually clean shaven to perfection. He must be extra busy with work.

"It's a erm, beautiful dress." He stands still for a moment before picking up his hand and patting me on the head several times, the last one lingering a bit too long. I raise my brows and he pulls away, hands down at his sides. "Sorry, don't know why I did that. I should head back downstairs."

"Aren't you having pizza with us?" Adamma is loving this interaction and cannot keep one ounce of glee from showing on her face.

"Right, sure, yes. I'll be back in a moment." Henry shuffles downstairs and I just shake my head as Adamma gives me a grin as wicked as an evil queen. She puckers her lips dramatically, then molds her hands together into a heart and pumps it at me from her chest.

20

. . .

Henry

"HOW LONG IS THE DRIVE? You're not taking me to Tijuana, are you?"

Lucy's been peppering me with questions about today's destination ever since I had to drag her body out of bed this morning. When I asked her last night if I could take her out for a surprise she seemed very excited, well, until I mentioned the five a.m. call time. But paddle boarding at sunrise is remarkable. She's going to love it.

Her first guess was an Alaskan cruise, then a trek through Yosemite. Now that we're in the car and dressed for a swim, she's starting to narrow it down to the southwestern coast. Latigo Beach is only a short drive from the house, but I've told her to bring plenty of snacks for the road trip. I like to keep her on her toes.

Once we park she finally notices the paddle board strapped to the roof of the car. I'm not quite sure her eyes were actually open when we left so she is genuinely surprised.

"Henry, you've seen me stand for like thirty seconds on a

surfboard, on my best day. What makes you think I'll be any good at this?"

"Relax Luzu, we're sharing. I'll do the paddling; you'll do the sunrise watching. Does that sound reasonable?" She beams, confirming that this was an excellent idea. Well done, Henry. "And if you're up for it, I might just let you paddle on the way back."

Once we get down to the water I explain to her that she can sit in front while I'm standing behind her. I show her some different options to help her balance, though she's not the most coordinated if I'm being honest. She decides to sit cross legged and once we're steady and moving she leans back until she's laying flat on the board with her head at my feet. Can she see up my trunks? I try to dispel the thought and focus on her instead. And then I realize focusing on her means staring at her half naked body, tan skin glowing ever so slightly with the rising sun, and am again, and more heavily, concerned about her seeing up my trunks.

That damn yellow bikini.

It's my favorite color now too.

"Lucy, sit up straight if you can. You know, balance and . . . stuff." Fucking hell.

She gives me a strange look before sitting back up and facing away from me. I miss her face immediately.

"This is amazing. I've always wanted to go paddle boarding. Jack used to go with our friends every summer at the Vineyard. I didn't even know I could share the board with him." I follow her gaze to the horizon where the faintest line of gold is starting to glimmer.

"You do seem to love the water, do you mind if I ask why it scares you so much?"

"Well, I was in Bermuda, my Junior year of college for Spring break. Went jet skiing with my bo—with Jack, and umm, I fell off. The undertow was really strong that day, I remember them warning people not to swim out too far. It sucked me down really hard. I honestly thought I was going to drown." There's a long beat of silence and I wonder if her story is over. "A lifeguard from the beach ended up saving me, not before I smashed into a huge piece of coral of course." She motions to the subtle scar along the outside of her thigh, and then another one on the back of her neck. "Twenty-two stitches. And I haven't been out past my waist since then. Well not until recently. It feels good to be out here again, even if I'm still mildly terrified."

"I'm impressed."

"Impressed? That's not the reaction I was expecting. Whenever Jack or I explained to his friends why I didn't want to join their ocean activities, the typical response was 'awww.'" She looks back at me and scrunches her face in annoyance.

"I'm sorry you got hurt, but you're not a child, Luce. I'm impressed you're out here, with me. I'm impressed that you've been out surfing with Graham almost every day for the past month. I'm impressed that you didn't let one tragic experience take something joyful away from you forever."

She stays silent for a while and I wonder if I've said something wrong. I know what it's like to be scared. For most of my life I've been scared to leave the house, and even now I rarely socialize with anyone outside of HAAAM, and now Lucy.

I decide to stop for a beat and sit with her; the water is exceptionally calm at the moment. I kneel down to balance back on my heels and tap her on the shoulder.

"Hi, care to turn around?" I offer a hand to help her maneuver toward me.

"Oh, hello Maestro, how kind of you to join me down here."

"So, what do you think?" I gesture toward the horizon, the sun slowly rising up above the hills, a ball of flaming orange wrapped in a glowing halo. No matter how many times I do this, I always find the view breathtaking.

"It's amazing. Thank you for bringing me. I'm sorry you had to drag me out of bed. You really should have told me what we were doing—I *might* not have been so difficult."

"But that would have ruined the surprise." I give her a quick wink, feeling a bit more confident than I did earlier.

"Touché."

"I'm just glad you came. It's nice having someone to talk to out here. I've only ever come alone."

When she smiles at me like this, I have to remind myself to breathe. The sun reflects off her emerald eyes, and they glow an unearthly shade of amber. Her hair catches the same light, glittering in the breeze. She looks like an angel.

I realize I'm staring at her and promptly clear my throat. "So, I finished *Throne of Glass*." She swiftly turns her gaze from the sky to me, eyes wide.

"What? You actually read it? Just the first one? It gets so much better the further you get in the series. Like a million times better."

"Yes, I think you mentioned that once. But no, I read them all. I finished the series."

"No way, you read all of them in six weeks? That's like . . . really impressive. I mean, when do you have time to read? You're always working."

Of course I read them.

"Well, I've always liked to read, and I do take breaks, you know. Reading always helps clear my head, or rather, gets me out of my head when I'm stuck on something. You saw my Kindle's permanent spot by the futon." I'd be lying if I said I wasn't excited when I found out Lucy was a voracious reader.

Books were my only friends as a child, besides my mum and dad. Getting lost in a made-up world was always the best way to cope with my frustrations, my lack of normalcy. Until recently, all the song lyrics I've written were mused from stories I've read. When your own life is void of emotional drama—the good kind, the relatable kind—you have to improvise.

"Okay, so . . . what'd you think? Did you like it?" Her face is all squished up now in anticipation and I know she's hoping I say yes. Luckily, I don't have to lie to her.

"It was brilliant. Really. I can see why you love it so much. I finally understand that jumper you're always wearing that says *Rattle the Stars*. It'd be a great name for a song, by the way."

"Oh my God, please write it. *Please!*"

"Happy to." I boop her on the nose before I can stop myself. *Jesus, Henry*. "And I see why Rowan is your favorite."

"Oh, really? Because of his big muscles? Immortality? Ability to fly?"

"Erm, I guess those might be qualities you appreciate, but no. I think you like him because of all the men in the books, he's the only one she can truly be herself with. She never has to pretend to be something else, and he loves her no matter what, even when she's well, you know, on a murderous rampage?"

Her face changes now and I'm not sure how to read it. Did I say something wrong? I really thought I had understood her for a moment, understood her insecurities that she tries to keep so close to the vest.

She's told me more than a few times how special these books and characters are to her. I could see that connection when reading them, like I knew all the emotions she went through in each book of the series. It's what I've always loved about books. How you can get so consumed by a story that you feel yourself living it, can be transported directly into the ink.

But Lucy's eyes are getting glassy and I wonder if I'm right about any of it.

Finally, she speaks. "You're very intuitive." Her eyes haven't changed but her lips have turned up just slightly at the edges.

"I like to think I've gotten to know you pretty well, Luzu. And thank you, for recommending the books. I saw a bit of myself in the characters as well. I've always desired a relationship like that, where all of my faults don't scare them away." She laughs at this, though I'm not sure why. And I swear she's moved slightly closer to me. I hope I'm not imagining it.

"Faults? Henry, what do you think is your deterrent? Working too hard? Being too handsome? Playing the piano *too* beautifully?" She tips her head to the side, still smiling like we're in on the same joke, like I don't actually believe there's anything wrong with me.

How does she not realize how mistaken she is? How does she not see the grown man in front of her who's never had an actual relationship with a woman beyond one night?

"I'm . . . awkward. You know I am. You've seen it. I struggle, sometimes."

"Oh, shit. You're serious." Her smile drops instantly. She reaches her hand out toward me but starts to lose her balance and places it back on the board. I grab on to her arm to steady her and we share a knowing smile. "That's not a fault, Henry. It doesn't make you any less lovable, not even a little. Trust me."

It doesn't make me any less lovable. Does that mean she thinks I *am* lovable? Could *she* love me?

I feel brave when I'm with Lucy, when her sincerity shines this brightly. It makes me want to tell her everything.

"I'm sorry I've never really explained my—issues. It's been like this since I was a child. Well, actually it was much worse when I was a child, but—" Am I even making sense right now? No wonder I've never tried this before.

"I've never been able to talk to people. You think I'm shy, but it's much worse than that. I just freeze up. It doesn't matter how much I *want* to say something, my body won't allow it. It feels like all my muscles are contracting and everything gets so tight I wish I could break something. The more I try to relax and work through it, the more tense everything becomes. Sometimes it's subtle, easy to hide, but other times it can get so bad I just want to scream.

"It usually takes weeks, months sometimes, before I can communicate with anyone new. Medication helps, but I hate how it makes me feel. Anything strong enough to sufficiently dull my nerves ends up dulling every other part of my brain as well, so I rarely take it anymore. I decided a while ago that my music was more important than having a social life."

The same music that brought Lucy to me.

"Instead, I just sort of deal with it. I never go out, or socialize, which I'm sure you've picked up on. I basically forced HAAAM into living with me so that I don't have to deal with anyone at studios and embarrass the team. Honestly, I never would have spent so much on a house, but I figured it was the best way to get their agreement."

Lucy's watching me intently, never interrupting. I wonder if she can tell this is the first time I've ever spoken these words aloud. Even Graham had to infer half of it.

"So, I guess I just wanted to be honest with you. In case you ever wanted to go golfing or something. I'm not exactly sure you'd want me to tag along."

"Huh, that's too bad, Henry. I bet you'd be an excellent golfer." She grins, like I didn't just give her every reason to dive off this board and swim away from me.

"I'm glad you told me though," she says. "I like knowing

you better. I'm just wondering, why doesn't it happen around me? And don't just say I'm special. I really want to know."

She's biting the inside of her cheek, awaiting my response. I don't think now is the right time to confess my feelings for her. Besides, I'm not sure those feelings have anything to do with it.

"But you are special, Luce. You are my anomaly."

21

• • •

Lucy

I'M SPEECHLESS.

I've known for weeks that Henry struggles with some sort of anxiety. I never wanted to press him about it because I know exactly what it's like when people ask invasive health questions.

Whenever someone sees Rowan's service-dog tag I get asked what I have, or what he does for me, like it's their God-given right to know my personal medical history. It enrages me every time.

But Henry offered it up to me. He wanted me to know what he's dealing with. And if I wasn't already melting a little more for him every day, this seals it.

You are my anomaly.

It's not exactly a romantic sentiment, but man did it feel like one.

It felt like Henry was calling me his soulmate.

"I'm really glad you told me, Henry. Thank you. I'm sure it's not easy to talk about, but I hope you know you can tell me anything. I'll never judge you."

The side of his mouth tilts up and I can tell he's done sharing for today. Instead, he's just looking at me.

He's *really* looking at me.

He's been looking at me like this for a while now, like I'm a bowl of ice cream he wants to lick clean.

I don't hate it. I don't hate it at all. It makes me feel sexy, and I can't remember the last time I felt that way. Ever since Jack left, I wondered if I'd ever feel desired again.

He brushes back a tendril of hair behind my ear and leans into me just a little closer. He looks so dreamy, his thick hair gently swaying in the breeze.

I feel an urge to lean in and kiss him. I think he *wants* me to kiss him. But what would that mean? It's obvious I have feelings for Henry, but I'm not sure I want to risk our friendship like that.

"You're so easy to talk to, Luce. This may sound strange but sometimes, well, you remind me a bit of my mum." He rakes his fingers through his hair as he blows out a breath, clearly embarrassed. "She's just the kindest person I've ever known, until I met you. You'll make a great mother one day."

I clear my throat, swallow the dense lump forming there, try not to react to his words. *Friends.* Henry and I are friends, and that's all we can be.

"Do you think we could head back now? Sorry, I wanna get back to Rowan."

"Happy to—under one condition." I squint at him, curious about what he's after. "You're paddling."

Henry shows me how to balance on my knees to make it easier than standing. Balance has never been my strong suit but he's so patient with me, so encouraging no matter how frustrated I get with myself.

I used to think Jack was the perfect partner, never asking me to go in the water with him after my accident in Bermuda.

He never pushed me or made me feel bad for not joining him and our friends when they would go water-skiing, surfing, or any of the other numerous activities I missed out on. I was glad he didn't push me, glad I didn't have to explain my fears all the time. But I was stuck, always sidelined, missing out on the fun everyone was having around me.

Henry is the complete opposite. He knows I'm scared of the water, but he doesn't want me to give up. Graham too. They've both given me a chance to do something I love that I avoided for years. It feels like they're on my team, like I can depend on them, like I don't have to worry about their disappointment, the way I've disappointed everyone else in my life.

Henry was right about the books. All I want is to be myself, my truest self, and have that be enough for someone else.

When I think about my time with Jack, I know it wasn't all bad. Most of it was really good.

After meeting him at the beginning of my freshman year we became fast friends. Sarah, Jack and I hung out all the time, and while he flirted with me a lot, he never made a move or asked me out. I knew about lots of girls he hooked up with and I figured he knew I wasn't into one night—or one week—stands. Or maybe he just wasn't attracted to me.

But then junior year, right before our spring break trip to Bermuda, everything changed. He pulled me aside one day and said the craziest thing: "Okay, I'm ready. Let's do this."

"What are you talking about?"

"Us. It's time, don't you think? We should be together."

"Jack, I don't understand where this is coming from."

"Liar." He smirked, like he knew exactly how this conversation would end. "Lu—I've been in love with you since freshman year. You know this." I didn't, but my face revealed nothing. "I knew that as soon as I asked you out, that would be it for me. I'm ready now."

I looked at him incredulously but was betrayed by the giddy feeling inside me. I never wanted to admit it, but I'd had the biggest crush on Jack since that very first day.

"I'm serious, Lu. I'm gonna marry you one day. But for now, be my girlfriend?"

The smile I was desperately trying to hide stretched wide across my face. He kissed me then. Not just any kiss. The perfect—grab my face with both hands, dip me just enough to kick a heel off the ground, sigh with relief into my mouth—*fairy tale* kiss.

That first year was perfect, but there were signs, and then there were more signs.

When we graduated, there was no question whether or not I'd move to Boston, a city where I had zero friends or family. That's where he got a job, so of course we went. I'm not sure he tried applying anywhere else. He always acted like my job as a writer was just a steppingstone to being a housewife, so I don't think he ever gave any thought to where I'd prefer to live after college.

When I wanted to take some time to travel, to work on my book somewhere new, he acted like I was trying to have an affair. As a professional writer, having a change in scenery can do wonders. To Jack, he only saw me wanting to get away from him. I never wanted to hurt him, so I didn't go anywhere.

Even for our honeymoon, I was desperate to go to Europe, to visit old libraries and be surrounded by history. But he'd already been to all the cities I suggested, so we went to Napa instead. I never really cared about wine, but he spent the whole week educating me so I'd be more knowledgeable at dinner parties.

The worst was when I opened up to him about my endometriosis. Sarah was the person who had always helped to take care of me, who went with me to the hospital so I wouldn't be alone, who laid with me in bed and swapped my heating pad when it cooled too much to alleviate the pain.

But once we moved to Boston, I needed Jack to be more involved. He was mostly just . . . uninterested. Always asking if I could just deal with it myself since "it's just bad periods, right?" Telling me it was a "girl thing" so he shouldn't be obliged, how he'd rather avoid going to the doctor with me because he felt awkward at a gynecologist. He was really encouraging when I asked for his opinion on training Rowan as a medical alert dog, but it was easy to tell that he saw Rowan as another way for him to avoid my illness.

Looking back, even that magical day when our romantic relationship began, it was completely on his terms.

None of these things were so bad on their own. I liked how decisive he was. But when I look at them all together, I realize he was molding me. Like I was never enough of what he wanted, not on my own. Change this, ignore that, pretend this doesn't exist. He had to make these little adjustments all the time to fit me into his life.

And then came the day when no adjustment could be made, and that was the beginning of the end.

I KEEP TRYING to pinpoint what's made me so happy here in Malibu. The weather? Surfing? Sharing these magical moments with Henry? Spending an entire month pain-free?

Maybe it's just feeling like I might finally be enough.

I'm grateful to be back in my bed with Rowan curled up next to me and giving me lots of puppy kisses. Petting his soft and shaggy fur is my favorite form of self-care. There's so much happening in my head right now, I need some time alone to think. I run my fingers through the extra silky fur on his belly while he licks at my elbow. He's in full submissive position with his paws tucked into his chest and his hind legs butterflied out. "Love you Row. Thanks for always being there for me. If you're really good this afternoon, we can play hide-and-treats later." I drop my head to give him a quick peck on the nose but instead get a wet tongue across my mouth.

Everything Henry told me today is running on a loop through my head. So many questions I had about him have finally been answered. I should probably apologize to Adamma because it sounds like she was right. He wasn't explicit about romantic relationships, but I'm going to infer he hasn't had many.

And there's still so much more I want to know about him. Like how music saved him, how he became so close with Graham, what happened in his childhood to cause the struggles he told me about, why the one person who's somehow immune to his anxiety is *me*.

But what I also want to know, if I'm being honest, is what he looks like naked. And this I've probably thought about the most. When I lie in bed at night, I'm assaulted by images of him, usually on the piano, but he's never playing. Sometimes I'm straddling him on the bench, hearing random notes as we both try and fail not to hit the keys. Sometimes I'm lying on top of the lid with Henry between my legs. Sometimes we're just curled up together on the futon, tightly pressed against each other.

Ever since I've been here in Malibu, Henry and I have shared these . . . moments. I've never been sure how to label them, but today, it felt like a switch was flipped. My attraction to him isn't one-sided. I can't just keep pretending I have some silly crush. Being with Jack might have stunted my maturity for the last ten years but I'm a grown woman, and I know what I want.

I want Henry.

His confession today didn't deter *me* in the slightest. But the problem is, he won't want me anymore if I offer the same insights into my own past.

My endometriosis has always felt like this invisible disability. I can be in excruciating pain—physical and mental just ping-ponging back and forth for days—but no one around me ever understands what I'm actually going through.

Pop some Advil, suck it up, get the surgery, move on.

It would have been easy to tell him my own story today. To explain about my divorce, why this past year has been so somber. But I'd rather keep Henry in the dark; then I never have to hear what he might say about it.

As much as my body might want something physical with Henry, my heart is much too fearful.

I'M STILL LYING in bed, thinking about Henry, when I hear a soft knock on my door.

"Come in!"

"Hey Luce, are you busy?" Preston's hanging on the threshold like he's afraid to enter. I realize he's never actually been inside this room before, at least not with me. He's so polite. Jayce and Graham never even knock.

"Hey. You can come in, you know." I motion for him to sit but he only moves a few steps.

"I, umm, I had a favor to ask you, if that's okay?"

"Of course. What's up?"

"Well, I want to do something special for Adamma." Of course he does. This is a favor I know I'll be happy to help with. "I don't exactly know how to cook, but you're so good at it. I thought maybe you could teach me a few things? I want to make her a big Italian dinner this weekend, something to remind her of our first date in Chicago."

"That's so sweet. Of course I'll help! Do you just want me to cook for you two? I'm sure I can get the rest of the guys out of the house for a bit so it's more romantic."

"No, I want to do it myself, at her place. But I thought maybe we could do a practice run together? You could show me how to do everything and I'll just take lots of notes. I'm a quick learner. At least I am with music . . ." He has his hands in his pockets and he looks down like he's not actually confident at all. It's adorable.

"This is gonna be great. Wanna do it tonight?" God knows I could use the distraction. "If you want we can go to the store now and get everything."

We menu-plan on the way to Whole Foods. Preston tells me all about their first date, right before they graduated high school. The restaurant wasn't fancy but he said they both loved it so much that they always get Italian for their anniversary, even if it's pizza. He's hoping to take it up a notch for this meal, he wants it to be extra special. I asked him what the occasion is but apparently there isn't any, he just loves her that much. I don't want my mind to go to Jack, but of course it does. Did he ever go through the effort to do something like this for me, just because? I can't think of anything. And then my mind whirls to Henry, because even something as simple as his butter cake surprise was sweeter than anything I can remember from Jack. It wasn't lavish but it was personal, it meant something to me.

After a lengthy discussion, we finalize the menu: prosciutto and melon with basil oil to start, then eggplant caponata with burrata and for the star of the show, meatball lasagna (because I know he won't be able to mess it up). Since he has zero experience with baking, I convince him to pick up Tiramisu from a bakery for dessert. I don't trust him to make it and it's truly the only way to end a delicious Italian dinner. There's no way Adamma won't be impressed by this romantic feast. Honestly, my mouth is watering just thinking about it and I'm very glad I'll get to eat the practice round.

I'm pleasantly surprised by how serious Preston is taking this. Once we're back in the kitchen he is laser-focused on everything I'm doing and is actually taking notes—and lots of photos—on his iPad. We start preparing all the vegetables for the eggplant salad because we have to cook everything and then have time to chill it before it's served. I let him know he can do this the day before to save some time.

After we make the basil oil and start preparing the prosciutto, we decide to have a taste. It's really the best part of cooking.

"This is delicious. What if I don't pick out a melon that's this sweet though? How did you choose one again?"

"Why don't you just let me go shopping with you the day before you cook? I promise it's not cheating, and it'll take some of the pressure off of you."

"Yes, thank you. That would be amazing. You're seriously the best."

"That's sweet, it's really no problem though. Plus, you know I love Dami—there's no way I'm letting you screw this up for her." I shoot him a wink right before I go to the fridge and start grabbing everything to start the lasagna.

"She loves you too. You know, she almost never came over here before you moved in. I owe you, it's been so much easier with work now that she'll stay here. A lot less driving back and forth from Culver City." I remember Adamma saying something like that too but it still doesn't make any sense to me. She obviously loves her boyfriend—she definitely doesn't need me to hang out with her.

"She said that too. But I don't get it. This house is amazing, why wouldn't she want to hang out here?" I put all the different ground meats in a large bowl and show Preston how to mix everything with his hands.

"This feels so weird." His face is half smile half scowl as he blends the mixture together. "And umm, things have just been different with you here, more relaxed. Especially with Henry. We never really hung out together before. It was just work all the time, and if anyone wanted to do something . . . fun, we'd go out."

He pauses, like he has more to say but isn't sure if it's appropriate.

"This place looks like a party palace, but it's our office, and I think she always felt like she was intruding on work when she came over. It's just, Henry's our boss, you know? So if he's always working, it kinda feels like when we're home, we should always be working too. Graham's the only one that isn't scared of him and just surfs all day until he has something due." I laugh at this, because I can't imagine Graham being scared of anyone. "It just never felt like we were supposed to have fun here, until you showed up."

"That's so nice of you, but I really can't take any credit. You don't feel like you guys are . . . friends? You all seem so close to me."

"No, we are. We definitely are, it's just different now. Henry never hung out with us before. The only time I ever saw him was when we were working. I'm not sure what you did to get him out of his shell, but having him join in when we have dinner or just chill at the pool, it's really nice. I'm finally getting to know him. He's like, surprisingly funny."

I think about everything Preston's saying as I walk him through the lasagna process. Henry may have explained a lot today, but I still have a million questions. Do I really have this much of an effect on him?

Preston seems more than willing to divulge all the information, but we're interrupted when Jayce comes in and tries to grab a ball of burrata with his hands.

"Ow! Did you seriously just slap me, Luce?"

"We're not done cooking. If you want to partake you'll have to wait until everything's done. I need to show him how to present it all." I flash him a satisfied smirk as he backs away and sits on one of the stools at the island. Good boy.

"When will it be done?" Jayce bats his eyelashes at me. "It smells so good and I'm fucking starving. Crystal and I just did five miles and it was steep as hell. Thanks again for letting me take Row."

"How many times have you gone out with her now? Is this the longest relationship you've ever been in?" Preston's definitely mocking Jayce but I don't see the grin I'm expecting from him.

"I'm so screwed. I really like her, like *really* like her." He slams his head down on the granite and moans.

I laugh at him. "Jayce, what's the problem? It's okay to have a girlfriend, you know. It won't kill you to be monogamous."

"I'd give monogamy five stars." Preston holds up five fingers to emphasize his proclamation. I have to remind myself to tell Adamma, it's too cute.

"Guys, I *want* her to be my girlfriend. That's not the problem. I've lied to her so much that I don't know how to come clean without her hating me. I mean, unless you think you could let me keep Rowan forever?"

"Not a fucking chance. Wait, what else have you lied to her about?"

"Well, I didn't lie exactly. But she might have assumed this was my house and I didn't really correct her." He's massaging his temples the same way Henry does when he's stressed about his music. I shouldn't feel bad for Jayce but I do.

"Okay, what else? Just tell me everything and we'll put our heads together. If you're actually ready to be in a committed relationship I'm not going to let some silly white lies get in the way."

"Umm, I told her we . . ." He winces. "I'm sorry Luce. I told her you were my cousin." Preston and I are both staring with our mouths open. "Hey, don't look at me like that. My mom was half Swedish, it's not impossible."

Okay, that last one was a doozy, but I'm undeterred. After a quick brainstorming session with the three of us, we come up with a plan. I reluctantly agree to name Jayce as Rowan's godfather. I'm not sure if this is actually a thing, but it does make me happy knowing that if I experience an untimely death, Rowan will be in good hands. Jayce works out the whole conversation for how to explain this to her and I don't see how she could be upset. As long as she doesn't find out I met Jayce the same day he first asked her out.

The house is a bit trickier. We decide it's best if he just comes clean. And if it's really that big of a deal to her, she might care a bit too much about his financial assets anyway. She knows he has roommates, so he just needs to clarify that they share it. The Henry details aren't important—I tell him he can leave that out for now.

As for his biggest mistake, yikes. No wonder she kept asking me about my family last time she was here. No one's ever inquired so much about my "heritage" before. I don't think it's feasible to keep pretending we're related. He said he just wanted to make sure Crystal wasn't jealous when she found out I lived here. I guess it's understandable, but still annoying. We decide that all the guys in the house use the term to describe me, just as a way of saying we're "like family," completely platonic. Preston says he'll make sure to call me "Cuz" next time she's over to help sell it. Why the hell not?

"All right, I've done all I can for you. Can you go tell Graham and Henry there's tons of food ready if they're hungry?"

I TAKE my last bite of lasagna and look around the table. Henry and Preston are laughing violently together and I think about our conversation from earlier. It's wild to me that this friendship between them is so new. I still can't believe I'm in any way responsible, but it makes me happy nonetheless. Jayce gets up to clear the table but stops to give me an aggressive hug first. He thanks me for dinner and for the advice with Crystal, and says he's going to see her tonight to come clean. I really hope she forgives him. Graham scoots closer and puts an arm around me before leaning his head on my shoulder. Then he mumbles something about a food coma.

I lean my head on top of Graham's and think about this morning, the moment Henry and I shared out in the ocean. I really did want to kiss him. I wanted to do more than kiss him.

But tonight, this reminds me that what I have now is the best I can hope for. I know there's no romantic happy ending for me. And in a way, this is perfect. This is like having a family again, a family I love. I can't mess it up.

22

. . .

Henry

"LUCY, there you are. Come sit down, I need to tell you something." I watch her descend the stairs with careful precision, her hair looking extra glossy today, almost glowing. Having her here with me in the studio has become a luxury; just her presence brightens up the room I spend my life in, the one that used to feel like a cave.

"Sure. You can tell me anything."

I take her hand and lead us both to the futon. Our eyes connect as we sit down and my nerves make me feel breathless. Am I really going to do this? I feel like an aggressively shaken champagne bottle.

"Luzu . . .Lucy. I—" Her eyes follow my lips expectantly, and I could swear, almost...encouragingly. A piece of hair falls down across her cheek, strands of molten honey. She's perfect. "Lucy. I love you. I—"

Her mouth crashes into mine before I can get another word out. The kiss is—is this our first kiss? It doesn't feel like it. Lucy's arms are wrapped around me as tight as a snake trapping its prey. She's kissing my neck, sucking on my ear, running her hands through my hair and moaning softly. She's fulfilling every fantasy I've had about her since the day we met.

"Say it again, Maestro."

"I love you. I lo—" My words are swallowed up by more kisses.

We're tangled up in each other, rolling until I'm hovering over her. I feel her tug on my shirt as her nails rake against the skin on my back and I shudder. I peel my lips away from hers just so I can look at her, so I can remind myself this is finally happening. She grasps the back of my neck, all soft skin and sharp nails and pulls me back down against her.

Now she's on top of me, her lips trailing down my chest to the plane of my stomach to my hip. I can feel her mouth against my skin as she speaks.

"Henry, I love you too. I've loved you for years. Why did it take you so long to finally say something?"

Did she just say *years*?

She rises, straddling my hips and raises a finger full of tiramisu to her mouth. I watch her tongue lap up every last bit of cream as the sound of her "mmm" rumbles through our bodies. She puts the same finger to my lips as she lowers her head back down to my waist. I savor the taste of her skin and her favorite dessert all at once.

My pants are off and my brain feels foggy from Lucy's kisses. Her hands grip my thighs and her mouth is around me, and moving, and—and she feels so good I may have forgotten my own name at this point.

She's still nestled between my legs when she speaks. "I can't believe this is finally happening. I've waited so long for you to say something. Why are you such a coward?"

"What?" I sit up to look at her but she's gone, a blur. I can still taste the sugary espresso on my lips but Lucy's a ghost, a sexy apparition. "Lucy!?"

. . .

I WAKE WITH A START, grabbing at my sheets as if I can hold on to the body that was never actually there. I sit up abruptly and look around the room before slamming my head back down on the pillow.

Fuck.

"I'VE FINISHED the theme and a few other pieces, here." I pass out the pages I've written to each of the guys. "Can you all get this done in the next week?"

"When did you do all this? Three days ago you said you were still tinkering with the opening frames?" Why does Graham always have to be so damn observant? It's like every time I pull an all-nighter, he just *knows*.

"I've been quite focused recently. Inspiration strikes, you know . . ." What I'm not saying is this is the only thing I can do to stop thinking about Lucy. Lucy . . . God, if I could only get her perfect face out of my head.

Even my dreams aren't safe anymore.

I'll never be able to compose an entire season of warring dragons when every note I play sounds like bloody rainbows and unicorns.

"I take it paddle boarding was a bust then?"

"Paddle boarding was lovely. Why don't you get to work, Graham. All of you, actually. I'd like to have something finished to share with the producers next week. And Preston, thank you for filling in on brass while I look for Craig's replacement."

"Not a problem at all. I actually think I'm better with

horns. You know I love the sax but you always have to jump in to change my flute parts." True, though I've never minded.

"Well, if you feel that way I see no reason to take it from you."

"Yes, definitely. Hire a flautist. I've got horns." Jayce starts snickering at Preston's comment.

"Shut up, Jayce," Graham jumps in, "you can laugh now but we all know you're thinking about how to use that as a creepy pick-up line."

I LEAVE them to it and head upstairs, I feel like I need fresh air or something. I'm about to make my way toward the pool when I see Lucy and Rowan outside. Is she training him? I see a bag of treats in her left hand as she makes different signs with the other. Is she . . . ? Yes, she is actually training him to give kisses. My God, I can't decide which one of them is more adorable.

"Hello there, may I have a kiss?" I step outside and kneel down on the ground. Starting a conversation with Rowan seems easier than approaching Lucy. Although, I wish asking her for a kiss was this painless. Rowan attacks my face instantly, licking every inch he can.

"Row, oh my God, enough." She snaps her fingers at him a few times and he sits, staring up at her expectantly.

"Sorry, once he gets going in a make out sesh, he just refuses to stop." She has a bashful look on her face, like she wants to be embarrassed but secretly loves how affectionate Rowan is.

I'd like to show her the same affection if I can ever get the chance. It felt like there was a moment the other day, out on the water. I'm probably just imagining it.

Lucy moves to sit on the ground next to me. Rowan

immediately plops himself on her lap, belly up, pawing at her hands for rubs.

"How's the book coming along?"

"Ugh, I'm kind of stuck actually. You know every book I've written I started with the ending? I always wrote the last chapter first. But this time I took the linear approach, and I have no idea what the ending looks like. The whole story has just sort of unraveled as I've been writing it and now I'm basically waiting around to see how it ends, like I'll just wake up one day and know. Is that crazy?"

"Not at all. I understand what you mean completely. Sometimes when I'm writing a new score I read the script and plan everything out, but other times I just start to play while I'm watching clips and see what happens. You don't have to stick to one creative process. The best of us don't." She blinks at me in surprise. "Would you like me to round up HAAAM and have them act out different scenarios for you? They're required to do anything I ask, it's in their contracts."

I nudge her shoulder playfully but I'm not sure it has the intended effect. I've been watching endless romantic comedies on my iPad these last few days, every time I'm alone. I thought it would help me learn flirting tactics but everything I do just comes across as awkward and creepy.

"Hmmm, can I get back to you on that? I don't think it'll help me write but I wouldn't mind pretending just to screw with them. Just gotta come up with something really good first." The twinkle in her eye has me dumbstruck for a moment.

"What are you doing tonight, Maestro?"

"Oh, busy, lots of work to do as usual." Wait, was she going to ask me to spend time with her? Did I just completely blow it? Fuck. "Erm, what about you? Did you want to get out of the house, go do something?"

"No, I'm gonna stay here, Jayce said he'd hang out with me.

He wants to get drunk and teach me to play the bongos." She chuckles before rising to her feet and making more commands to Rowan.

"WHAT'S GOING on with Lucy and Jayce?" I've seen Graham in one of the recording rooms for the last hour but he's finally taking a break, so I jump at the chance to talk to him.

"What? Nothing's going on with them. Henry, are you getting paranoid?"

"She said her plans for tonight were to get drunk with Jayce and learn to play the bongos. Don't tell me I'm paranoid."

I know she and Jayce spend a decent amount of time together. I've heard them talk about their hikes with Rowan and I've kept my jealousy at bay, but making plans to get drunk together?

Now I'm wondering if Lucy thinks I'm too dull for her; I rarely have more than a glass of wine or cocktail. I explained to her why I avoid substances that cloud my brain, but even if she's understanding it doesn't mean she won't consider me a bore compared to someone like Jayce.

"Henry, calm down. Lucy hangs out with all of us. I'm probably the only one who's seen her topless, but who knows?" I feel rage brewing in me at his comment and my face must match the feeling. I've never seen Graham look scared before. "Okay, sorry mate, wrong thing to say, just messing with you. Please don't murder me."

"I don't care if she wants to spend time with everyone else in this house. I'm worried because it's Jayce, and alcohol, and we both know what he's like."

"Charming?" Graham is really testing me right now.

"Henry, there's nothing going on with them. I promise you. Didn't he just say last night he's been hanging out with that Crystal chick? Plus, Lucy is not interested in him like that, not even a little. If he tries anything, she'll shut him down immediately. I'd quite like to see it actually."

My mind is spinning. What if he did try something? Maybe I should join them, say I need a night off from work. Jayce would see right through me, he's never seen me drink as an activity before. Maybe I could make an excuse to use the piano in the living room? At least that way I could have eyes on them if they're outside by the pool. Bongos? Did he really offer to teach her the bongos or is that a euphemism that I pray I never discover the meaning of?

"Henry, I can actually see the hamster wheel turning in your head. Let this go, do *not* spy on them. Lucy's a big girl, she's been stressed about her book, she can get drunk with her friend for a night, okay?"

It's 11:25. I haven't gone upstairs in three hours, terrified of what I might find. Is it possible Lucy is interested in Jayce? I've seen his effect on women, how easy it is for him to flirt, to date them for as long as he chooses to. I don't think I've ever seen him rejected. He's always the one to break their hearts, never the other way around.

I'm trying to work, but I just keep playing the same notes over and over, and they sound menacing. In my head, it's the soundtrack to me strangling Jayce and ripping off each of his limbs. Actually, maybe this is usable. I remember a dismemberment scene in the script—something at the end of episode two . . .

"That sounds spooooooky." I turn to find Lucy stumbling quite clumsily down the stairs. She's sporting a wide grin and I wonder who it's for.

"Hello there. Where's Jayce?"

"Well, Jayce..ss..ss." She lingers on the end of his name like she's a snake before continuing, "Decided to ditch me for his hot date. I guess my Crystal plan worked. He supplies me with numerous tequila shots, and then leaves me here to go to The Bungalow. Hmph." She doesn't seem angry but her words give me pause. Is she upset he left to be with another woman?

"Lucy, come sit down. You seem a bit wobbly." She giggles as she attempts to repeat "a bit wobbly" with a horrendous English accent several times. Eventually she lets me help her onto the futon. I sit down beside her and brush several pieces of hair out of her face. She looks like she may have taken a tumble.

"You're pretty." She says it as she stares straight into my eyes. I scoff and offer a mild "thank you."

"No, like really pretty. You're like so beautiful it's not even fair. How am I supposed to look at you every day? Are men even allowed to have lashes that long? And your cheekbones, *come on.*" I know she's inebriated, very inebriated, but I can't help but enjoy the compliment. I've never been told I'm unattractive but hearing these words from her feels like I've won some sort of prize. She hiccups quite audibly into my face but doesn't seem to notice.

"Okay, Luce, I think maybe you've had a few too many. Let's get you to bed, eh?" I fold an arm around her waist to help her up. I'm debating just tossing her over my shoulder at this point.

"Mmm." She hums as she leans into me and wraps herself around my chest. "You smell good too. And you're so warm. How are you always so warm? Are you a werewolf?" She looks up at me, eyes wide as saucers. Was that a serious question?

She's clinging to me like some sort of woodland creature. I'm pretty sure if I stand she'll still be attached. I so want to kiss her, but I know it's not the right time. I could never take advantage of her in this vulnerable state, no matter how badly I may want to.

"Lucy, how about you lie down, sleep down here, okay? Want me to play you a song? I might be able to whip up a lullaby if I really put my mind to it."

"Nooooo." She clings harder. "Stay here, your shirt's soft." Another hiccup. She all but forces me down to use my chest as a pillow.

I know I should leave, should peel her perfect little hands off of me and leave her be. If only I were a stronger man. I lie back and start running my hand through her hair before I can think better of it.

I remember the first time we shared this bed together. I was terrified of getting too close to her, worried I'd scare her away with even the briefest touch. But at some point in the middle of the night she reached for me. I'm sure it wasn't intentional, maybe she was just cold, but I remember waking to her arm draped over my chest, her hair tickling my skin. What I would give to lie with her like this every night. Once she starts to snore I finally close my eyes and let myself enjoy her drunken embrace.

23

• • •

Lucy

TODAY IS A GOOD DAY, a really good day. All the guys are taking a break from work to go to the beach, Adamma is here, and I've been splitting my time between hanging with her at the pool and in the kitchen making a special family dinner: fajitas—because I discovered they're Henry's favorite.

"Almost done!" Adamma yells over the blender. She's making me her famous hangover cure which only sounds mildly disgusting. I know I drank way too much last night, but I don't feel horrible, probably because I seem to have gotten a lot of sleep. I was a bit surprised to wake up on the futon again, but at least I was alone this time. Henry told me how I came down to the studio last night and drunkenly asked him to play me a lullaby, and once I passed out, he figured it best to leave me there. I must have spent all night dreaming of snuggling with him, because I could not get the image out of my head this morning.

"Here you go. It's best to chug it fast, trust me." Adamma hands me a glass full of brownish goo and I do as I'm told while trying not to gag. Thankfully it tastes better than it looks.

I start bringing everything out to the patio and bump into Henry.

"Are these the famous Luzu fajitas?" He smiles at me like we have a shared secret.

"Steak and shrimp, just like last time. I doubled the salsa verde though so no one has to fight Graham for it."

Henry circles me until he's directly behind me. He balances his forearms on my shoulders while he drops his head on top of mine. He's been doing this a lot lately and while I'm used to guys wielding me as an armrest, the gesture from him makes me melt every time. It's like he's claiming me.

"Fajitas are my favorite food
I like the way they sizzle and I like the
way they groove
I like them extra spicy and the salsa
very green
but what I like most is the chef who eats
with me"

He drops a kiss on the top of my head before pulling out the chair for me. "Sorry, that was lame. I just always want to sing for our food now. You know, in case it gets jealous of our last meal? But this may have been even worse than my fish and chips rap."

I start to giggle, and I don't miss Adamma's smirk as she watches us. She flashes the slightest head tilt as she raises her brows. No one else will pick up on the gesture, but I understand her perfectly. For weeks she's been claiming she knows something is going on with us. Maybe she's right, it's hard for me not to want to be close to him, especially after getting serenaded like that.

"So, I hear you're writing a book about us. You better make

me the hot one." Graham gives me a seductive wink, followed by a purr and hand gesture to match. "Ahh I can't reach, can someone pass me the salsa?"

"It's not about any of you. Henry, what did you tell them?"

Preston is giving me his best impression of puppy dog eyes. "He said it's about a girl who moves into a big house with some guy she thinks is perfect and it turns out he and his housemates are all evil psychopaths. Lucy, what are we supposed to think!?"

Adamma laughs hysterically beside him.

"I think it sounds sick," Jayce says. "Can I be the *really* bad one though? And Luce, I'm happy to pose for inspiration, you know, whatever you need, girl." Jayce winks at me but the look Henry gives him could cut glass. What's going on there?

"Guys, stop. It's not about you, not any of you, I swear. It's a *Beauty and the Beast* retelling, just kind of, in reverse, with vampires. It's a hundred percent fiction, only inspired by a fairy tale."

I feel Henry's knee accidentally bump up against mine before he speaks. His voice is soft as he leans over, and I realize he's just talking to me.

"Should I be worried? I know I wasn't supposed to say anything, but it slipped out. Are you going to kill off my character now?"

"Oh my God, it's not about you!"

"Would you like it if I were more . . . beastly?"

Our knees bump again and I pull my leg away. Henry's definitely flirting with me. I feel butterflies playing racquetball in my stomach as I try to formulate a response.

"If you're a beast, I'm a beast." I say it with an awkward laugh, not quite sure what I even mean, before I stand.

"Adamma, wanna come help me make some more margs?"

. . .

"Have you even had one drink yet? Why are we making more?" She followed me into the kitchen and now we're just standing at the island while I try to figure out what's happening with Henry.

"No, I think your magic hangover cure actually made me feel worse. Maybe I'll have one. Tequila could help at this point."

"Amen." She pours us each a small shot and we throw them back.

"Are you gonna tell me what's going on with you and Henry?" She motions to pour another shot but I decline. Last night is still fuzzy and I'm worried I might have embarrassed myself. Did I honestly ask him for a lullaby? Yikes.

"I told you, we're just friends. Nothing has changed, really." She cocks her head and just keeps looking at me like I obviously have more to say. "Okay, maybe we flirt a little. And, I don't know. We sort of had a . . . *moment*, the other day."

I wince. I've been wanting to talk to someone about this but I'm already regretting it. What if I'm wrong? What if it's all in my head? No, I know it's not. He was overtly flirting with me tonight.

Beastly.

God, why is that such a turn on?

"What do you mean, a *moment*?"

"Well, we were paddle boarding. And he sort of, opened up to me. It was really sweet. I just noticed him looking at me differently, like maybe he—" I bite my lower lip hard, embarrassed from how childish I sound. "Like he wanted me."

I squint at her in shame trying to gauge a reaction. She *snorts*.

"Luce, *of course* he wants you! I can see him pining after you all the way in here. Are you the last person to notice this?" I look over to the window to determine if Henry's in my line of sight but he's completely hidden. "I wasn't being literal. Jesus Lucy, you obviously want *him*. What's the problem?"

"I . . ."

"Dami, what are you two doing in here? I missed you." Preston interrupts us with a big pout before sliding up next to Adamma and wrapping his arms around her. "We got a fire going, nice and warm. Come back?"

Adamma looks down at Preston. She kind of towers over him, especially in her heels. They're so sweet together, just gazing into each other's eyes. I realize I should probably let them be alone and make my way back outside. They follow me anyway and Adamma runs ahead to whisper in my ear, "Don't be an idiot, he wants you."

The guys have all moved to the firepit and there's an empty chair for me next to Henry. When I stumble into it, I notice his gaze on me, locked and unmoving. And after I sit, he reaches down to the chair's leg and tugs me toward him. I'm not sure if it's cold out here, or if he's giving me actual chills.

"Want a bite?" Henry holds up a perfectly roasted marshmallow a few inches from my face. "I toasted it for you." I take a mouthful, savoring the burnt sugar on my tongue.

"You look beautiful tonight," he says. I squint at him and raise an eyebrow. I'm wearing my three-sizes-too-big Nantucket sweatshirt as a dress over my bikini and my hair is messily thrown into a topknot. I don't get dolled-up often, but I know this isn't exactly my best look.

"You do. You look vibrant. Like the sun. Like everyone else is just orbiting around you."

I feel our knees touch and know it's not an accident this time. I wonder if it was ever an accident before. He leans closer, like he's ready to whisper something directly in my ear, but he doesn't speak. He wraps an arm around me and pulls me closer.

"What are you . . . ?"

"You're shivering, Luce." His hand starts traveling up and down my arm and I resist the urge to nuzzle into him. I can feel the warmth radiating off of his body and I'm reminded of last night's dream. I close my eyes for just a moment and I'm back on that futon, wrapped around Henry while his fingers comb through my hair. The dream was so vivid it feels like a memory. Henry tightens his hold on me and I open my eyes with a start. I can sense my pulse quickening. I feel . . .

"I'm gonna go grab some chips!" I'm not sure why I need to exclaim this quite so loudly to the group, but I'm up and out of my chair heading toward the kitchen before anyone can respond.

Am I really hiding in the pantry?

I'm walking in tight circles, quickly trying to sort through everything happening in my head. I've already told myself not to pursue my feelings for Henry; I know it will only end in disappointment for both of us. I can't let one little compliment get to me.

But was it just a compliment? I *did* feel good tonight; I felt like the woman I used to be, confident and fun, never thinking about my failures or who I was currently disappointing. Sometimes it feels like he can see right into my soul.

"Luce, you okay?" Of course he followed me in here. He's looking at me so intensely, his expression unreadable, like he's waiting for something to happen. I feel him lightly gripping my wrist. When did he do that? He inches closer and his hand starts to slide down until only our fingers are entwined.

"Lucy." One word, just him saying my name and I'm under a spell. His voice has dropped at least an octave. He licks his lips and I think he might kiss me. I can't stop staring at his mouth.

Please kiss me.

What am I doing? I should walk away but I'm frozen here

in the damn pantry praying to the Tostitos and cake mix that he'll kiss me before I have the sense to run out of here.

"Lucy." It sounds different this time, like a prayer, like a question to which I have all the answers. He moves closer. His eyes are the darkest I've ever seen them, and I imagine the deepest depths of the ocean. He's moving so slowly, giving me every opportunity to bolt.

I'm a statue.

Suddenly, I need to know what his lips feel like, if he'll be gentle and timid like he was when we first met. Or maybe his self-assurance will take over and he'll grab me forcefully, a man in control.

I close my eyes, lost in a fantasy of all the ways Henry might feel, and then his lips are on mine, pillowy soft and so gentle I can barely breathe. He tastes like tequila and burnt sugar, and unadulterated lust. I feel him slide a loose lock of my hair through his fingers and hold it steady just below my chin. The kiss is chaste, but languid, meaningful. When he pulls away, I instinctively lean toward him and he kisses me again, a whisper of lips and breath.

He's moving so slow, so decadently, painfully slow.

I place my hands flat against his chest ready to push him away, stop this before it goes any further. Two kisses, that's all, that's fine. We can definitely go back to normal after two kisses. Blame it on the margaritas, laugh it off like it never happened. But my hands betray me, start fisting his shirt, drawing him in closer to me.

Apparently, this was the sign he needed. His fingers move through my hair greedily and his mouth is on mine in a possessive, seductive way that makes my toes curl. His hands trail down to squeeze my ass as he pulls me up and wraps my legs around his waist. My back is pressed flat against the closed door, Henry never once breaking the kiss.

This is . . . *hot*.

Somehow, he's everything and also nothing like I'd imagined. He's gentle and firm, tender and wild. He's utterly intoxicating.

"I dream about this, about you." He's nuzzling the slope of my neck as he says it. I can feel his lashes tickle my skin, his lips barely brushing against my throat, his thumb fiddling with the bikini string on my hip. And then his mouth is back on mine and the kiss is filled with so much warmth I feel my entire body start to melt. This doesn't feel like just a kiss. It feels like the start of *something*. "Tell me this is real. Please?"

"It's—" I'm suddenly pressed harder against the door, maybe a little too hard, actually . . .

"What the hell!?"

The voice comes from the other side of the door—Jayce. Henry sets me down instantly and we pull away from each other with lightning speed. The door swings open and I see Jayce staring at us, mouth agape like a fish. We may not be pressed up against each other anymore, but I can see how disheveled Henry's shirt and hair are looking, I'm sure it's even worse for me.

"Sorry, too much tequila, couldn't decide on a snack. I think I'm just gonna go to bed, actually," I murmur quickly as I make my escape.

I hear Jayce's bewildered: "It's only nine thirty," but I'm already gone, grabbing Rowan, and heading upstairs to a room that isn't mine.

I'm hiding.

I'm actually hiding in Graham's room.

When he came up for the night, he was more than a little shocked to see me and Rowan in his bed. I told him that he couldn't ask any questions but Row and I needed to spend the night with him. In return, he gets to pick the dinner menu for a month. I'm going to overdose on red meat.

I'm still here in the morning, and he's being surprisingly cool about this, barely inquiring at all as to why I haven't left his room. I guess Graham just gets me, or maybe he doesn't really care. Either way, I'm grateful. I have no idea what I'm feeling after last night. I keep going over every moment in my head. It was incredible, intense, more than any one word can describe. I can still feel Henry's lips against my neck.

I dream about this, about you.

That kiss. I never knew kisses like that even existed.

I want to regret it, but I don't. I can't. I just need to figure out how to stop it from happening again, and not lose Henry in the process.

We're eating donuts in bed, Rowan's favorite. Graham ducked out for them while everyone else was still asleep, and now we're starting our fifth straight episode of *Below Deck Mediterranean*. Graham and I clearly have very different tastes in men, and we've been fighting all day over whether the second stew should hook up with the rugged South African bosun or stay with the deckhand from New Zealand that has a few too many tattoos for my liking.

"Seriously though, what is it with you and Kiwis? You're from Australia. Doesn't that automatically make them less exotic?"

"Dear Lucy, you naïve little lady. Have you ever seen the All Blacks?" I often have to translate Graham's words but, what did he just say? "Don't look at me like that. NZ's rugby team. You take one look at those blokes and tell me you don't want to take a tumble with them. I'll wait."

I'm googling New Zealand All Blacks when we're interrupted by loud knocking on the front door. It's followed by a hauntingly familiar voice yelling my name. A voice I haven't heard in months.

This cannot be happening.

"No, no way. Not possible. This isn't happening right now." As if to prove me wrong I hear my name again, louder this time.

"Luce, what's going on?" Graham points to the window facing the front drive. "Do you know that bloke?"

I mouth *"Jack,"* too shaken to say his name aloud and Graham's face turns stormy.

Rowan may be a lap dog, but Graham is a Doberman, ready to go to battle for me. It makes me feel brave. I may have fallen down on that surfboard hundreds of times but I'm standing now. I just had to push through the fear. I can do anything. I can face Jack.

Luckily, everyone who's home is in the basement working and unlikely to hear what's going on, but I also know that my luck can't last forever, so I need to go shut him up as quickly as possible.

I head down the stairs, open the door and step onto the threshold—I do not want him inside this house. This is my sanctuary, my safe haven, my special place where nothing bad happens and no one abandons me. I won't let him ruin that for me.

"What the hell are you doing here?"

Jack has always been objectively attractive. Six feet tall, sandy blonde hair, so perfectly preppy that he could easily live inside a *Vineyard Vines* catalog. Nothing gives me more joy than how little I feel for him in this moment.

"Whoa, hey to you too, Lu. What is this place? Apparently, you upgraded after you left Boston. Don't tell me you're dating someone new already?"

"Okay, first of all, no. And if I was it would be none of your business. *You* left *me*, remember? And don't call me Lu. What do you want?"

"Lu. Lucy, I'm sorry. I made a mistake; I know that now. Do you know how hard it was for me to find you here? You haven't answered any of my calls." He plasters on one of his perfectly polished grins, like that's all it should take for me to come crawling back into his arms.

"I don't care. And I don't care if you miss me. We're divorced, or did you forget?"

I do wonder how he found me here, I haven't told anyone where I'm living except for my agent and Sarah.

"Okay, I wasn't expecting you to be this angry with me. I thought we understood each other. I never wanted to break up, but at the time I didn't think I had much of a choice, you know? I realize now that maybe we ended things too soon, so I'm willing to talk, have a real discussion this time. I think we could make something work."

"Maybe? Willing? Jack, you're delusional. You *hurt* me. When I had *no one, nothing,* you *left* me. I wasn't the only one who got bad news that day. And I couldn't just walk away from it. There's nothing to discuss, not now, not ever." I turn to go back inside and Jack pushes through the door with me, with more force than I was ever expecting.

"Jack, what the hell! Get out of here."

"Not until we talk about this. I'm your husband. Was your husband. I'm not ready to give up on us. Just hear me out, we can make this work again."

"It's too late for you and your white horse." The lyric flies out of my mouth. I always loved that song. *And I was never a princess.* "This was never a fairy tale." I say the last line almost under my breath, but his look of confusion tells me he hears every word.

“Huh? What are you talking about, Lu?”

“Taylor Swift is so wise. Too wise for you, Jack. Now please, just leave.”

“Fuck Taylor Swift. I’m here for you.” He reaches out to grab my shoulders but never gets the chance.

I hadn’t realized Graham had been hanging behind me just out of sight until he comes charging through the foyer and shoves Jack out the door so hard, he topples to the ground.

“Get the fuck out, mate. No one wants you here.” A loud huff escapes Graham’s mouth. “And Taylor Swift is a damn hero!”

He slams the door shut, locks it, and makes a motion of wiping the dirt off of his hands.

“Well, that was fun. More Bravo, or do you plan on bringing any more drama to the house yourself?”

24

. . .

Henry

SHE HAD NO ONE, *nothing, and he left her?* What did she mean by that? It's only been a few hours since I overheard the Jack incident, and I can't get those words out of my head. She told me she was going through a tough time. I knew she needed support, a mate, something, but did I actually ever know the extent of what she's been dealing with?

I want to kill him. The pain in her voice when she spoke to him, it made me feel physically ill. I almost chased after him once Graham tossed him out, but I didn't want Lucy to know I'd been listening. I'm a coward. I know I'll have to tell her eventually, though considering she's avoiding me like the plague, I'm not sure when that will occur.

I just can't make sense of *why* she's avoiding me. I didn't push her, or pressure her. She kissed me back, wrapped her legs around my waist so tight I barely had to hold her. I know she has feelings for me. I refuse to believe it's all in my head.

That kiss was magic.

I've been sitting at the piano for hours when she wanders

in. "That sounds really beautiful. Is it for the new show? Doesn't seem very dragon-y."

"No, just tinkering a bit." I hadn't even realized I'd been playing. Every time I think of her, my hands have a mind of their own. I stop and look over to see her face turned down toward her feet. Her fingers are fidgeting with the hem of her shirt. She must still be upset over her unexpected visitor.

"Could we talk? Grab dinner, maybe? I was thinking Fish Grill. I really want something deep fried." Her eyebrows knit up while her mouth pinches sheepishly.

After the day she had, she deserves all the fried food on the planet.

"Let's do it."

I've determined Lucy likes to ramble when she's nervous. She spends the entire car ride talking about Graham's obsession with the rugby team from New Zealand, and his apparent fetish with tribal tattoos. But once we get to the restaurant, her mood abruptly changes. Quiet Lucy is one I don't know how to read at all.

We grab our fish and chips to go and cross the street to walk down to the beach. Once we've chosen a spot to sit down, she starts attacking her chips with a fervor I've never seen from her. She must be starving. She eats through half her plate, with her head down, barely acknowledging me. It's strange, so unlike her typical effervescent self. I wonder if I should bust out the rap we came up with on our last trip here. Finally, she looks up and then swallows several times before speaking.

"So, I just wanted to say I'm sorry. About last night. We obviously had too much to drink and—"

"Lucy, what are you talking about? You weren't even drinking. I probably had half a margarita."

Her mouth opens but nothing comes out.

There's a long pause, and I have no idea where this is heading.

"Lucy?"

"Sorry. I don't know why I said that. Look, I'm just trying to say it was obviously a mistake and I hope that it doesn't ruin our friendship. You mean so much to me. Can we just forget that it ever happened?"

Forget? I could never forget that kiss, nor would I ever want to.

"What if I don't feel it was a mistake? What if *I* think we like each other, as more than friends?"

"Henry, I don't want to be anything more than friends with you. And if I led you on, I'm sorry, truly. I just hope you can forgive me."

"Led me on? Lucy, why are you saying this? We shared that kiss, both of us. You know it wasn't a mistake."

Is it really possible she's that good of an actress, or that I'm just hopelessly delusional? I can still feel every bit of her body pressed up against me, can still hear the sighs she made when I raked my fingers through her hair. I've never felt anything like this before. It can't be all in my head, it just can't.

She must notice the pained expression I'm trying to hold in. "I'm sorry, I'm so sorry. I just need—I need us to go b-back, to before, to . . . to being friends. I c-can't lose you. I can't—"

She starts to cry and my heart plummets. I move to wrap my arms around her; I can't stand seeing her sad. I'm just so fucking confused. Of course I won't do anything to diminish her presence in my life, even if it means she wants us to stay platonic. But I wish I understood why.

"We'll always be friends, no matter what. Just tell me what's going on. I can see this isn't really what you want. Why are you pretending?"

She's still tucked in my embrace, and I aggressively fight the urge to kiss her. To my dismay, she takes a deep breath and pulls away from me. Her tears cease rather abruptly, and she expels a long, slow exhale to compose herself. It looks like she's putting on a mask.

"I'm not pretending. I was just lonely, okay. I don't feel that way about you. I'm just sad because I was worried I messed up our friendship."

Well, then.

I promise to follow her wishes, no matter how much it kills me inside. I drive us home in mostly silence, not knowing what to say to her. I promised we'd stay friends and I meant it, but now that she knows I want more than that, how am I supposed to act? I've never had a girlfriend. Hell, I don't think I've ever had a crush. I've definitely never had whatever the fuck this is. I just need to get to work, get Lucy out of my head and focus on something else for a while.

I give her a hug before we go inside, trying to touch as little of her as possible, and I wonder if there's anything in the world that could make this day any worse.

25

. . .

Lucy

I FEEL SICK, empty.

I hated lying to Henry. I could see the hurt in his eyes; I swear I could feel his pain deep in my gut. Maybe it was just my own pain, shattering the best part of my life right now. In my head, I know I made the right decision. If I let this go any further, how could we hold on to our friendship? But my heart is aching, I just want to curl up in a ball and weep.

Just as we walk into the house, he gives me a hug that's more of a side-squeeze and it feels brother-y. I hate it. What have I done?

"Lucy, I am *so* sorry. I swear to you we're going to find him."

"Preston, go back out there I'll take care of th—"

"No, I have to . . . I'm so sorry, I'm *so sorry*."

"Guys, where the fuck is the peanut better? I can't find anything in the pantry and I already used up all the treats. Oh! String cheese—"

The scene in front of us is absolute mayhem. The guys are

all running in circles, yelling over one another. I can barely make out what anyone is saying.

"What the hell is going on here!" Henry bellows into the house.

Graham speaks first. His eyes are down, refusing to look at me and his words are clipped. "It's Rowan. He got out just a bit ago, we're having trouble finding him."

"Lucy, I swear I just let him out the side door like I always do." Preston is basically hyperventilating, eyes red as he looks at me apologetically. "He's never run like that. I'm so sorry. I'm going back out to look for him now."

I know I should say something but I'm frozen. This might be my worst nightmare coming to fruition.

I feel myself falling but don't seem to register what's happening until my knees hit the ground. Graham is at my side instantly, helping me onto the couch. "He's really gone?"

"We're going to find him. He probably just wanted to check the surf, roll around in some sand. Don't panic, okay, love?"

"It's almost dark. There are coyotes, and mountain lions and snakes. Oh my God, why did I bring him here? What have I done? I was supposed to take care of him. I . . . I can't lose him. He's all I have left, he's . . . everything. He's the only family I'll—"

Strong hands land on my shoulders before cupping my face and holding it up. I see Henry's sapphire eyes, blurred by my tears, looking back at me.

"Lucy, I swear to you I will find him, okay?" I struggle to keep my eyes open, can barely comprehend him, lost in thoughts I wish I could vanquish. "Lucy, look at me. I don't care if I'm out all night, Rowan is coming home, okay? You stay here with Graham, try to relax. I'll be back as soon as we have him."

"No, I'm coming. I have to go find him." I attempt to stand but sway right into Graham's open arms.

"Luce, you can barely stand. I think you're in shock. Let them find him, okay? No one is going to let Rowan get hurt."

Minutes pass that seem like hours. Graham is trying his best to keep me calm. He suggests we go for a swim, says it will help calm my nerves to float in the water. I didn't even realize how much I've been shaking. I feel numb anyway, so I change into a swimsuit and throw on my paper-thin bathrobe that Rowan loves to sleep on. It smells like him.

When I get back to the living room, Preston and Jayce are there. They look defeated, red-eyed and sullen. Preston tells me they've looked everywhere, but it's almost nine-thirty now and the sun has completely set. They both came back to the house assuming someone else had found him.

A few more minutes go by that feel like years. I'm curled in a ball on the floor surrounded by pillows the guys keep tossing at me since I refuse to move to the couch. I just want to stay on the ground; it feels like I'm closer to Rowan. The only sounds I hear are the guys calling neighbors, the police station, anyone they can think of to help with the search. Preston went back out with every flashlight he could find, but I already know it's a lost cause.

I'm still lying on the ground, crying into a pillow when I hear the door open. Somehow, I know it's Henry, and I'm not ready to hear the bad news. I bury my face into the pillow, unable to stop weeping. I feel Graham shaking me, speaking to me, but I can't hear anything other than the ringing in my ears.

"Lucy!"

"Look!"

I hear voices but I don't, everything muddled together with the screaming in my head. I feel Graham's hands take hold of my face, pulling me up from the floor.

"Lucy, look! He's home. Rowan's fine, he's home."

Rowan's safe. He's here. He's home. Home. When did I start thinking of this as my home? When did they start thinking that?

Rowan is licking my face and now my tears have turned joyous, but falling freely, nonetheless. What the—

God, he's covered in sand.

"He gave us quite a fright but turns out he just wanted to do a bit of digging on the beach. Isn't that right you sneaky little minx?" Henry is on the ground with me and Row. I'm afraid to look at him. I'm afraid of all the emotions that will overwhelm me if I take a single peek at his gorgeous face.

I'm not sure how long we all lie there, just petting Row, constantly reminding myself he's not lost anymore, but Graham interrupts the silent snuggling.

"Luce, how about I give our little jailbird here a bath? He's . . . disgusting, and you deserve to relax, go for that swim we never took, hey? I'll watch him like a hawk the rest of the night."

"Thanks, that actually sounds kind of nice. I'm way too wired to sleep yet anyway."

Henry grasps my hand and I finally meet his eyes for the first time since he returned. "Mind if I join you?"

After Henry changes his clothes, he meets me outside where I'm lying down on the pirate raft. It's not in the water, but it's the most comfortable thing out here. The pool is illuminated by nothing but the hazy light of the moon, a gleaming orb suspended above us. I'm exhausted and exhilarated by tonight's events and I want to properly thank Henry, especially after our conversation from earlier. I look at his face, his brutally perfect face, the chiseled jaw, those deep, lustrous blue eyes. Where do I even begin?

"Henry, I . . . I know that thank you doesn't even come close to what I need to say to you." He tries to interrupt me, but I place my hand over his mouth, willing him to let me do this. He kisses the pads of my fingers and gently takes my hand in his, tracing small circles over the back with his thumb. This loving, intimate touch feels so natural it takes me a minute to realize this is far beyond our normal. I should pull my hand away but I can't. "You were out there for hours, and you've already done so much for me, and I feel like such a shitty person for what I said to you tonight, and I just need you to know how grateful I am, okay? I just, I—"

"Lucy, listen to me. You losing Rowan was never an option. I would never have come home without him." He tugs on my hand until he pulls me up to sit directly in front of him. His other hand comes up to land on my shoulder before he starts fiddling with a loose lock of my hair. "Do you understand how important you are to me? Being *just friends* might not be my first choice, but it doesn't mean I won't do everything in my power to make you happy. I'd sell my soul to see you smile."

I move before I even know what I'm doing. I kiss him, and it's not friendly at all, it's deep and delicious, and . . . what am I *doing*? I pull away.

"I'm sorry," slips out and I wish I could take it back.

I'm not sorry at all.

I only wish I could get my feelings in check, get back to a place where every look he gives me, every word he speaks, doesn't make me want to peel his clothes off and climb on top of him.

Henry clears his throat, and his voice comes out deeper, raspier than usual. "Lucy, I want to be respectful. I heard what you said earlier and more than anything else, I want you to be comfortable living here. But am I mad? I feel like there's something here, something . . . magnetic between us. Don't you feel it too?"

I can't lie to him. It was hard enough a few hours ago. After everything that happened tonight, I just can't do it. I nod my head slowly and watch the corners of his mouth twitch slightly.

"Henry, of course I feel it. I just—"

"Don't. Please don't finish whatever you're planning to say right now. You are all I think about, Luce. You're my favorite person. Every time I see you sad it kills me that I can't hold you, can't touch you and comfort you how I want to. It kills me that it's not appropriate even though it feels like the most natural thing in the world." He moves his hand from my shoulder, gently cupping my chin, forcing me to look at him.

"Let me kiss you, please? Let me kiss you under the pretense that we're not just friends; that for me, at least, I want to be much more than friends."

How am I supposed to deny him when he looks at me this way? "I mean, you do owe me you know; I saved your pup tonight. That has to deserve at least one kiss." I laugh just a bit. I don't have the energy to resist this anymore. I pull his face toward me and lock my lips with his.

The second I lie back on the raft, Henry's mouth glued to my own, I know this isn't just a kiss. It feels like I'm finally letting go, like I can breathe again. I've been pushing all my feelings for him deep inside, and now that they've broken free, I'm consumed by them.

He keeps making the same "mmm" sound and each time I hear it my body vibrates. He's pressed up against me in only his swim trunks and I'm finally able to marvel at his perfectly sculpted body. My hands roam greedily across his shoulders, his chest, down to his abs. But he seems to be only touching my face, his fingers grazing my neck. I arch slightly and tilt my head back, hoping it sends the message that I'm ready for more than a kiss.

26

• • •

Henry

I AM COMPLETELY and utterly ruined. Kissing Lucy feels like heaven. No—it feels like home. It's nothing like it was last night. No hesitation, no fear, no hard door at her back. This entire evening was wholly unexpected, but we are so perfectly in sync, it's like this moment was fated.

God, she feels good. I smooth my hand down her hair until I'm fisting it at the ends. She tilts her chin back and gives the sweetest, smallest moan I've ever heard. I decide to take advantage of the new position and drop kisses along her neck until I reach the spot just below her ear. I'm rewarded by another breathy sound but this time the note is clear to me, a perfect G4. I linger there for a moment, wondering what other notes I can coax out of her.

I wish I had more experience with this. I want to know what she wants, what she needs, but I've always had a complex relationship with sex. When I was younger, girls just saw me as the awkward bloke who never uttered a word. I wasn't exactly wooing them with my charm. Then I got to LA, a twenty-five-year-old-virgin, and suddenly I couldn't keep them away. The women here are so aggressive. The first date I went on, set up by my agent of course, I decided to hire a limo for the evening. I thought it'd be romantic and gentlemanly. Instead, I got my first blowjob before we reached the restaurant.

After that first date, I didn't bother with a limo, decided it was better to meet them instead, usually at a bar. Didn't make a difference. Apparently, women here don't mind if I say two words over drinks; they think I'm mysterious. Or maybe it's that they can google my net worth. I can't think of a single time I wasn't invited back to their home after, and sometimes it wasn't even after. I've been dragged into the loo more times than I care to admit. I'm equally ashamed that I rarely declined the offers. For years I had fantasized about what it would be like to be with a woman. I so badly wanted to experience the love and affection I'd seen with my mum and dad. I also wanted to feel the immeasurable difference between a woman's touch and my own. The reality was always so disappointing.

Until now. Until Lucy. *This* is what I've been chasing after all this time, the connection I've always desired. And now all I can think about is how inexperienced I am with this part. I don't know how to seduce a woman. I only know how to say yes, to perform, and to leave.

What kind of man does that make me?

I realize I've almost completely opened her robe. I've been tugging at the neckline to expose more of her throat and shoulders but now even the waist is starting to come apart. She doesn't seem bothered by it. I'm not sure where this is going, considering she told me earlier tonight that she only wanted to be friends, so, am I taking this too far? I pause and pick my head up to look at her, try to gauge what she's thinking. She slowly drags her teeth over her bottom lip as her eyes lock on mine.

She's panting. Fuck. I reach for the sash on her robe but decide I want to be one hundred percent sure.

"Is this okay?" My voice sounds so gravelly I barely recognize it. I see her nod once before I pull it loose and lower my mouth back down to her body.

Her bikini covers most of her breasts, but the skin I have access to is so supple I'm afraid to scratch it with my stubble. I'm still not sure what I'm doing, but I'm dying to hear that note again and feel desperate to get it out of her. I reach to tug on her bikini strings after she gives me another silent nod. At the sight of her I feel myself stiffen immediately. There's no way she doesn't feel it too. This is one area I've never been in doubt of. At first, I'm worried how she'll react, but she leans into me and hooks her ankle around my calf.

I drag my hands along her ribcage, feeling her soft skin pebble with goosebumps, and lower my mouth to the peak of her breast. I want to be gentle with her, touch her body as sweetly as she feels in my arms, but she arches into me, silently urging me to do more. I appease her with a nibble, though I'm not sure if it's enough. Now I'm wondering if she can sense my insecurities, because she grabs my hand and slowly leads it lower, down to her navel, and then further, in between her legs. She's guiding me. She wants this just as much as I do.

We work together in a slow rhythm, her showing me exactly where she wants to be touched as I memorize every inch of her skin, every place that makes her shiver or sigh. I love the way her body responds to me. I wish I could bottle up the sounds she makes and create my own personal symphony from them. Her moans rise toward a crescendo, but I stop and pull away.

This isn't how I want to do this. I have three master's of Music from Juilliard, two for *performance.* Lucy may see me as the awkward bloke who needs help ordering wine at restaurants, but I'll be damned if I require her help here. I know I have skills; I just need to show her.

I grip her thighs deliberately and begin to press into her with each fingertip, strumming her skin like I would a guitar. Her light gasp lets me know this is good, unexpected but good. I move my hands up and down her legs, while I lower my mouth to the place she led me earlier. I use everything, my lips, my tongue, my teeth, and when her lovely little whimpers quicken, I start to hum.

Hearing her call out my name as her entire body trembles is the sexiest thing I've ever experienced. That is until she grabs onto my shoulders and pulls me against her, drawing our lips together as her legs shake beneath me.

After a few blissful moments wrapped around Lucy, once her breathing has slowed, she stands up, gloriously naked save for the gilded rainbow gleaming from her neck, and says, "How about that swim?"

"You're . . . stunning." A shy smile skates over her face before she reaches out her hand. I take it instantly and as soon as I'm standing I kiss her again. I don't know if it's possible for me not to touch her anymore, it feels like an addiction.

I reluctantly peel my lips away from her when I feel her fumbling with the tie on my trunks. And now she's dragging them down. I did not expect this to happen but, fuck, she can do absolutely anything she wants with me tonight. She must notice the startled look on my face. "What? You expect me to go skinny dipping alone?"

She helps me shimmy out of my trunks completely and I watch Lucy eye me up and down.

"Just *look* at you."

I chuckle, a bit embarrassed but pleased with her assessment. "No, Luce. Look at *you*." I scoop her up and walk us down the steps into the pool, kissing her along the way.

I'm a junkie for those lips; I'll never get enough.

"Henry?" she asks, stepping back into the water. "Want to make up a song? We could really branch out with a sea shanty." She eyes the pirate ship raft.

"No."

I grab onto her hips and kiss her again.

27

. . .

Lucy

AFTER OUR SWIM we decide to take advantage of his outdoor shower. He pulls me by the hand, and we shuffle quickly through the house and his room. My legs are wrapped around him before he even gets the water on, and he holds me up against the wall.

"Can you be gentle?" I really don't want to explain about my endo right now, and luckily he doesn't need me to. So far, Henry is excellent at taking directions.

"Anything you need. Just tell me, okay?" He starts to kiss my ear as he presses into me and begins whispering softly, "Anything you want . . . fuck . . . please tell me what you want . . . is this okay . . . fuck . . . Lucy, you feel . . . amazing." This might be the most I've heard Henry say all at once. I guess I finally figured out how to get the man of few words to ramble as mindlessly as I do.

Sex with Henry is euphoric. He's slow, reverent; never once letting his lips or fingertips leave my skin. His body is pure muscle, holding me up easily with one hand while the other caresses every part of me. It might be the best sex I've ever had.

Every movement, every kiss, sends more heat into me until I'm nothing more than a molten puddle.

As he finishes, I feel his teeth sinking gently into my neck. It's the most possessive thing I've ever experienced during sex and reminds me of all the Fae novels I obsess over. Maybe fictional men do exist.

When he sets me down, he moves us directly under the waterfall shower. The droplets send tingles from my scalp, past my neck and down to my bare breasts. He never stops touching me, his hand between my legs, his teeth dragging against the back of my shoulder. I brace my hands on the wall as I come, Henry behind me, holding me so tight I'm not sure if my feet are still on the ground.

After we dry off, he takes my hand and wordlessly leads me to his bed. We've spoken so little all night, and I'm not sure what this all means, how I'm going to fix *this*, but he lies down next to me and starts slowly stroking my hair. I've never felt such pure bliss. Even though I know this thing between us will be short-lived, I lean into his touch, wishing I could suspend this moment in time.

"Thank you for the kiss."

I scoff when he says it, knowing we've clearly gone beyond a *kiss* tonight; but he is stoic, no hint of amusement on his face.

He closes his eyes and drops his voice to barely a whisper. It comes out guttural and thick with emotion. "I think about kissing you all the time. I keep trying to write this battle scene—dragons, monsters, it's bloody intense—but all I can see in my head is your lips, your smile, the flutter of your eyelashes, and the notes turn much too lovely. You may be the end of my career as I know it."

Words escape me, so I snuggle in closer to him. He kisses the tip of my nose and I feel like I might physically melt into his sheets. I don't remember ever feeling this way with Jack. Loved, yes. Jack definitely loved me. He told me all the time, he did all the things a boyfriend, then a fiancé, and then a husband was supposed to do. Well, except the leaving me part. I guess he wasn't supposed to do that.

But tonight, in Henry's bed—in his arms—I feel adored, treasured, like my body is sacred to his own personal religion.

I must have dozed off at some point but wake when it's still pitch-black outside. Henry is lying on his back and presumably sleeping. Suddenly all the dark thoughts start seeping into my brain, depleting the joy I felt earlier.

I need to go back to my room. *My* room.

I live here. This is already getting way too complicated. I can't deny my feelings for him but where will this actually go? I know what kind of future Henry wants, and it's not one I can give him.

Suddenly I'm picturing Jack. When he told me that I had put him in an impossible situation, that it was over. How he was young, he still had options, how could I not understand? I remember apologizing then, somehow empathizing with him in the moment instead of myself. Who does that? I remember how small I felt the next day. I never fought for us, for me. He left me after one year of marriage and I never even got to yell at him. Until yesterday. Somehow it didn't make me feel any better.

Henry may seem perfect tonight, but I know better. Jack was perfect, until he wasn't.

I slowly slide out of bed and tiptoe across the room, realizing my bikini is still outside by the pool and I have absolutely nothing to wear. With four other men in this house, walking around naked is not an option. I feel around for a drawer and open a few at random, find a pair of boxer shorts and throw them on. I can cover my chest with my arms if needed, I just have to get out of this room. I'm just turning the knob when I feel Henry's hand on my shoulder.

"Where are you going?" He sounds hurt. I turn to face him but can barely make out his features in the dark.

"Sorry, I didn't mean to wake you. I thought it'd be best if I went back to my room."

"Why?" Such a simple question. It's so unnerving when he speaks like this. So matter-of-fact, like my answer should be just as effortless.

"Umm . . . I . . ." He places his hands on each side of my face and laces his fingers through my hair, pulling all the way to the back of my neck. I shudder at the touch, goosebumps covering my arms. I try to speak again but he starts trailing kisses across my jaw and all that escapes is a breathy moan. I arch into him and his hands elegantly slide down the sides of my body.

"Stay." A command, a plea, a prayer. "Please." Why are such simple words able to have this effect on me? I nod slowly, knowing my heart is going to betray my head for the rest of the night.

He lowers his head and starts dropping kisses onto my neck, then my chest. I feel his teeth gently tug on my nipple and I grab onto his shoulders for support. I thread my fingers through his hair while he slowly, so slowly, moves his lips lower. It's like he somehow memorized every place I like to be touched. Each press of his lips feels tactical, like he's following all the x's in a treasure map. After pressing the warmest kiss just below my navel, I feel him drag his mouth against the boxers I've stolen and pull them down with his teeth. His hands grab my hips firmly, and I feel his tongue glide between my legs as my knees buckle and I almost collapse into his arms.

He quickly picks me up and carries me to the bed. It feels different this time, frantic, hands and lips quickly covering as much ground as they can. It's like we both know this is the last time we'll be here. The sex is clumsy and sweaty, not purposeful like before, yet he still remembers to be gentle with me. He flips us over, letting me on top, telling me to set the pace. Straddling his body that is twice the size of mine makes me feel powerful, strong, *sexy*.

And seeing the way he looks up at me, for just a moment I believe I am completely worthy of a man like Henry.

"You're perf—"

"Don't. No one's perfect. Especially not me." My words are whispered, an attempt to mask my emotions. It may seem like a compliment to him but it only reminds me of how little he really knows about me.

"You're *my* perfect."

This time, after we finish, he isn't soft or tender. He holds me firmly, sensing I might make a run for it.

28

. . .

Henry

I WAKE to a wet tongue stroking the side of my face and my eyes open lazily. Sunlight creeps through the blinds, dappling the room like a motionless disco ball.

I'm not alone. I've only ever woken up in this bed alone. But Lucy is here, cocooned in my arms. I'm so fucking happy.

"Luce? Are you awake, love? Rowan must have snuck in here and he's having his way with my ear at the moment." I gently slide my hand up her arm, reveling in her smooth skin against my palm, but she stiffens. Then she half-stifles an extremely fake yawn before popping up and holding the sheet up to her chin.

"Sorry, I should take him out. Can I, umm, borrow a T-shirt or something?"

I grab her a bathrobe that looks utterly ridiculous on her. She's so tiny it's actually dragging on the ground when she walks toward the door. She's so damn adorable. I fight the urge to pull her back to bed.

"Row, be a doll and make it a quick wee, eh? I'm going to need your mum back in bed, *tout suite*."

I give Lucy a sly grin, amused with myself, but she barely picks up her head. I can see she's clearly embarrassed but about what, I'm not sure. Does she regret what happened last night? I may not have that much experience with women, but I know I'm not the only one who enjoyed it. She spent the entire night tucked into my arms, using my bicep as a pillow.

She leaves without a single word.

29

. . .

Lucy

THIS TIME I know Graham's room is still too close, so I escape the house entirely and head to Adamma's. She's the only person I confide in about my night with Henry, and she gladly invites me to stay with her until I'm ready to go back, as long as I give her all the juicy details. Her two-bedroom apartment in Culver City isn't bad, but I'd be lying if I said I wasn't missing the Malibu mansion.

"You promise you didn't have sex in the pool? I mean, it's his house, but just . . . I need to know before I go back there. And there's no way you just *swam*."

We're sitting at her kitchen island while she peppers me with never ending questions about last night's tryst. She should honestly work for the CIA. It's becoming impossible to keep any details to myself with her relentless interrogation.

"I promise. No pool sex. I swear I would tell you. I've told you everything else!"

"Okay, but like, what *did* you do in there?"

"Umm, just a lot of kissing, really."

Kissing, splashing, climbing all over him until I felt every single one of his corded muscles with my hands. Henry guiding me to the edge and grabbing my thighs.

I can feel my face warm up and from her expression the blush must be visible. I'm not sure why I left this part out, maybe it just felt gratuitous. I've never had a man be as generous as Henry.

"Kissing? Like the kind of kissing where poor Henry has to hold his breath the entire time?"

"Oh my God, no! That sounds . . . terrifying." She's giving me that look, eyebrows raised and silently urging me to fill in the blanks. "Okay, so no he wasn't underwater. But at one point he stayed in the pool after he lifted me—out." Effortlessly. My skin heats up just thinking about his strong grip on me. I can't get the scene out of my head...

"Henry, what are you—" He sets me down on the edge of the pool and holds up my leg, pressing kisses from my toes to my thigh.

"You said I could kiss you. Have you changed your mind?" He looks up at me with a wicked grin, his face dangerously close to my hips. "Please don't change your mind. I don't want to miss a spot." He presses his lips to my sensitive skin until goosebumps cover my leg. "I want to taste every inch of you. I want to hear every sound you make. You are my favorite melody." His mouth starts moving again. He gently bites at my inner thigh and then sucks on the same spot. My arms turn to jelly while I try to hold myself up.

"You really don't have to do that. You already—wow." He grabs both of my ankles and knots them around his neck, silencing my words with a deep press of his tongue. My entire body goes limp and I fall back onto the ground.

. . .

I CLEAR my throat and stare down, embarrassed, partially from where my mind has wandered and partially because of Adamma's need for information. I don't think I've ever talked to a girlfriend about my sex life in this much detail before. I guess all my friends back in Boston I knew through Jack, so there was no way I would even think about talking like this.

Or maybe it just wasn't as interesting to talk about. *You are my favorite melody.* Who speaks like that? Henry, apparently. I've never been with anyone who could be that sexy and equally romantic in the same moment.

"Okay sweetie, I'm gonna need you to be more specific. When you were *out* of the pool, can you tell me where your legs were?" She's clearly mocking me and I don't love this probing, but I did promise her details in exchange for lodging.

"His shoulders." My voice comes out as barely a whisper.

I wince at my own words as Adamma stands up from the couch and starts wagging her finger at me vigorously.

"Lucy, that man is *hot*, and he is *clearly* into you. Why the hell are you hiding from him!?"

Of course, she thinks I'm foolish for not wanting to see Henry, but she doesn't know the full story. I just don't know if I'm ready to tell her, or anyone, exactly how things ended with Jack. I hate to admit it, but deep down, I'm always afraid of people saying that they understand his decision, that he made the right call, that I shouldn't be so upset with him.

I tell her I'm just not ready for a relationship yet, that I've only been divorced for ten months. I tell her how Henry has become one of my closest friends, and how I'd be devastated to lose his presence in my life. And even if this isn't the whole truth, it's a huge part of it.

"Is that really your problem? You're afraid of losing your friendship?"

"He's not just a friend Dami, he's—"

"Umm, obviously. I don't have any friends giving me multiple orgasms." She lifts her brows tightly, but I shake my head at her.

"I don't mean it like that. He *is* my friend, but it's more than that. Before I met Henry, and came to LA, I was . . . well, I was in a pretty bad place. There was just nothing good left in my life. I lost all my friends except for Sarah, and you know what ended up happening with her. I thought moving out here was a place to start but I never expected to be as happy as I've been. I never expected to be *happy* at all. I'm so fucking scared of going back to where I was. I don't ever want to feel that hopeless again."

Adamma wraps her arms around me just as my tears start to fall. Then she pulls back and places her hands firmly on my shoulders.

"I hear you, okay? I just think you'll be even happier if you give this a shot. What do you have to lose?"

In a way she's right. What haven't I lost already?

"Did you know I was supposed to get a hysterectomy a month ago?" I blurt out.

"What? Of course I didn't know that. What happened?"

"I think I've mentioned to you that I have endometriosis." She nods, sitting back down on the sofa. I follow her lead and nestle myself into the corner. "Well, I probably didn't explain how bad it is. Mine is like, really severe. I'm in pain all the time and—well, that's why I have Rowan. Thanks, by the way, for never pressing me to explain what he does." We share that distinctive smile between friends who don't always need words to communicate.

"So, my doctor back in Boston had been pushing me for a while to get the surgery. It would basically cure all of my symptoms and I won't have to be in pain all the time. And after the divorce, I figured I should just go ahead and do it. But then

Sarah called and asked me to move here. I told myself I had to help my friend, and I would just reschedule the surgery. But I think I was really looking for any excuse not to do it."

"Damn, Luce. I wish you would have told me. I had no idea you were in this much pain. But, I'm sort of confused. What does this have to do with Henry?"

"I found out a year and a half ago that I'd never have kids. That's why Jack left me, by the way. I don't think I ever mentioned that."

"*By the way*? Don't just skip over that bomb, Luce. What the actual fuck?" Her jaw tenses as she mulls over everything I just said.

I wait for the head tilt, the realization that maybe he had a point, but it never comes.

"Next time he shows up here I want a crack at him. Tell Graham to get in line." I keep waiting for the rest of her reaction, but I see nothing on her face other than anger. "So, this is your issue with Henry? Jesus, Luce. That's a lot to carry on your own. Why haven't you talked to me about this? Why don't you talk to *him*? God knows, he has his own issues. I'm sure he'd be supportive. Sounds like it wouldn't take much to be more supportive than Jack."

I start to chew on the inside of my cheek, unsure of the proper response. Luckily, she isn't finished.

"You need me to pull a Phoebe and surrogate for you? All you have to do is ask. Have you seen these hips?"

I chuckle. "I appreciate the offer but I can't even do a retrieval or freeze anything. This whole playground"—I wave a hand over my lower abdomen—"has been under construction for years. It's officially condemned."

She laughs at my joke, but her eyes are slippery with emotion.

"I'm a mess, Dami. I just turned thirty and I'm already an

old crone. If I'm smart, by my next birthday, I'll be dealing with a severe case of menopause. Why the hell would someone like Henry want *me*?"

"He wants you, Lucy. He's made that abundantly clear. Or do we need to recap your sex-a-thon from last night?" She tilts a brow at me. "You honestly think sharing all this with him will change that? I don't mean to diminish your feelings because they are valid. But come on. Give the man a chance to prove you wrong."

I let her words roll over me. "But what if he doesn't even realize how he feels?"

"I'm not following."

"Okay, look. I read about this scientific study a few years ago where they tracked all these strippers."

"Excuse me?"

"Hear me out!" I continue, tucking my heels underneath me and sitting up straighter. "They tracked a bunch of strippers over twelve months to see when they got the most tips. After the study ended, their findings showed that strippers who were ovulating always got more tips than those who weren't. They even got more tips than the ones on birth control."

"Jesus, now we're punished for taking the fucking pill? Can women have *one* thing? Just one?"

"I know, right? But it's such an interesting study. Because of course, none of the men actually knew who was ovulating. They weren't consciously thinking 'hmm, she looks impregnable. Let me add another dollar.' But they were just innately more attracted to them. I'm already infertile. Once all the plumbing is gone, I'll probably be invisible. I'd be the most poorly paid stripper out there."

"Lucy, this is fascinating, and I absolutely want to read that study. But also, you're wrong. You'd make an *amazing* stripper." She makes a motion of ogling me. "Those boobs alone would get you a few hundreds each shift. And Henry gave you how many orgasms last night? Do you honestly think he would have gone another round if you'd been ovulating?"

I roll my eyes. "Ha-ha, you're hilarious. I don't mean it that literally. And I know he's attracted to me now, but after the surgery and everything else, what if he's just . . . poof . . . repulsed by me?"

"You know you sound crazy, right?"

"Of course I do!" I sink back into the pillows. "But I also know it's not that far off from my reality. Look at Jack. He was definitely in love with me, and it wasn't enough. There are zero guarantees it won't happen the same way with Henry. He absolutely wants a family."

My mind goes back to the day we went paddle boarding. *You'll make a great mother one day*. Of course that's how he sees me. Once I break that spell, it'll all be over.

"I'm sorry, Dami. I'm being selfish just showing up here out of the blue and throwing all of this on you. Can we talk about you? How are things with Preston?"

"Luce—" I give her a pleading look to change the subject. "Yeah, we're great actually. We're going to Chicago soon to visit his parents. They're a lot of fun."

"That's great you get along with them so well. Do your parents still live in Chicago too? Will you see them?"

"Hah, no. They moved to Toronto a few years ago, and if I do visit, Preston isn't exactly welcome."

"He's not? Why?" Preston seems like every parents' dream for a son-in-law. Who wouldn't love the man who gives monogamy five stars?

"He's not Nigerian. End of story."

"Seriously? I'm so sorry."

"Luce, I'll be more than happy to tell you all about my

parents another day. Right now, please be selfish. Let me help you work through all this."

Adamma and I have only known each other for two months. I felt close to her immediately but I'm so touched by how much she cares. When I first talked to Sarah about the divorce, she had this strange attitude with me. At one point I remember her saying "well, I guess you can't have everything."

I feel so lucky in this moment; to have a friend like Adamma, to have met Henry and everyone else in the house, to have this support system that I've been missing for years.

"I appreciate you, I do. I should probably start seeing a therapist again. This isn't your job."

"You've been dealt a tough fucking hand," Adamma exclaims. "Don't ever feel like a burden, especially not with me. A therapist might help, but you need your friends just as much. Plus, I will gladly have Rowan here any time. He is the best snuggler!" She reaches for my hands. "Come on, let's drink wine in bed and watch *The Vampire Diaries*. Times are tough, but at least you've got a beating heart. It's important to remember that."

MY FIRST MORNING waking up in Culver City isn't exactly pleasant. As someone who rarely sleeps in, seeing my phone blink 10:23 is almost as jarring as Adamma yelling at me to "get the hell up!" My pink wine hangover is in full force, but I jump in the shower, get dressed and obey every other order my new landlord gives me.

Adamma's goal today has been clear: distract me. First, she took me out for waffles (and thankfully, mimosas), and now we're heading to a "very special bookstore," whatever that means. But when I see the sign for *The Ripped Bodice* I realize she's deceived me. It shouldn't surprise me in the slightest for her to lure me with the promise of a bookstore, but instead trick me into buying some scandalous lingerie. Maybe she has Henry hidden inside a dressing room with a bottle of Champagne.

I glare at her when we near the door and shake my head. "Not cool, Dami! You said books! And you were right that it was probably the only way to get me off the couch, but still. Take me to a bookstore—I'm not in the mood for a sexy fashion show today.

She starts to chuckle before pointing a finger at the window. "Lucy—it is books. I swear! I just thought maybe you could use a sexy story, you know, as a distraction? Come on, you'll love it."

Wow. I think I have actually died and gone to heaven. An entire bookstore dedicated to happily ever afters? And even better, they love my dog! Nothing makes me happier than Rowan's love of bookstores. He always gets the most pets—bookish people are the best.

I make Adamma promise not to mention my author status, but that doesn't stop her from finding my latest book and screaming about it to the whole store. Then she promptly pushes me in the direction of steamy paranormal romances.

"I told you, I'm more of a fade-to-black kind of girl. Can we go back to the cartoon covers please?"

"Lucy, this is the inspiration you need! Your new book sounds amazing, and definitely adult considering all the bloodshed. Can't you add in a little dark romance? Please? For me?"

Actually, it's not a bad idea. I've been itching to add in a romance subplot, and with all the murder taking place, I don't think my typical dreamy kisses and longing looks will cut it.

"All right, grab a few. I definitely will need some ideas if I'm going to go this far out of my comfort zone."

"Come on, it can't be that hard. Just picture your night with Henry but throw some fangs on him." I choke at the vision. "See, you're halfway there!"

Adamma throws her arm around me.

"All right, Luce, let's go home and read about some sexy monster-men."

𝄞♪♫♬

I'VE NOW SUCCESSFULLY AVOIDED Henry for two whole days and the knot in my stomach is turning into physical pain. The worst part of it all is that I miss him—*terribly*. I pull out my phone to see thirty-one missed calls and a string of his unanswered texts.

Maestro:

8:57

Come back to bed love

xxx

9:33

Whered you go you sneaky girl

xxx

2:49

Are you all right Luce?

10:07

Have I done something wrong?

6:28

I'm going mad Luce - can you call me please?

And then I see a couple from Graham as well, as if I could feel any worse right now.

Teddy Graham:

3:16

What happened with you two?

11:05

Really Luce? I thought we were closer than this.

I know I have to go back, have to fix things with both of them. I have no idea what to tell them, how to explain my behavior. I don't even know how to explain it to myself. All I know is that I can't lose them, I can't lose this new life I've built. I feel like there's this thread holding everything together and it's so delicate, I could make one wrong move, and it will snap into pieces.

It's clear Henry has feelings for me, but there are too many secrets between us. And maybe it's selfish, but I don't want to be honest with him, because as soon as I am, everything will change.

This thing between us feels as fragile as a snowflake.

I grab Rowan, get into the car I now realize I stole from Henry, because I've actually become the worst person ever, and head back up the coast.

I'm not sure what I'll find when I get back to the house. I creep in like a mouse hoping I can make it to my room before anyone spots me. The first one I see is Jayce as I make my way through the kitchen. He walks straight by me with a big smile and a high five. I guess at least one person didn't notice my absence. But as I turn toward the living room, I see Graham sitting on the sectional staring back at me and the look on his face is anything but welcoming.

"Nice to see you again. Plan on staying a while?"

"Graham, I'm sorry I went dark on you, okay. I just needed some time to think." I can feel Rowan against my ankle pressing hard enough to get my attention, but I ignore him.

"To think? Did you use any of that time to think of someone other than yourself? Henry almost lost his mind, coming up with all sorts of outlandish possibilities. At one point he thought you and Row fell off a cliff together. If it wasn't for the missing car and Preston's call to Adamma my head may have gone there too. How selfish are you, Luce?"

I feel a sharp stab of pain in my gut and can't tell if it's real or just the guilt I'm feeling. It steadies to a low throb.

"I'm so sorry. I wasn't thinking. I just—things happened so fast with Henry and—" The look we share lets me know he's been debriefed on the Henry situation. "Look, it was horrible of me. I just needed to get out of here and figure out how to tell him it was a mistake. Please don't hate me, Graham."

"I could never hate you, but I can still be angry. Just, please don't scare us like that again. And stop saying it was a mistake, I see the way you two look at each other—what's the problem? He loves you, Luce, you know he does."

"Don't—don't say that. Please don't say that." My lower back starts to ache now too. "We can't be together, not like that. We just can't."

Rowan starts to bark but Graham ignores him.

"What do you mean, you can't? I know you, Luce. I know you wouldn't sleep with someone you didn't care for." Half of my body is pulsating with pain and Graham is looking at me like he doesn't actually know me at all, like he's trying to puzzle together everything when he's missing half the pieces.

Rowan gets louder, more determined. He's pressing into my leg as hard as he can. I know I should go lay down, but I can't just walk away from this conversation.

"Graham, please, just try to unders—"

The pain gets sharper and now I'm positive it has nothing to do with my emotions. It's in my back, my legs . . . I can feel myself doubling over right before everything goes black.

30

. . .

Henry

GRAHAM and I are weaving through cars up the highway, racing to the hospital, and he's not answering any of my damn questions. Lucy's eyes started blinking open right when the ambulance arrived and the paramedics stole her away from me before I could find out what happened.

"What the hell do you mean she just fainted? What were you doing? What was she saying? What was—"

"Henry, I don't fucking know, okay? We were talking. About you, actually. Then she winced like something was hurting her. I think she might have grabbed at her hip?"

"You think!? Graham, can you be a little more specific right now? What was hurting her?"

He tries to explain every moment he can but I still don't understand what the hell happened. I've spent the last two days replaying our night together over and over in my head until I thought I might lose my mind completely. I still have no idea why she left the house, why she refused to answer any of my calls or texts, none of it. But if I was missing her before, I'm terrified now. I can't even stop the tears from coming.

It feels like an entire lifetime passes before we get there, my thoughts growing darker every mile no matter how hard I try to push them away.

Graham slams on the brakes and the screeching sound brings me back to the present. "Okay, we're here. Try to calm down. Go find her while I figure out where to park."

I can barely think or see when I enter the hospital. I finally find the reception area, but before I can ask where Lucy is, I freeze.

No, not now, come on Henry, not NOW.

This hasn't happened to me in weeks, but I realize Lucy isn't here. She's been my anchor, better than any drug, keeping my anxiety at bay. Now that I'm alone again, it's like nothing has changed. The nurse looks at me questioning, but I just stare back at her. It's a stalemate and I want to murder my own fucking brain right now for failing me.

"Hey, did you find out where she is?" Thank God, Graham is here. I meet his eyes and he immediately knows what's going on. I really don't know what I'd do without him. He was the first person other than my mum or dad who truly accepted me, encouraged me to have a real life. He takes care of asking all the questions but unfortunately, they tell us to sit and wait anyway.

Thirty minutes, thirty *excruciating* minutes later, a nurse finally tells us Lucy has been moved from the ER and is seeing a doctor on the eighth floor. We get up there as quickly as we can and run in a few circles before finding someone who can give us a room number. All the nurses up here are wearing pink when I could swear it was all blue and green scrubs down below.

I hear someone tell us we can't go into her room unless we're family but Graham and I charge through the door before anyone can stop us.

31

• • •

Lucy

NOT AGAIN. I had my last surgery less than a year ago and that same pain is already back. I can't believe how sudden it came on this time. I came-to in the ambulance, feeling mostly embarrassed. I didn't need to be rushed to an emergency room. I knew exactly what was wrong. Once we got here, I explained everything to the staff and after a few tests and scans they moved me upstairs, so that I could explain everything again to another nurse.

I hate hospitals. I should just wear a list of my medical history around my neck.

"So, Lucy." I see the doctor reading over my chart. "I hear you're already a pro at this. How many laparoscopies have you had now?"

"Five."

"I'm so sorry, hun. I'm giving you something for the pain now. Do you have a primary gynecologist we should notify?"

"Actually, no. I just moved here from Boston about two months ago." I haven't exactly gotten around to finding a new doctor in LA yet, which surprises me. It's probably irresponsible but I have a feeling it's also contributed to how much lighter I've been feeling.

Dr. Wasserman tells me she'd be happy to see me in her office later this week to establish care. Then she continues poring over all the paperwork that came upstairs with me from the ER.

"Okay. I want to get you an ultrasound today. The CT SCAN showed a pelvic mass and I'd like to take a closer look."

Graham and Henry crash into the room breathless, like they ran here all the way from Malibu.

"Do you know these men, Lucy?" Dr. Wasserman looks like she's about ready to throw them out if I say the word.

"Yeah, they're my roommates, they're fine."

"Lucy, what happened? Are you okay, are you hurt? What is that sticking out of your arm? Is she hurting y—"

"Henry, I'm fine. Calm down, okay? You're freaking me out."

Dr. Wasserman completely ignores him as she makes her way toward the door. "All right Lucy, I'm going to send in the nurse to get some more vitals from you. Then we'll get you down for an ultrasound, just to rule out anything that will require surgery today."

"Surgery!?"

"Henry, chill out!"

He finally focuses his eyes and starts to resemble himself instead of a wild animal. I had no idea he'd react this way. It's kind of sweet, but also a little annoying if I'm being honest.

Really though, I should be grateful. The last time I went through this was right before Jack left me. The day of my follow-up when they showed us all the test results that meant our future family was an impossible dream. How some women can get through this unscathed, but I was just one of the unlucky ones. It would be so much harder to be alone right now. Having him and Graham both here means the world to me.

What's the best way to tell my housemates I have severe chronic endometriosis? That every so often, my medication fails me and I suffer excruciating, debilitating pain throughout the whole lower half of my body. That getting a minimally invasive surgery once a year is really not the worst part of it at all.

Well, there really is no smooth way to deliver that so I just blurt it out. And I'm received with blank stares, unsurprisingly.

The nurse comes in and asks if I have any questions about the next steps. "No, I've been through all this before, thank you."

"Okay, is there any possibility of pregnancy?" I start to laugh, and apparently it's joyless because she looks down at me like she just found out I'm terminal.

I think this is the fourth time I've been asked this today since waking up in the ambulance. I can't fault them, not really. I'm a thirty-year-old woman who fainted unexpectedly. But every time I hear the question it's like driving a tiny dagger into my heart. I wish I could just get a stamp on my forehead that says *not pregnant* and maybe I would never have to hear that aching question ever again.

I turn my gaze to Henry and he still looks so confused, like his mind is in a million different places. He hasn't been paying attention, his concern for me clouding his thoughts. I can tell he's been crying and knowing I've hurt him is almost as painful as my ovaries. But when my eyes move to Graham, I could swear he knows everything. The look he gives me breaks my damn heart.

The next twenty-four hours are a blur:

Move to wheelchair, elevator down, Henry tries to follow.

New nurse, new room, get in stirrups, light pressure, watch the screen.

"Oh, dear."

"Twisted ovary."

"No blood flow."

"O.R."

Out of stirrups, back in wheelchair, Henry's hand.

Elevator up, hospital bed. Henry being dragged away.

More doctors, more questions, more drugs.

No more pain.

"Count down for me."

Fade to black.

-

-

Blink.

Blink.

Blink.

New nurse. "How's the pain?"

"Henry."

More black.

Blink.

New room, new wheelchair.

Warm hands. Henry.

Sign this, sign that, take this prescription, schedule follow-up.

Elevator down, sliding doors, cold air, black sky.

Back seat, Henry's lap, lips on my hair.

Floating.

Bed.

Warm hands. Henry.

Soft fur. Wet tongue.

"Rowan."

Black.

-

-

Blink.

Blink.

Henry.

-

Water.

-

Rowan.

-

Apple Pie.

-

Black.

32

. . .

Henry

LUCY'S BEEN HOME from the hospital for three days now, and I feel like an absolute and utter failure. All I want to do is take care of her but I have no idea what she needs. She mostly lies in bed with Rowan and says she's fine but her mood seems to have regressed back to the night we met. So without any other bright ideas, I've been supplying her with copious amounts of sugar, hoping to lift her spirits.

I want to heal her, get her back to the place she was at just days ago, but today my only goal is to get her fed.

"Luce, are you awake?"

"Mhmm." She doesn't open her eyes but stretches just a bit.

"How's the pain? Do you need any more pills?" I brush some fallen hair off her face and help her sit up in the bed.

"I'm okay, thanks. How long have I been out for?"

"Just a couple of hours. You should really eat something. Are you hungry at all?"

I notice her bite the inside of her cheek, like she's debating what she wants to say. "Yeah, I kind of am."

"That's great. I think Graham finished all the Tiramisu, but we have some coffee ice cream left. I could make you a sundae. That's . . . Tiramisu adjacent?"

"Actually, I'm sort of craving salt. Do you know if there's a Jewish deli around here? I would kill for a bowl of matzo ball soup right now."

"Matzo ball soup?"

"Yeah, it's a Jewish thing. My mom always made it for me when I wasn't feeling well. I must be having some sort of Pavlovian response."

"GRAHAM, are you—oh, all of you are here. Does anyone know where a Jewish Deli is? Lucy wants matzo ball soup."

"What's a Jewish deli?" Graham asks.

Well, we're equally clueless.

"I think I've been to one in Westwood," Preston says. "No idea if they have soup though. Want me to call Adamma?"

"I googled it. It looks like chicken soup with really big croutons." Jayce shoves his phone in my face. "Here's a recipe—let's just make it for her."

The ingredients look relatively simple but none of us know how to cook.

I raise a brow at him. "Erm, alright. Who's up for helping out? We'll need to go to the store and—maybe we can find a YouTube video or something?"

We all pile into the Range Rover and head to Whole Foods. Luckily when we get there someone immediately offers to help us. We must look ridiculous, but I'm thankful because I doubt we would have ever been able to find matzo meal on our own. And once we're back at the house, we divide and conquer.

Everyone seems scared of the major task at hand: the balls. I've got no clue what they're supposed to look like but I've apparently drawn the short straw so I watch a few videos and get to work. Preston and Jayce start chopping vegetables, something I honestly didn't think they'd be able to do. Apparently, Lucy's been teaching them. And Graham is, well, Graham isn't really providing any help at all. He's just sitting at the island cheering us on, or maybe mocking us. Better than nothing, I guess.

For a minute I thought I had the hang of it. In retrospect, rolling matzo balls is nothing like biscuit dough. I can't seem to get a single ball-shaped anything, and most of the mixture is stuck to my hands. I'm very glad we thought ahead and bought about three times the amount of ingredients we needed. By the second batch, I'm finally making a bit of headway.

"Henry, you did it! They look like balls!" Preston beams with pride and I'm not sure if I should feel offended. He obviously had little faith in me.

"Okay, so this says they should double in size and then they're done. They just grow? In the pot?" Jayce looks like he's about to witness a magic show but soon enough all three of our heads are hovering over the stove waiting for a miracle to occur. "Does anyone know a Jewish prayer?"

"Guys, she's awake." Graham has been slyly checking in on Lucy every fifteen minutes. "It's go time."

We have all had a taste and were pleasantly surprised. The fluffy balls are actually quite enjoyable, and I made sure they were well salted for Lucy. Even so, I'm a nervous wreck as I make my way to her room.

"Hey Luce, you still hungry? I hope this tastes okay for you."

She sits up further and looks at me incredulously. "You cooked?"

"We all did—don't give Henry all the credit."

"Oh, come on Jayce, he made the balls. You were too scared." Preston interrupts and I can't help but enjoy Jayce's frown.

"Guys, this is awesome. I can't believe you cooked for me. I'm so excited to try it."

I convince HAAAM to leave us for a moment and help Lucy get situated so she can eat without burning herself.

Lucy grins. "You're kind of amazing, you know." Her eyes find mine and for a moment all I can think about is kissing her. I bring a spoonful of broth to her lips instead.

She coughs. Fuck.

"That bad?"

"No! It's really good actually. I just wasn't expecting that much salt, especially after the sugar diet you put me on." We share a quiet chuckle. "This is perfect. I can't believe you made it." She pauses and frowns at me. "I, umm . . . I—"

"Just enjoy the soup, okay? I'm going to go clean up and leave you be, but I'll be back to check on you in a bit." I lightly kiss the top of her head, I can't help myself.

"Wait. I haven't tried the matzo balls yet."

Oh lord, I'm positive they won't be up to the standard of her mum's cooking. I carefully watch her take a large bite.

"Well? What's the verdict? Keep in mind it was my first time. It was much more difficult than rolling the biscuit dough." She takes a second bite while I ramble on, which must mean it's not completely horrible.

"Henry, I'm impressed. This is really good! And your balls are the perfect size this time." She winks while my mouth hangs open. I should walk away but . . .

"Do you like my matzo balls?"

I start to sing.

"Are they the perfect size?
Do you prefer them in your mouth or
against your thighs?"

Now her mouth goes slack. "Did you just sexualize matzo ball soup?"

"Come on, Luce. You were asking for it."

33

. . .

Lucy

IT'S BEEN over a week since my surgery and Henry has not left my side. He's also brought me every possible dessert I could ever think of. And while there's a constant loop in my head of Henry's lips on mine, all he seems to care about is how I'm recovering.

He even refused to let me drive myself to my follow-up appointment yesterday. There was no way in hell I was letting him come in with me so the poor guy just sat in the waiting room for over an hour. On the way out I'm afraid he might have heard the doctor tell me I should strongly consider the removal soon. Luckily, it seemed as though he had no idea what she was referring to.

I know he wants me to talk about this with him, to share all the details, and he's so supportive that it's tempting. I just can't get the images of Jack out of my head, of his disappointment, of him asking for a divorce as soon as he realized what a life with me would entail. And Henry still won't talk about our night together. I've tried to apologize numerous times about going to

Adamma's, about running away, but he won't even hear of it. It's like he's afraid of what I'll say, and honestly, so am I.

So for now, I'm focusing on my book. It's a bit ironic but I'm definitely channeling Henry. Life is too much to handle right now, so I'm directing all my energy to my work. And getting pages to my editor on time is a very added bonus.

I finally figured out my ending, or lack thereof, I guess. I'm going to leave it open, maybe even write a sequel. If it can't have a happily ever after, why does it have to end at all? And Adamma was right; adding in the romance was exactly what it needed.

I'm proud of myself. I wrote something dark and gritty and *compelling*. And so what if the reader isn't smiling and giddy at the end? Their jaws will drop—because surprise! The female lead *is* the beast (thanks, Henry)—and somehow that's even more satisfying.

I keep wondering why I've always been so focused on the ending. Every book I've written before this one, I started with the final chapter. It seems so childish now. I think I treated my own life the same way, always focusing on the finish line. But I'm starting to realize that finding the perfect partner or having the perfect family isn't an ending at all. It's more like the prologue. What happens *next* is the story. And I'm finally feeling like my story isn't over, that maybe it hasn't even begun.

We're just finishing breakfast at the kitchen island when Graham asks Henry if he can talk to me alone for a bit. I don't think Henry has ever been away from his piano this long—and he seems to trust Graham not to break me—so he shuffles down to the studio to give us some privacy.

"How you feeling, Little Lu?" He wraps me in a toasty hug before I can respond. Graham is my rock, such a huge source of comfort for me. I hate that I hurt him. He guides me over to the sectional where Rowan is lounging, and we sit down to snuggle with him.

"Thank you for getting Henry to detach for a minute. I'm really fine. I told you guys I've done this before. It's not a difficult recovery. I could go skydiving tomorrow, really."

"You? Skydiving?" He looks at me like I've lost my mind, and well, he's right. I would never, ever go skydiving.

"You know what I mean."

"Just let us baby you, Luce. Especially Henry. I'm not sure why but I think he needs it." Row chooses this moment to aggressively lick my hand, like he's showing Graham he's part of my caregiving team as well.

I agree to let them dote on me a little longer, even though I'm starting to develop a sugar addiction worse than before. But now there's an awkward silence hanging between us. We haven't been alone together since right before I went to the hospital. There's so much that's been left unsaid.

"Graham, I'm so sorry. You were right about everything. I shouldn't have let things get that far with Henry, I just—"

"It's because you can't have kids, isn't it? The divorce, the way you refuse to admit you could have a future with Henry."

I'm not sure how to respond. I know I'm just staring back at him and now my eyes are starting to burn. I haven't explained anything to him because I didn't want to explain it to Henry, but now it feels like I'm hiding. I don't think I want to live like that anymore.

"Yeah, it is. It's also—well, it's more than that. I'm getting a hysterectomy. Before the end of the year." A strange sound pours out of me and I can't tell if I'm laughing or crying or both, but Graham just watches me, urging me on. "I'm going to go through menopause before I turn thirty-one. So yeah, it's probably not the ideal time to start a new relationship."

"Luce . . ." He wraps his arms around me, tighter this time. "Do you want to talk about it?"

"Not really." I snuggle in closer to him, trying to steal all of his warmth.

"Want to talk about where we'll hide the body if Jack shows up here again?

I snort, but Graham's face is cold as stone.

"I won't say anything to Henry, but Luce—you should tell him."

We reposition ourselves on the couch and turn on our next episode of *Peaky Blinders*, Graham and Rowan both snuggled up against me. I'm not sure how much longer I can stay in this house, how much longer I'll have this family, but I'm not going to waste a second of it.

I feel like I'm somehow in an okay place right now, until my phone starts buzzing again.

Sarah has been texting and calling me consistently for over a week now. I'm still annoyed that she never responded when I first let her know where I'd be living, so I haven't exactly been in a rush to get back to her. Plus, her texts have been generally meaningless. Lots of "let's catch up" and "how's my LuLu?" Like she doesn't already know about the shit show I've been dealing with this last year.

But today I got a text that I can't ignore.

Sarah:

What's going on with you and Jack? Should I not have told him where you were?

Of course she's the one who gave Jack my address.

Sometimes I forget how close they were before he and I ever dated. She grew up in D.C. but her dad had a summer house on Nantucket right next door to Jack's. Our first week at Emory, Sarah told me she knew a guy that would be perfect for me. I always had the sense she had a thing for him, but for some reason she just never acted on it.

"So, who's coming over?" I'm filling in Graham on everything Sarah-related since he's the only one in the house who knows the details about Jack.

"Sarah. The girl I was supposed to be living with in Santa Monica, remember?" He nods, and he has a pissed off look on his face that lets me know he remembers exactly who she is. "She's been asking me to talk for a week now, and honestly I just really want to know why she'd send Jack here without telling me."

"Can't say I'm a fan of this one any more than dickhead Jack. Do I have to play nice with her?"

"No, you don't have to talk to her at all. It might be better if I just keep her to myself. She's kind of . . . boy crazy?" It sounds so childish when I say it, but I also know it's true. If she walked in here and saw Graham and anyone else, I doubt I could keep her focused on our conversation.

"All right. I'll tell the guys to give you some space. Holler if you need me, love."

When Sarah arrives, I immediately bring her out to the patio and grab chairs by the pool. Everyone in the house is working and I want some privacy for our conversation.

Whenever I see Sarah after a while apart, I'm taken aback by her beauty. I hate the feeling of jealousy, but it's hard not to envy her. Her completely natural copper hair glitters like rubies in the sunlight and her pale, freckled skin somehow has a gorgeous tan. But what really gets me is her body. She's five foot nine, and her legs seem endless. She wears the tiniest little cutoff shorts that undoubtedly look chic on her, and her sheer cream blouse hangs perfectly on her lithe frame. It wouldn't bother me so much if I didn't know about her diet. She survives mainly on Taco Bell, fried cheese, cookie dough and vodka. She never even works out unless she's specifically asked to for a booking. Such is the life of a model.

"Luce, this place is amazing!" She looks around from the pool to the firepit to the amazing ocean view. "I mean holy shit, how did you find this house?"

"I'm just staying here, as a guest, actually. I met someone on my flight out here and he offered to let me stay for a while." I watch her face twist into something that resembles jealousy. Really? "I would have told you all about it if we could have talked, you know. You just went dark on me."

I don't want to be bitter but I can't help it. She's acting like nothing is out of the ordinary, like she didn't abandon me as I moved to a new city to help *her* out.

"Well, it looks like I did you a favor." She smirks at me. I guess I shouldn't hold my breath for an apology. "Things always seem to work out for you, huh."

"What's that supposed to mean?" Resentment skates across her features as I try and puzzle out what her deal is.

"So, look. I take it things didn't go as planned when Jack came here? Should I not have given him your info? I figured you'd be so happy to hear from him."

"Happy? No, I definitely wasn't happy. I just don't understand why you'd do that and not even give me a heads up. He totally blindsided me."

"He told me it didn't really go well, but are you still considering his offer?"

Offer? What the hell?

"What do you mean, his offer? He just said he wanted to

have a discussion, but I threw him out. After the way he ended our marriage I have nothing to discuss with him."

"Oh. You wouldn't even talk to him? Honestly, I think you're being a little selfish, Lu." Selfish? *I'm* being selfish? What about Jack? Isn't he the selfish one? I can still remember every word he said when we finalized the divorce.

"Don't you see how lucky we are, Luce? How much better it is to end things this way? Do you know how many couples end up bitter and unhappy because of their failed efforts to create a family? We don't have to go through all that pain and suffering. You can focus on something else, like your fairy books. And we can still be friends. You know I love you. I'll always love you. I just need to do what's right for me. I can still have everything I want."

I can't believe this is happening again, with Sarah. It's just like Jack's mom, telling me how disappointed she was that I hadn't warned her this was a possibility. That I had somehow deceived them even though this happened *after* the wedding. Jack knew about my endometriosis before we even moved in together. He just chose to ignore it.

Why is everything my fault? Will anyone ever be on *my* side? I suddenly wish I had Graham next to me again.

"How am I being selfish? He chose to get a divorce and I gave him what he wanted without any protest. Are you saying I'm supposed to just wait around in case he changes his mind and wants to get married again?"

She flips her long hair behind her shoulder and tilts her head back. The move screams *I don't actually care about any of this.*

"Hon, he doesn't want to get married again. That's really what you thought? You know you can't have everything, Lu. He just wanted to talk to you about trying an open relationship." Her condescending tone makes me want to scream. An open relationship? How would he ever think I'd agree to something like that?

And how is the girl in front of me my best friend? How did I ever consider her to be my person, my *sister*, when she doesn't seem to care about me at all? *I can't have everything*? What exactly does she think I have? "I need some water, wanna come inside for a sec?"

"Sure, got anything stronger?"

We walk into the kitchen and I fill up two glasses of water, ignoring her question. I can tell it wouldn't be her first drink of the day, and I don't plan on supporting her habits when I know she's driving herself home.

I hear a few notes before I realize Henry is playing the piano in the living room, and he's surrounded on all sides by HAAAM, I guess working on something. I have a feeling Graham suggested this to keep an eye on me. I'm about to introduce Sarah to everyone but she beats me to it, sprinting over to the piano and plopping her perfect self onto the bench next to Henry.

"I *love* the piano! Wanna play hot cross buns?" She playfully nudges his arm before he turns to flash me an equally annoyed and confused expression. And then it quickly evaporates into concern when our eyes meet. He mouths something to me, a question, but I can't make it out. I just shake my head.

Once she realizes Henry is not amused and is not going to be playing a duet with her she swings her legs back over the bench to face me. "Luce, you didn't tell me how hot these guys were—I would've come sooner!" She looks toward them now, her radiant smile beaming. "I'm Sarah, Lucy's roommate."

"Roommate? Luce, you're not moving out are you?" Jayce looks toward me and the frown he's flaunting makes my heart squeeze a little.

"Of course she is! Lu was the best roomie in college, I can't wait to have someone in the house again who cooks!"

Henry continues to look between us, his gaze feverish but tough to read. He still hasn't acknowledged Sarah and I don't know if it's because she's a stranger to him or if he can sense that I'm not her biggest fan right now. He looks like he's struggling to get the words out, but when he finally speaks it's to Sarah, though his eyes never leave mine. "Lucy already has a home, with people who take care of her. Why would she go live with you?"

Sarah scoffs and jumps off the bench. I can tell she's ready to defend herself to the end but I cut her off before there's any need for an argument.

"He's right, Sarah, I'm not moving in with you. I like it here, and honestly, I can't trust you. I'm assuming you and Emmett broke up again or you wouldn't be here, not that you've even mentioned it. But I don't wanna be kicked out of my home every time you decide to give it another shot."

"Okay, that is so unfair. We're obviously done for real this time or I wouldn't be here. I thought you *wanted* to live me with me." Indignation pinches her cheeks before she looks around the house. "But I guess you've moved on to bigger and better once again."

"Again? Sarah, I honestly don't know what's going on with you lately but—are we still friends? You're acting like . . . I don't know."

"I'm acting fine. You're the judgy one." She huffs. "So you're really not gonna talk to Jack? You won't consider the open relationship thing?"

Henry and Graham both flash me shocked and appalled expressions. They know me better than Sarah does after two months of my living here. It's kind of wonderful to have friends who understand me so well. "Of course not, no way in hell. Feel free to tell him that for me if you talk to him."

"Okay. Well, I actually had a question for you then."

I mumble a "sure" hoping this is quick.

"Okay, so there's this thing you do, this position." She leans in to whisper to me but we're close enough that I know all the guys can hear anyway. "I guess it's like, when you're on top, but you kind of twist—"

"Are you asking me for sex advice right now?"

"Well, yeah, kind of. I mean I just need to know how to—"

"Wait. How do you know about anything I do? Were you talking to Jack about our sex life? Were you—"

I'm dumbfounded for just a moment.

I look around the room to see every guy staring in anticipation, or fear, of what I'm about to say. I don't even have to ask her, I already know. Of course she slept with Jack. As if I needed any more evidence of her disloyalty.

I'm not confused anymore. She can have Jack and his open relationship.

Now I'm pissed. I'm pissed at everyone I thought I could depend on that has shown me how incredibly wrong I've been. I'm pissed at Jack for thinking he can get whatever he wants from me. At Sarah, for using me like a fucking puppet. Mostly, I'm just pissed at myself. How did I ever trust these people?

"You have got to be kidding me. You slept with him? And what, you're talking to him about what I did in bed? You're disgusting."

"You just said you're not getting back together with him. Why do you care so much if you don't want him back?"

"We were together for ten years! And you literally *just* asked me if I was considering his offer." Her open mouth lets me know she has no comeback this time. "Is he still here, in LA?"

"Yeah, he's been staying with me, just until he decides what to do next. He lost his job and he's kind of figuring things out, you know?"

Now it all makes sense. He needed me again. He didn't think he made a mistake. He was just out of options. And now he's what, crashing with Sarah waiting to see if I'll take him back? I figure it's not worth mentioning to her that I've had at least five texts from him a day since he showed up here, all professing his love. I'm not even sure if the open relationship is his idea or hers.

"I'm sorry, I must not be understanding things correctly. You came here thinking I was going to move in with you, when my ex-husband is currently staying at your place, and you're *fucking* him?"

"It's not like I'm dating him, Lu! It's just sex. You wouldn't understand. You've never had casual sex. Actually, I bet it'd be good for you."

"Yeah, I'm gonna need you to leave. I really have no desire to talk to you or see you ever again."

She protests as I guide her toward the door. "Okay, but can you just tell me how you do the twist thing, it's really important for hi—"

"Are you guys role-playing me or something? What is *wrong* with you?"

"Luce, I'm sorry, you know I've always needed more attention than you do. You just don't understand. You never have." I've finally gotten her outside the front door, I can't fucking listen to this anymore. "See! You're being judgy again. Can't you just get off your high hor—"

"Just shut up for a second, okay?" I let out a deep breath, trying to gather my thoughts. I'm angry but I think more than that I'm just . . . sad.

"Damnit, Sarah, you were my *best* friend, my family. Why

are you doing this? Why now? I've always been okay taking the backseat in our relationship. Your life is glamorous and full of drama, and I was fine being the supporting role. That's how much I loved you. But this year? You couldn't give me one fucking year of being a good friend? Or I don't know, just a decent human being?" She tries to cut me off, but I won't let her, not this time. Besides, my questions are rhetorical. "You blow me off when I move here, for *you*. You make a fucking joke of my marriage. I honestly don't know who you are anymore. I've been missing you so much, but I'm not sure why. Get out of my life, okay?"

I slam the door in her face, and I don't think anything in my life has ever felt better.

"Holy shit, that chick was crazy. And, like super hot, like *stupid* hot. But is she seriously banging your ex and asking you to live with her?" Jayce looks amused and excited, clearly enjoying the drama that is my life.

"Yup. That was Sarah." I fall down on the couch and cover my face with my arms. "You guys are cool with me staying a while longer, right? I really don't want to see her again."

"I wish Adamma was here. She would have seriously fucked her up." Everyone looks at Preston in shock; he never swears. He beams with pride just knowing hypothetically how protective his girlfriend is. I wish she was here too. I'm so happy to know I have a friend like her in my life now.

"As far as I'm concerned, you can stay forever, but there's something I need you to do before we shake on it." Graham scoops me up, takes my spot lying down on the couch and sets me on top of him. He grabs my legs and starts placing them in different positions. "Alright, love, show me how it goes. I've got to see this magic move of yours."

The guys all start hollering with laughter, I think Jayce even falls onto the floor as I kick my way off of Graham's body. I make the briefest eye contact with Henry and the expression on his face is nothing I've ever seen from him before.

He is undeniably smug.

AFTER DINNER TONIGHT, Henry and I wordlessly make our way to my room and collapse on the bed, somehow perfectly parallel to each other.

"Hi." A lazy smirk is painted on his face.

"Hi. Sorry about all the drama with Sarah. And thank you. For being so . . . you." He eyes me quizzically. "Seriously. If it weren't for you, I might actually be living with her. And even if I wasn't, I'd probably be as unhappy now as I was the day we met. You brought me back to life, Henry."

I watch his throat move but he doesn't speak. We're just . . . gazing at each other, so much unsaid between us. It's been weeks since we slept together, but I can still taste him on my lips, still feel his hips rocking against me. We may not have spoken about that night together but I know it's on both of our minds.

"Can I tell you something?" His expression has turned serious, and I mentally brace myself after giving him a nod of approval.

"I'm quite tired." Tired? I'm physically and mentally exhausted, but his eyes are shining brightly. "I'm so tired of trying not to kiss you."

Oh.

"So kiss me." My words surprise me but they shouldn't. I may pretend—even to myself—that I want to squash this thing between us, but every kiss we've shared runs on a constant loop in my head.

"I'm thinking about it." He licks his lips and I see his eyes roam over my face, from my eyes to my mouth, to the bob of my throat. Why is he teasing me like this? I inch closer to him but he holds his hand out between us, lightly pressing into my chest.

"If I kiss you, will you run away? Go into hiding again?"

"No." My lack of hesitation seems to shock him, but it's true. I'm done hiding from Henry. I only want to be closer to him.

"Are you sure? I worry you could get terribly lost if it's dark out. Maybe I could put a bell on y—"

I move quickly, grabbing his arm and tucking myself underneath it while I press my mouth against his. At first, I'm afraid he won't respond, but his lips part almost instantly, inviting me in for something deeper.

Every kiss we share is so distinctive, and this one might destroy me. With each soft stroke of his tongue I feel my whole body liquify, my skin turning to vapor underneath his touch. I pull back to create the tiniest sliver of space between us.

"I think I was tired too. Of not kissing you. Let's just never stop kissing each other, okay?"

"Lucy," It's just my name, but he says it with so much longing, like those two syllables cause him physical pain. "We should—"

"Don't say talk. Please? This day, this week, this . . . can you let me enjoy this a little longer?"

His lips find mine again, but the frenzy is over. His tongue moves slowly, his lips finding each corner of my mouth before searing a trail down my throat and licking at my collarbone. It's fucking torture. He nips at my shoulder before nuzzling his head into me.

Henry is like a magician the way he communicates. His lips let me know how much he wants me, and somehow also how much restraint he has. And now his fingertips start tracing every part of my body, like he's worshiping me, showing me how deep his feelings run.

"You're so beautiful." His words fall like petals onto my skin.

"You're more beautiful."

He scoffs. "Lucy—your beauty is suffocating. When you smile, it could light up an entire continent. When you laugh, the sound is more vibrant than any music I can make." His fingertips follow the curve of my waist down to my hip, and I'm unable to suppress my audible reaction to his touch. "That little whimper—God, Luce—I've been trying to find the right note, the right key to recreate that perfect sound you make. It's impossible." He doesn't stop tracing my skin, following the path down my legs before trailing back up again. "Everything about you is exquisite."

At first, his touch made me tremble, but I'm finally sinking into it, finding its comfort. I used to think Henry's music was a drug to me, but now I realize it's just him. Being in his presence, physically connected by nothing but a fingertip, and I'm as relaxed and content as I've ever been.

"Henry Turner, I think you should be a songwriter." I giggle just a bit, but I don't expect him to respond. I'm learning to love his silence, to read it just as easily as ink on a page. His fingers sliding through my hair tell me everything I need to know.

"Please be here when I wake up," he whispers.

And with that, he silently folds me into him, our bodies tightly pressed together. One kiss behind my ear, some hushed words I can't make out. I easily fall asleep, more attached to Henry than ever before.

finale

Where words fail, music speaks.

-Hans Christian Andersen

34

• • •

Henry

LUCY MAY THINK I've been overprotective since she came home from the hospital, but endless bed rest (her term) has given her a lot of time to work on her book. She sent the final manuscript of *Beautiful Beasts* to her agent this morning, and she's been diligently working on an outline for something new. She seems quite eager to be doing her take on *Alice in Wonderland* for her next novel. We've been watching it constantly in bed together—every version.

She hasn't wanted a bit of distance from me lately, and even though she's been spending most of our time together writing, I'm addicted to the feel of her body curled into me every night as we fall asleep. I might as well turn my room into a library for her. I live here now.

I've just finished reading her newest outline for *Wonderlust*. It was not easy getting her to show it to me but I have sworn to write an entire score for the book to use as she pleases. Her extortion feels a bit extreme, but there's not much I'd deny her these days. Though now that I've read through it, I'm feeling a bit guilty for how vigilant I've been as her caregiver. While I think Sarah's visit was enough drama for ages—I'm still trying to wrap my head around it—it seems Lucy may need a bit more excitement, something I've known for a while I need to work on if I'm to have a real chance with her.

I've gone back and forth about ways I can show Lucy we'd be great together. I'm still unsure if golf is something she's actually interested in, but I do know she loves to travel. She seems to have been everywhere along the eastern seaboard but has never gone further than Mexico or Bermuda. Traveling: something else Graham may have brought up to me, something that *normal* couples tend to do together. Something that I typically require copious amounts of drugs to handle. But I'm different when Lucy's around, I'm not scared of wandering out in public. I suppose I could take her to a country where we don't speak the language, that might be a safe bet to ease my way into it. But that would interfere with the other plan I have brewing, the one that will get Lucy to finally understand how I feel about her.

"I think we should go somewhere, take a trip. Are you up for an adventure, Luzu?" I set down my tablet and roll toward her. Rowan is curled into her side between us. At my question he pops up and starts kissing my face with vigor. I wonder if he's also in need of a change in scenery.

"Row, enough! An adventure? Really, Henry? I'll be happy to go outside of this house. Are you actually gonna let me do anything?"

"Look, I'm sorry for being overprotective. I just want to keep you safe, but I get it. You're feeling cooped up. You're literally writing about a girl doing wild and reckless activities just to *feel* something. I'm not daft." The story does sound quite interesting, but it doesn't take a genius to draw parallels to her current situation.

I slide closer to her, reveling in the fact that I no longer have to fight against every impulse to stroke her hair and catch her lips between my own. So I do. She tastes like sugar and cinnamon and I notice the slice of apple pie on the nightstand. The one she said I should stop buying for her.

"I want to make it up to you. Have you ever been on a private plane before?"

THREE DAYS LATER—AFTER thorough approval from her doctors—we're on our way. I'm not sure if this little trip I've planned is the best or worst idea I've ever had. I've felt so close to her lately, but I know she's still keeping things from me. It just feels like I have so much to prove to her, and this seemed like the best way to do it.

"You're not scared of flying are you? You seemed fine on our flight from Boston."

"No, not at all, I don't mind it." She's been fidgety and scattered all day, I can't quite figure her out.

"Okay, Luce, why are you so jittery? Your leg hasn't stopped bouncing since we took off."

She looks down at her knee and the movement ceases instantly. "I guess it's just been so long since I've left the house." She raises her brows at me. "Are you gonna tell me where we're going yet?"

I wanted to keep this a surprise until we arrived but it's a long flight and I'm dying to talk to her about our plans.

"I'll give you three clues, okay?" She leans toward me, eager, her eyes dancing with fizzy anticipation. "First clue: big clock." I wait for a response but she just squints at me. "Second clue: fish and chips." I see a smile forming but she still doesn't say anything. "Third and final clue: the queen."

"You're taking me to London!? Are you serious?" I give her a satisfied nod. "When you said an adventure I thought maybe we'd be going to Santa Barbara or San Francisco. We're seriously going all the way to *England* right now?"

"Lucy, I did warn you it was a long flight."

"Well, yeah, but you told me we were going on a road trip when we actually drove two miles away to go paddle boarding."

"Can you really blame me for being a bit devious? You're adorable when I surprise you. Look at yourself right now."

She looks down and I wonder if she's even realized how she's contorted her body since we've been talking. She went from a normal sitting position to balancing on her knees, bracing her hands on the armrests and leaning so far off her seat I have a hand at the ready to catch her if she falls.

She frowns briefly before moving to sit next to me. And then her arms are wrapped around my shoulders, her face smashed into the crook of my neck.

"Thank you. Thank you so much. I've never been to Europe before. I'm so excited." I can feel her mouth curve into a smile—it makes me shiver—and then we're interrupted by the flight crew asking if we're ready for dinner.

Our arrival in London is a bit dreary. We land early in the morning but the sky is so full of clouds that the sun is a distant stranger. Well, this is England. Lucy and I both slept for most of the flight, so we decide to quickly drop off our luggage at the hotel and get to exploring before the rain comes down. It's only a matter of time.

I let her lead the way for a bit of sightseeing. I know she has a list of places she wants to visit: bridges, towers, the usual. Honestly, I think she enjoys our trips on the tube as much as each destination.

"So, there's really no circus? I was hoping for elephants."

"Lucy, I warned you that you would not be impressed. I specifically said it's just an intersection. You refused to listen to me!"

"But you're always messing with me. I thought you just wanted me to be surprised." The frown she's sporting makes me want to kiss her with abandon, but I resist. The only reason I agreed to this stop on the tour was because it's a few blocks from our planned destination and we're already late for our reservation. Luckily I have an afternoon surprise that she's going to love.

I've been thinking about taking Lucy to Sketch since she first told me her new book would be inspired by *Alice in Wonderland*. I've never actually been here before but my mum loves it, and her friends never shut up about it. Dining out isn't exactly a favorite hobby of mine, but a restaurant with a Wonderland theme? Lucy's going to go mad for it.

There are quite a few different rooms, but I made sure to reserve our lunch in The Glade, the one they describe as their garden party room. It's captivating, extremely whimsical. The walls and ceiling are decorated so heavily you feel like you're really outside in a garden, a magical one. But the only thing I can focus on as we enter is Lucy's bright-eyed twinkling face, grinning like a damn Cheshire cat.

"This is unreal. I feel like a talking white rabbit is about to pop out at any moment. Whoa, I didn't even notice the floor. Is that real moss?" We've finished our meal now but she's still looking around the room in wonderment. I don't think I've seen her smile like this since before her trip to the hospital.

"Do you feel inspired?"

"I do. But I doubt I'm going to get much writing done while I'm here. Will you take some pictures?"

"Of course, anything you want." I notice Lucy starts to bite the inside of her cheek, like she's trying to stop herself from saying something. But there's a sparkle in her eye she can't hide from me. "What is it, Luce?"

"You brought me into wonderland, and
fed me lots of English tea
The crumpets were delightful, and the
cakes were très petits"

She pauses, waiting for me to join her. Every meal with Lucy means another song.

I will never get tired of this. *This* is what I've been missing in my life: *joy*. I love my work. I'm proud of what I've accomplished and the life I've built for myself. But none of it compares to the feeling I get when Lucy grins and our gazes find each other.

"I hope this makes up for the circus,
even though the animals here
are fake
If you use a little imagination, this
could be the perfect date"

Our lunch *is* perfect. We sing, and laugh, and sing some more. The table next to us decides to join in around the fourth verse and we laugh even harder. My fingers itch for a piano and I start strumming them on the table.

It feels like every bit of tension has dissolved between me and Lucy. Maybe I'm still holding back too much, pretending to be normal when it's not the truth, but I don't want to do anything to ruin this. It feels too good to risk. And after tomorrow, Lucy will know exactly how I feel about her. Then I can tell her everything.

AFTER LUNCH we decide to wander aimlessly. The rain has held out and the temperature is quite pleasant. And when Lucy hooks her arm through mine, I decide nothing can ruin this day. That is until the clouds open up with vigor and pelt down on us until we're completely soaked.

"This way! Come on, Luce." I find an awning to duck under and realize it's actually a hotel. After shaking out my jacket and hair as much as possible I guide us both inside to wait out the storm.

"Oh, hello! Just in time. The event is to the left, straight through those double doors. And there's toilets to the right if you need to change. Welcome!" A sprightly woman with a short blonde bob greets us at the entrance, but Lucy and I look at each other in total confusion. Then she winks at me.

"Great, thank you! Let's go, Henry, we don't wanna be late." She takes my hand and pulls me toward the double doors.

"What are you doing? Do you have any clue what she was talking about?"

"No, but it sounds like a party or something. Let's crash for a minute—it could be fun." Well, this is it. The moment Lucy realizes I don't do spontaneous *fun*. Is it possible I can keep this perfect day going? Be normal in a room full of strangers? What if she wants to . . . mingle? God, even thinking that word makes me shudder.

"Erm, are you sure? What if it's some stuffy English thing?"

"Oh, come on. Let's just check it out. We can always leave."

All right. For her, I'll try.

We open the doors into what looks like a ballroom, but what we find inside is, well, unexpected. There must be at least one hundred people, probably more, but they're all dressed in costumes—animal costumes. I see Lucy's gaze float across the room and then she turns to me with a startled grin.

"Oh my God—do you know what this is?" I am unequivocally clueless. I shake my head at her, still holding on to her hand tightly. "I think it's one of those . . . yep, holy shit. Look at the sign." She points to a banner on the far wall that reads 'ConFuzzled 2023.' "It's a *furry* convention." She whispers the last two words and I'm still a bit dumbstruck. I'm not exactly a socialite, but am I supposed to know what that means?

She sees my still very confused face and pouts at me like I'm a naïve little boy. "They're all like, really into dressing up as furry animals. I think sometimes it's a sex thing. But not always." What in the world . . .

"I think we should go." I'm not sure she even hears me as her attention is elsewhere. She removes her hand from mine but uses it to start nudging me over and over until I finally see what she's gaping at. Holy shit. "Is that man dressed as a . . . ? He looks just like a giant-sized . . ."

"*Rowan.*"

It's almost remarkable, the similarities. It's like he took a picture of her dog and made the costume to match. Same white shaggy fur, same gray ears. Even the tongue lolling out of the costume head hangs slightly to the side, just like Rowan. It's fucking eerie. But Lucy looks transfixed, and then I realize she is slowly moving us toward this imposter.

"Luce, what are you doing? You're not thinking of engaging with this creature, are you?"

"It'll be fine. Maybe they just really love sheepies." She's so cute when she gets like this, her eyes sparkling while she bounces on her toes. I can't stop her, but I'm determined not to let her out of my sight either, so I stay very, very close and keep a hand at her back. The only thing she'll be cuddling tonight is me.

"Hi, umm, 'scuse me." Lucy is so short the giant sheepdog probably doesn't even see her. She pokes at it to get its attention. The deep voice that responds is startling.

"How ya doin' lassie?" I can tell Lucy is struggling a bit with his thick Scottish brogue. I think she might choose to finally walk away, until she pulls out her phone.

"I just had to show you, you look just like my dog, Rowan. See?"

I turn away slightly, I can't believe she's doing this. Holy hell, she's as comfortable talking to strangers as I am avoiding them. We could not be any more different. I want to interrupt her, break her away from the furry Scot before he gets any ideas, but when I try to speak, nothing comes. And then I realize she doesn't need me. He is showing her photos of his dog as well.

I finally convince her it's time to leave, but not until after they exchange emails and Instagram handles (for the dogs of course). I hadn't seen until now, hers is @RowantheSnugWarrior.

I am so, helplessly, in love with her.

35

. . .

Lucy

HENRY WILL NOT STOP APOLOGIZING about the accidental furry convention. I love seeing this embarrassed side of him, constantly running his hands through his hair, down his face. It's so endearing.

"Henry, stop apologizing! It was fun!"

"But this day was supposed to be perfect, romantic. If it wasn't for the damn rain . . ."

I can tell how much thought he put into this. It shouldn't surprise me considering how thoughtful he's always been. High tea at a Wonderland-themed restaurant? It *was* romantic.

Maybe too romantic.

I keep meaning to talk to him, to tell him everything I told Adamma. And if it ever slips my mind, her constant text reminders are always there for me. The one from this morning is my favorite to date.

Adamma:

Ask him how much he'd pay you to strip. Great

conversation opener and I bet his answer's in the thousands. That's how you know it's real love.

I promise myself I'm going to do it. I should have on the flight. I should have *before* the flight. I'm just too scared to end this, to end all these perfect moments we have together.

"Henry, this whole day was romantic, and I like the rain. I'm just excited to be here, in London! With you. It doesn't matter where we go or what we do. It's already perfect."

He sighs, slowly takes my face in his hand and tips my chin up toward him. And then his lips are on mine. God, he kisses like a man heading to war. I feel drunk on his affection, the care with which he cradles my face, the smooth, barely there touch of his thumb tracing the line of my throat. We're stopped in the middle of a bridge, people all around us, but I can't stop whimpering like a baby bird. I want to feel the weight of him, all of him. I'm starving for his lips to be everywhere, just like our night at his pool.

I pull back, worried if this kiss keeps going I'll just strip down in the middle of the street. "Want to head back to the hotel?" Henry's eyes are wild, his lips red and swollen. He looks completely out of his mind and it might be my favorite version of him. But he shakes his head. "What?"

"Sorry, this will have to wait a little longer, love." He kisses my nose, which is turning into another one of my favorite things. "I have one more surprise for you. And, erm, are you hungry? It's almost dinner time."

Hungry? Ravenous, but not for food. I think I've lost the ability to say no to this man, so I loop my arm through his and let him lead the way.

When I see the sign reading Tiramisu Café, which happens to be right where Henry brings us to a stop fifteen minutes later, tears threaten to spill from my eyes.

"I know it's subjective, but I did a lot of research. This is supposed to be one of the best in London. They have sandwiches too, just in case you want a real dinner first. Are you okay? What's wrong, Luce?" He wraps his hands around my neck, peering into my tear-drenched eyes.

"Can we get it to go?"

"Of course. How about instead of PJ's on the couch we eat it in robes on the bed? I'll make sure it's extra cozy for you." There's a rush of emotions making a home in every corner of my body. For me, it's always been the most simple acts that feel profound.

"That sounds perfect."

We finish the Tiramisu in the back of a cab, feeding each other every bite. After a short ride, we arrive at the hotel and the anticipation of getting into bed with Henry has me practically climbing him in the elevator. He carries me to our room and doesn't let go until he lays me down on the bed. I peel off my purse and jacket, kick my shoes across the room. I'm so incredibly needy for him right now and I'm not even trying to hide it.

"Luce . . ." He's sitting on the edge of the bed, very obviously *not* on top of me like I'm hoping for.

"Kiss me. Please?" He laughs, enjoying this moment much more than he should. "Henry?"

"Sorry. It's just nice to be on the receiving end of that. I'm usually the beggar with you."

"Is that what you want? For me to beg? I'll beg—"

Finally, his body hovers over mine, but in true Henry fashion he takes his sweet time. He smooths all the hair out of my face before leaning down to press his lips to me, carefully, softly. I can't take it—this pace is making me crazy.

I grab onto his arms and flip us on our sides before reaching my hand under the back of his shirt and pressing him closer to me. His skin is so warm, his muscles hard under my touch. I hook my leg over his hip, trying to bring us as close as physics will allow.

His hand grips the back of my head as he starts to gently suck on my bottom lip. There's a sultry humming sound coming from deep in his throat that makes my whole body tingle.

"Henry, I need—"

"I got you." He rolls me onto my back as his hand slides up my thigh, bunching my dress at the waist. He teases the lace on my hip, twirling it between his fingers as his mouth moves to my ear.

"Care for a song?" His warm breath on my neck brings out an audible sigh and I can feel Henry's smile.

"Lovely Luzu shivers
She pants and moans and quivers
She wants none of my laughter
My touch is what she's after"

The first time we were together he seemed nervous, unsure of himself. But now, he's playing with me. It's maddening, and I kind of love it. I reach for him, but he takes hold of both my wrists and knots them above my head. An extremely frustrated sound escapes my lips.

"Relax, Luce. I'll take care of you. I'll always take care of you."

He unties the straps of my dress and tugs until my chest is completely exposed. He takes one nipple in his mouth, then the other, twisting gently with his teeth, as his hand slides between my legs underneath the lace.

"I have another song for you."

"*Henry.*" His name comes out as a strangled breath.

His lips move back to my ear and he starts to hum, a melody I faintly recognize. Then his fingers follow the same rhythm, stroking, tapping, adding and releasing pressure. It may just be a game to Jayce, but I *am* an instrument right now. And Henry is playing me like the master musician he is. By the time he reaches the bridge, I shatter completely.

I'm not sure if seconds or hours pass before I come back down to earth. When I do, Henry is sliding my dress back into place and dropping chaste kisses along my jaw. That just won't do.

I press against his shoulder until he's flat on his back, and I reach for the buckle on his belt. To my frustration, he grabs my hand and pulls it away. He speaks softly, directly onto my skin.

"No. Not now."

"It's okay, Henry, the doctor said it's fine. I'm all healed, I promise."

He has this tortured look on his face as he starts to trace the outside of my ear with his fingertip. I move my hand lower again but he catches it mid stride.

"Not until I know."

"Know what? What do you mean?" I'm still trying to maneuver around his belt, but his grip is getting stronger.

"Why you ran, why you're scared. Not until you're ready to tell me everything."

I stare back at him, not knowing what to say. I can't fault him for this. To say I've been giving him mixed messages would be a severe understatement. I can't help it. I want him—so badly that part of me is willing to suffer the heartbreak just to spend a little more time with him like this.

Luckily he saves me from myself, whispering softly this

time. "It's okay. I know you're not ready yet, just let me know when you are. I'm not going anywhere."

He brushes his lips against mine one last time before folding his arms around me and tucking me into him. We lie like that for a while, our breaths harmonizing together. His embrace always relaxes me, but I'm not exactly sleepy.

"Henry?"

"Mm?"

"For next year's convention, let's not forget our costumes. What should we dress as?"

"Please don't make me go back to one of those. It was a bit creepy if I'm being honest. If you require me to wear a costume I'll be happy to do so any time, in our home."

Our home. I smile at his slip of the tongue.

"Hmm, what about a koala?"

"Am I not cuddly enough for you already?" He tightens his hold on me and nuzzles his face into the crook of my neck. It tickles and I start to squirm. He must mistake my movement for wanting space and pulls away from me. "Sorry."

I want to correct him, but maybe a little space is good. If he kept holding me like that I'm not sure I'd have been able to keep my hands to myself.

I roll over to face him again. "Actually, you should probably be a giraffe. You're too tall for anything else; you might look deformed."

"Ahh, well in that case you'll have to dress as an elephant."

I scoff and smack him lightly against the chest. "Rude!"

"A baby elephant. They're adorable, and wobbly, just like my Luzu."

"Wobbly? That's how you're choosing to describe me?" I refuse to acknowledge the "my Luzu" because my heart cannot handle that right now.

"Well, yes. It's cute, endearing really. You trip quite easily, love. Sometimes I do wonder how you're able to balance on the surfboard at all. Low center of gravity must help."

I can't argue with him. I stumble more often than I care to admit—and baby elephants are ridiculously cute.

"All right, it's decided then. A giraffe and a baby elephant for Confuzzled 2024."

"Graham will want to come. Should I pencil him in as a kangaroo?"

"No, I don't think that really suits him to be honest. Maybe a crocodile? No, a gorilla! Or maybe one of those flying monkeys from *The Wizard of Oz*. Wait a second . . ."

"I definitely don't think he'll be on board with a gorilla cos—"

"Oh my God, Henry! That was *Over the Rainbow*. What the . . ." His eyes peek at me under thick lashes while he bites his lip. "You seriously just got me off to *Somewhere Over the Rainbow*!?"

His lips seal shut but he isn't able to suppress his amusement. "Is that, erm, okay?" He looks nervous now, like he's in trouble. But I can't hide my smile any longer. It's not long before we're both breathless with laughter, Henry entwining his fingers with mine. "Ahh, I thought you'd like it."

He pulls me back into his arms, where I gladly stay for the rest of the night.

36

. . .

Henry

EACH TIME I wake up next to Lucy feels bittersweet. This lovely girl whom I can't seem to live without is so close I can touch every inch of her, and yet, she's still out of reach, taunting me, like a mountain I can climb but can never get to the crest.

She rolls over to me and smiles lazily, before reaching for my waist and pulling me toward her. "Good morning, Maestro."

"How'd you sleep, love?" I give her a quick kiss but try to keep just enough distance between us. I think I used up the last of my self-control last night.

"Like the dead. This bed is heavenly, it's so fluffy it feels like I'm lying in the clouds."

She does a little twist and roll movement before stretching out her limbs like a cat. Her golden hair is absolutely everywhere, an angelic Medusa lying next to me. I want to wake up like this forever.

I'm a bit nervous to tell her our plans for today. I've gone back and forth as to whether meeting my mum will be a good surprise. I feel like this is the one thing I can do to demonstrate how serious I am about her. I know there's something she's not telling me, but it has to be her fear of my intentions. That idiot husband of hers left after one year of marriage, and now he wants a bloody open relationship. God, hearing Sarah say that made me ill.

I may not know all the details, but she made it clear Jack abandoned her. I know exactly how that feels, and I'd never do it to Lucy.

Of course she's nervous about my commitment to her. If I can just prove that I intend to have a real future with her, that I'm nothing like Jack, I know that will set us on the right path, quell her apprehension. I have to believe that's the issue, because the only other option is that it's me, that Graham was right, that Lucy thinks being with me would be too difficult, that I'm not normal.

No, I know that's not it. She's never made me feel like I'm anything less than the man I hope to be. She's too kindhearted, too compassionate to think like that.

Sometimes it seems Lucy's like a sparkly jigsaw puzzle. I'm so determined to figure her out but I just keep getting distracted by all her glittering pieces. Maybe I don't need to fit them all together if I can love each morsel on its own. It's rather apparent I already do.

I should tell her where we're going now, before we leave the hotel. And yet, there's a twisted part of me that is yearning to see her reaction. Lucy gets so animated every time I surprise her and I'm a selfish bastard who wants to see her face light up like a firework.

"So, would you like to know our plans for today?" She's up and leaning back on her heels. I've got her attention. "We're going for a drive, going to get out of the city for a while. How does that sound?"

"Sure, I'm up for anything. Where are we going?" Her eagerness radiates from her face and I fight the urge to kiss her.

"I was thinking we could go to Oxford. Did you know they have over one hundred libraries there?" Her eyes flash brighter as she shakes her head. They're an intense shade of green today, like freshly cut grass glimmering in the sunlight.

"I would love to go there. Can we go to Blackwell's? It's been on my bucket list forever."

"Already on the itinerary." She gives a small shriek of excitement before jumping out of bed to go take a shower. I shouldn't lie to her so before she closes the door I add, "And after Oxford I think we'll spend some time in the countryside, show you my favorite part of England."

37

. . .

Lucy

HENRY IS TAKING me to a library.

Actually, he's taking me to several. The amount of history here in Oxford is staggering—I think I want to live here forever. I'm overwhelmed with everything there is to read, to learn, to see. He gets me. He knew this would be my ideal way to spend a vacation.

A few summers ago, Jack and I spent three weeks on Nantucket when his parents were in Hawaii. I went to the Atheneum every morning—the island's only public library—and usually stopped by Nantucket Bookworks every afternoon. Being surrounded by books, by stories and knowledge and magic and *possibility—that's* my happy place. Jack never joined me. He would tease me about being a book nerd, about being stuck in my imagination. But what's so wrong with imagination? Stories show us the way things *could* be, in an alternate life. One where I might still have my parents, or functioning ovaries, or the power to teleport.

Jack was never mean, and it didn't particularly bother me at the time. Books were my thing, never his. But now I think, I didn't know what it could be like to be with a man who truly supported me, who understood how my brain works, who cared enough to plan a day together like this.

Oxford is a dream, and so is my current headspace. I love picturing what a future with Henry would look like, but it's impossible for me to imagine it without the inevitable disappointment. My heart still believes in fairy tales, still sees the perfect ending playing out for me, again. My brain knows better. She's seen some shit.

Driving through the countryside now is so idyllic, I vanquish all the pesky thoughts rattling in my head and squeeze Henry's hand that never leaves my side. The air is scented with dew, the sweet earthiness lingering from the rain. I suck it in greedily through the open window, determined to hold on to my Oxford high.

Henry and I are in this perfect, mushy little bubble. I know I'm being selfish, but I've been throwing caution to the wind on this trip and just following the pleasure-seeking part of my brain. Who knows when I'll be back in the hospital, getting another surgery, the one I've been dreading, the one that will change me *forever*.

I know I'm way overdue to have this conversation with Henry. He deserves my honesty, and I don't want to keep anything from him anymore. It's painful to think about ending what we have together, but I think I need to rip off the Band-Aid now before I let anything get more serious than it already is.

If it gets any more serious, I don't know how I'll ever get over him.

I wish I could flip my own script right now, pretend that motherhood isn't so intrinsically tied to my self-worth. I wish I could focus on anything else in my life, things that make me feel good or sexy or *enough*. But no matter how much I try, it's just always there.

My own mom started talking about grandkids long before I was ever engaged. And when she got sick, she always said that wanting to meet her grandchildren kept her fighting the cancer every day. I want her back more than anything, but maybe it's for the best that she never got the chance to see what came of her wish. The thought of enduring her disappointment now seems unbearable.

And Henry's attraction to me, I know it's real. I feel it in my bones with every look he gives me, every time his lips brush my skin. But I'll never forget him telling me I'd be a great mother. It's all tied together: sex and fertility and motherhood and—God, I'm so *sick* of being a woman sometimes.

I just can't put this off any longer. As soon as we get to the hotel, I'll do it. I'll tell him everything.

And then I'll deal with the consequences.

"Umm, Henry. Are we staying at a bed and breakfast or something? This looks like a neighborhood."

We just pulled onto a long street dotted with homes, surrounded by fields and . . . not much else. Henry stops the car in front of a modest, Tudor-style house. He squeezes my hand just a bit tighter and offers a nervous smile.

"This is my home, where I grew up. I wanted you to see it."

Okay, this is unexpected. I guess I have been wondering what part of England he's from. I was surprised it never came up when he told me his plans for the trip.

Wait, he's getting out of the car. We're going in? Does his mom still live here? My mind is racing and I can barely comprehend what's happening in front of me. Henry is opening the passenger door for me, and walking me up to the porch, and the door is opening. And I am now *inside* his house and a tiny woman who looks nothing like Henry is staring back at me.

"Oh, Lucy! I'm so glad to finally meet you! What a treat this is. I'm Mary, Henry's mum, of course." She reaches out to give me a hug and we share a quick embrace. She's almost as short as I am. Henry's dad must have been a giant.

How did Henry not tell me this is where we were going? I am not prepared for this.

Mary is looking at me with a worried expression and I realize I haven't said anything yet.

"Are you okay, dear?"

"Yes, sorry. It's so nice to meet you. I'm just a bit surprised, I didn't know we were coming here." I shoot Henry a quick glance letting him know this is not the good kind of surprise.

"Henry, shame on you. You promised this lovely girl a holiday and didn't tell her about the visit to your boring old mum?"

Henry wraps his arm around me and whispers a quick "I'm sorry" into my hair, followed by a kiss to my temple. Another kiss to my nose, then my cheek and now my mouth. He's kissing me, in front of his mom, and she is positively beaming. What is happening right now? This is the opposite of my plan. Fuck.

I keep trying to get Henry's attention so we can talk alone. I don't know why he brought me here, or why he didn't tell me about it, but I feel like things are suddenly moving way too fast. I need to squash this before it gets bigger than it already is. Unfortunately his excitement about being here has made him much less observant to my subtle cues. He's entirely oblivious.

I let Mary give me the tour while Henry brings our bags in from the car and takes them upstairs. I'm surprised she still lives in this house when Henry could obviously buy her something bigger, newer, nicer. But she says she refused all his offers.

"This is the house where I fell in love with Fred—my late husband—and where I raised Henry. All my best memories are here. Why would I ever want to live anywhere else?" It's so sweet, and it makes me long for the family I've always wanted to create those kinds of memories with, the kind I don't get to have.

"Is this Henry's dad?" I point to a framed photograph leaning on the mantel, it's clearly Mary from many years ago—before her perfect bob turned silver—with a man dressed in uniform.

"Yes, that's my Fred. The best man I've ever known." She looks so wistful I'm afraid I may start to cry.

"I heard you lost him recently, I'm so sorry. You look very much in love."

"Three years ago. The man was always one for the dramatic, had to go out on March 29th, my birthday. He never did want me to celebrate without him."

Suddenly, all the air is sucked out of my lungs and I grab at my chest, my throat, trying to find a way to breathe. I'm numb, tingling all over, and can't move a muscle. I'm completely frozen in shock.

"Lucy, are you okay, dear? What's wrong?" Mary places a hand on my back and guides me to sit down on the love seat. She feels so motherly, it makes the pain in my chest ache even more. She rubs her hand up and down my back as she tells me to breathe. It feels like the wind was knocked out of me.

It takes a few moments, but the tightness in my chest eases. "I'm so sorry, I didn't mean to scare you. You just caught me off guard. That's umm . . . that's the same day my mom died. Three years ago."

We share a long and heavy look that carries so much meaning, how we both lost someone we loved, how it happened at the exact same time, how my mom died on Mary's birthday, the weirdness of it all. And then she hugs me fiercely.

When she finally pulls away, I can see her eyes are wet. "Are you hungry, dear? I can get some dinner together, or maybe we should just go straight to dessert?" This woman really understands me.

Henry comes downstairs to find us eating strawberry pie straight from the pan, light sniffles coming from each of us sporadically. "Erm, what did I miss?"

"We're having pie for dinner, Henry, grab a spoon."

"Whatever you say, Mum." Henry comes over and gives her a hug before grabbing the spoon out of my hand and taking a bite. Mary reaches out to take my hand in hers and Henry beams at seeing the gesture. He scoops up another perfect bite but brings the spoon to my lips instead of his own. He moves closer to me, eyes glued to my face. At first, I wonder if he can see I've been crying, but then his gaze turns starry-eyed and I know he's just enjoying the moment, the three of us together.

For a second, I can see it.

I can see a whole life with him: simple nights sharing pie, sitting by the piano, Henry surprising me with butter cake and impromptu vacations, visiting Mary in this quaint little town, feeling like a *family*. Henry's eyes connect with my own and I know he sees it too. His smile is so warm, so intentional, I swear I can see little hearts in his eyes.

It's too much.

"I, umm . . . need a minute." I hurry upstairs to Henry's room, the one Mary showed me we'd be staying in. I go to close the door before tears spring from my eyes but Henry beats me to it, stepping inside and folding himself around me.

"Hey, what's wrong? What happened?" His voice is so soothing I want to melt into him. But I can't. I break away.

"Henry, why did you bring me here? What is this?" I

gesture to the room around me, to the house we're in, to the town we traveled over five thousand miles to get to.

"I'm so sorry Luce, I wasn't thinking. I just, well I guess I thought you'd react differently. Is there a problem with my mum?"

"No, of course not, she's perfectly wonderful. But . . . Henry, I think you're giving her the wrong impression. You're acting like we're together and this all feels so serious and I—"

"I am serious. I'm serious about you. That's why I brought you here. I wanted to show you I want us to be together. I'm not like Jack, Lucy. I wouldn't leave you. I could never leave you."

"Jack? You know nothing about Jack or why he left. You have no idea if you're like him or not. We just—we can't be together like that."

"Why? Tell me *why*, Lucy? Tell me why he left. You're not making any sense. Look at yourself, you're a mess."

He's right. I can feel my chest heave as tears stream down my face. I'm horrible at containing my emotions, and sadly, I'm not a pretty crier.

"I just don't think we should get into it right now—"

"*No!* You don't get to say that anymore. Enough with your fucking excuses. We kiss and you tell me you were just lonely. We sleep together—no—we have the most incredible night of my *life* together, and you run away! I'm telling you I want you. I want something real, something that will last. Maybe forever." I see his throat bob and his eyes go glassy. In just a few moments he's gone from rage to despair. "I'm in love with you, Lucy. Just be honest with me."

His words spill over me like an enchantment.

He's in love with me.

I may have guessed it, but hearing him say it does things to my heart, to other parts of my body. He's right, he doesn't deserve this, doesn't deserve any of the lies I've spun. God, I've made such a mess of everything.

"I want you too. I want something real, but I can't have what I want. I couldn't with Jack and I can't with you. And he left because of everything I can't give either of you. I saw the way you looked at me downstairs, like we could be a family. I want it too, Henry, but I can't give you that."

I collapse onto the bed and hug my knees to my chest, cover my face in my hands because I'm so tired of him seeing me cry.

"A family? What do you m—" I see his mind work as he tilts his head up toward the ceiling, like he's finally seeing what happened in the hospital that he was too manic to understand at the time. "Lucy, that changes nothing for me. How could you think that?" He comes to sit beside me, takes my face in his strong hands. "Jack is a dick and I should have killed him when he showed up at our house." He knew about that? Did Graham tell him? "Please don't let that numbskull ruin our future together."

Future. I'm so sick of that word. I don't want to think about the future, it only makes me sad. I want to think about the past, when I had my mom, when I had hopes and dreams for a real-life fairy tale, when I used to plan what names my children would have and where we would take our family vacations.

I stand up, removing myself from his embrace, and start rubbing my necklace vigorously, pleading for the hope it's supposed to give me.

"I've disappointed everyone I've loved, Henry. *Everyone.* I couldn't even grant my mother's dying wish."

Saying this out loud breaks something inside me. I can't stop picturing her face from that final day we had together. All the promises I made that I'll never get to keep. Will I ever stop feeling like a failure?

"Henry, I'm not—I'm not good enough for you. You deserve

everything out of life. I'm getting another surgery in a few months, and after that, I'll barely be me anymore. I'm just trying to do the right thing here. You shouldn't waste any more of your time loving me."

"Do you honestly believe any of that matters to me? Because it doesn't." His voice starts to crack. "It *doesn't.*"

"Right now, you might think you know what matters most to you, but that will change. I can't disappoint you too."

"Lucy, I love you. *You*—not what you can give me. I couldn't care in the slightest whether or not you can bear children. It's inconsequential to me."

"Don't say that to me. Don't say it because deep down you have to know it's not true. Even if you think it is, it'll change. You'll resent me. You'll always be disappointed that you didn't have a child of your own—with your blood, and your brain, and your perfect cheekbones."

He looks like I've slapped him.

Good. He gets it. He knows I'm right.

"I'm sorry, Henry. You shouldn't have brought me here. I can leave. I can—"

"You're not leaving. I'll sleep in the other room, give you some space." His words are clipped, all the emotions from moments ago have been sucked out of this room.

"I really shouldn't stay here. I don't want to upset you anymore. I'm sure I can find a hotel, get a flight out in the morning."

"Just . . . stop, okay? If you want to go home tomorrow, we'll go. If you want to go back to London, we'll go. If you want to go to bloody Morocco, I'll take you there instead." I look at him incredulously. "Sorry. Just—stay here tonight, there's literally nothing around here and the trains have all stopped anyway. I'll leave you be, we can talk in the morning." He drags his hand through his hair, down his face several times. He looks horrible. And it's my fault. It's always my fault.

"I'm sorry, I'm so sorry, I never wanted things to end like this." I've lost control of my tears again, can feel the dehydration headache setting in. He places a hand on my shoulder.

"Nothing's ending, Luce. You're really fucking testing me here, but I meant it. I'll always be in your life, no matter how hard you try to shove me out." He gets up and crosses the room to the door. "I'll see you tomorrow, okay? No running. It's very dangerous out there."

And he's gone.

I'M ALONE AGAIN, and I can't stop crying, and I have no one to blame but myself.

Am I being irrational? I so badly want to believe his words, that it doesn't matter to him, that it *wouldn't* matter to him. No, I saw the doubt in his face, the look he gave me after everything was said. He sounded so full of conviction, but his eyes betrayed his confidence immediately.

What do I do from here? He told me not to leave, and I admit, I would have no idea where to go, but what about tomorrow? The next day? I have to move out now, have to sever myself from this life that I love. Will I ever stop running? I've never needed my mom as much as I do right now.

I grab for my phone. Graham has been texting me pictures of Rowan just about every hour since we left. I wish I would have brought him with us, even if Dr. Wasserman assured me it wasn't necessary. I need something to hold on to right now, something to tether me to anything other than my thoughts of Henry.

Me:

I think I may have fucked up again

Teddy Graham:

Well that was bound to happen. Fix it

Me:

I can't - I don't know how

Teddy Graham:

<<picture of Rowan with his nose covered in peanut butter>>

Me:

Is that supposed to be your advice? And please don't let him fall asleep like that

Teddy Graham:

Yes, my advice is to go find your favorite thing and stick your face in him

It ;)

Me:

This is not helpful

Teddy Graham:

Just do what makes you happy ok?

Do what makes me happy? I'm not even sure I know the answer to that. Planning ahead used to make me happy, thinking about what comes next, how to set myself up for my *future* happiness. Now it feels like I've just given up. But without a plan, without hope, without anticipation of what's to come, what is there really? It feels like time may as well be standing still.

I try to fall asleep but there's a supercut flooding my mind with every moment that Henry and I have kissed, every time he's smiled in my direction. I think about the night we met, how I was completely falling apart during that flight. I had no idea where I'd live, what I was going to be doing with my life once we landed. He saved me, like an actual prince rescuing a damsel in very serious distress. I never expected to fall in love with him, never even considered it a possibility. But I did, and now I'm right back where I started, broken hearted and alone.

38

. . .

Henry

I MAKE MY WAY DOWNSTAIRS, still unsure of what just happened. I've never seen Lucy look so . . . broken. Why is she so determined to push me away? I admit I'm still getting to know her, but how can she act like she knows everything about me, even my future decisions?

I've dealt with a lot of hardship in my life, but I always found a way to make it work. Hell, I hired HAAAM so I could find a way to have the career I knew I wanted. I always felt guilty for using them but we're friends now. From what Lucy says, they're grateful to me. Things always seem to work out, no matter how bad they start. My entire existence is proof of that. So why can't Lucy see it this way?

Her words are stuck in a continuous circuit in my head, making me feel dizzy and unsettled: *You'll always be disappointed that you didn't have a child of your own.*

I turn around to go back upstairs. I need answers. I give a slight knock on the door before it swings open.

"Mum . . . can I ask you something?"

39

• • •

Lucy

I WAKE up from the worst sleep I've had in months and there's a slew of text messages waiting for me. They simultaneously make me want to cry with joy and fall into a deep depression.

Jayce:

So turns out crystals a lying bitch - she's had a boyfriend this whole fucking time! I need you - when you guys comin home??

Adamma:

<<picture of hand wearing a diamond ring>>

I said yes!!!!! I know you helped him plan this - thank you! I'm so happy! ILYSM

yellow heart emoji

If you promise to be a bridesmaid I'll let you wear yellow!

SAY YES

Preston:

THANK YOU THANK YIU THANSK YOUIO

IM GETTING MARRIED *party emoji*

Teddy Graham:

<<picture of Rowan licking Graham's face>>

<<picture of Rowan in Graham's lap>>

<<picture of Graham kissing Rowan>>

Your turn *winky face emoji*

There's no way I can hold on to this family, not now. Not if I'm going to do the right thing and give Henry the distance he deserves. I respond to Adamma because I'm so happy for her—and I did spend hours helping Preston plan the perfect surprise while they're in Chicago. Then I turn off my phone and tip toe downstairs hoping to find coffee and reluctantly face Henry. To my surprise and delight, he's not there, but Mary seems to be waiting for me.

"Coffee, dear? I was just about to scramble some eggs."

"Sure, that'd be great. Is Henry here?"

"No, I think he went for a stroll. My fault actually, I may have asked to spend some time alone with you today. Care to indulge an old lady and have a girls' day out?"

"A girls' day sounds great, actually. What'd you have in mind?"

I take a sip of coffee as I try not to think about where Henry is right now. We both could use some time apart from each other. I doubt this was Mary's idea.

"Afternoon tea. There's a place in London I used to frequent with my mum and I haven't been in ages. I'd very much like to take you, though I have to warn you, it's a royal pain to get there." She smirks mischievously, and I wonder if there's some sort of inside joke I'm missing out on. But I love tea and all the cute little sandwiches they're sure to have, so I'm happy to oblige.

An hour later, we're out the door walking to the train station. She takes my hand and tells me how thrilled she is to do this again. I want to be as animated as she is, but I just keep thinking about my own mom, how I wish I could be here with her, doing something as simple as getting tea.

I wonder what advice she'd be giving me now that I'm divorced, if she'd suddenly tell me all the reasons she actually hated Jack but chose to let me believe otherwise. I wonder what she'd think of Henry and how she'd help me navigate the current situation. I wonder how she'd feel about me getting a hysterectomy, if she'd agree it's worth losing that part of myself to combat all the pain.

I'm always *wondering* and then I'm angry because I know that all I'll ever get to do with her now is wonder.

Mary must sense the direction of my emotions. She leads me onto the train but seems content to ride in companionable silence. After we switch stations in Hampstead, I'm feeling a bit more energized, so I ask Mary to tell me about this special place we're going to.

"Well, I don't want to ruin the surprise completely, dear. But I can tell you it's been around for ages, longer than me, that's for sure. It's very traditional, beautiful china, and *oh*, they have the most wonderful scones! I always wanted to bring Henry here as a boy, but he wasn't very comfortable going to restaurants."

She looks lost in a memory, and I think back to our night at Nobu. That feels like years ago, but I'll never forget that night. The bitchy waitress who I wanted to pummel. Then the amazing dinner we had at Fritto Misto. Falling asleep on opposite sides of the sectional, our feet brushing against each other, knowing he stayed just so I wouldn't feel alone.

"Lucy, this is our stop! It's only a quick walk through the park from here, let's go." Her excitement is palpable and I'm finally starting to feel its contagious effects.

Walking through Hyde Park is breathtaking. There's a small walking bridge that reminds me of being back in Boston Commons, but this place is immaculate; it looks so much like a fairy tale that I'm disappointed when a carriage drawn with white horses doesn't instantly appear. I want to come back here to write. As Mary leads the way, I see we're heading toward an actual palace.

"We're not having tea with the queen, are we? I don't think I'm dressed appropriately for that."

"Oh Lucy, don't be silly. The queen takes her tea at Buckingham palace. This is where the duke and duchess reside."

I see the signs for Kensington Gardens, and we walk through the most well-manicured flower beds I've ever laid eyes on. There's a small rectangular pond covered in lily pads, but it somehow looks like it's been cleaned just this morning. I make a mental note to tell Henry I'd like to see more of London, and then I realize I can't ask him things like that anymore. I try to erase the thought from my mind and enjoy the moment.

Mary has reserved her favorite table for us at The Orangery and we're seated in a beautiful all white room with the perfect amount of daylight shining through numerous window panes. She was right. It's special, idyllic.

Straight out of a fairy tale.

It feels like something I would have done with my own mom, if we could travel together today. But I'm not going to dwell on the what-ifs. And I'm happy to be here with Mary. I think I need this.

. . .

"All right Lucy dear, there are some things I need to tell you."

I guess I knew something serious was coming. At least she waited for me to have my first cup of Earl Grey and a perfect bite of scone with clotted cream and raspberry jam.

"Now, just listen, sweetheart. I know you're going to have a lot of questions for me, and I promise I will answer them, but for now, let me tell you a story, okay?" I nod slowly, fearful and intrigued.

"I got married very young. Fred and I were so in love and wanted a big family, we never saw the point in waiting. Well, we tried for seven years; and I mean tried. We went to every doctor we could find, east, west, we saw them all. They all said the same thing: we were both healthy and should have no trouble conceiving, we just had to keep trying. That word still haunts me, as if I just needed to try harder, everything would come to fruition. Well, I guess I didn't try hard enough." She must note my look of confusion. "Oh, I'm sorry, dear. I thought I knew how I wanted to do this today and now it's all coming out wrong. What I'm trying to say is that Henry is not my biological child."

She pauses a moment, probably to let the information sink in. I guess I know now why they look nothing alike.

"He actually came to us when he was about five years old. Just walked into the police station one night when Fred was working. Walked right up to him and handed him a letter." I see her eyes go glassy, but she only sniffs once and continues on. I decide right now, I want to be strong like her. Maybe one day I'll be able to tell my story without letting any tears fall. "Now, I've never told Henry the contents of that letter and I would never burden you with that either—some information is too cruel to be shared—but suffice it to say, his mother let us know she wasn't coming back for him.

"My husband, well, he was Chief Constable back then, he had a lot of connections. He knew how depressed I'd been, not being able to fall pregnant. We became Henry's foster parents that same night, and legally adopted him a year later." She smiles with so much pride my heart is bursting. I have a sudden urge to call Henry, to see him and hug him and hold him.

"I was obviously elated. I finally had my son. He may not have come from me, but I felt a connection to him right away. But it was almost two years before he ever spoke to either of us. I felt like I was in this endless cycle, back to see as many doctors as I could, to find a solution. He was finally diagnosed with selective mutism caused by severe anxiety. Apparently, it's not uncommon in young children, but without the right treatment and his obvious lack of parenting, it doesn't always go away. And of course, we had no idea what kind of trauma he'd experienced with that wretched woman, but it was clear he had suffered abuse from a very young age.

"So, I was back to *trying*. This time trying to get my son to speak. My goodness, the stories I could tell you, all the wacky ideas Fred and I came up with, all the different languages we tried speaking in. I still can't believe all I had to do was teach him to play the piano. As you can imagine, that was a success right away, and before long he was begging for any instrument he could think of. Every occasion, every Christmas, it was something new he needed to master. Thank goodness he made a career out of it; we must have spent up our whole retirement! First the violin, the cello, then so many guitars; the flute was quite a nice surprise, it does sound so lovely when he plays; I drew the line when he asked for a harp . . ."

She gives me a knowing smile, like we have some shared history together to laugh over.

I can imagine it though. I've seen Henry when he gets in the zone, flying from one instrument to the next. I've even seen him juggle two at a time, convinced he can harmonize alone before calling in the team to start recording. And then I think back to him saying I'd be a harp, that night at the pool. I wonder if he ever got one, if he learned to play. I still don't know why he chose it for me.

"Music seemed to make everything better. He could finally communicate with us, but it was still difficult for him. He was so frustrated with himself and it came out as anger. Fred started teaching him to box every day to help release all the tension. That became a whole new obsession, and before I knew it, Henry was twice my size. We did whatever we could to help him work it out. But no matter how comfortable he became with us, he still never spoke to strangers. It could take weeks, or often months for him to get acclimated to a new person. As he got older it became more problematic. He couldn't speak to his teachers or fellow students. As you can imagine, kids can be quite cruel. And with Henry suddenly becoming a prizefighter, well, we had to pull him out to be home-schooled."

Her eyes start to wander and I can see she's lost in a memory, a sad one. I had no idea what Henry'd been through.

"I'm so sorry, dear, I believe I've gotten off topic. What I wanted to tell you is that Henry's always known he wasn't 'ours.' He was around five or six when we found him so there was no point in pretending, not that we would have. But we've never discussed it. He's never asked about his birth parents, never questioned our relationship. He's alluded to it enough times that I'm sure he knows the reality of things. Used to make jokes to his dad and me about how much shorter we were, because we don't have his 'Viking genes.' But never, not once in almost thirty years, has he asked about our situation, not until last night."

I'm trying to absorb everything she's telling me, but it's so . . . *much*. I see her eyeing me like it's now my turn to talk.

"What did he ask you?"

Her pursed lips tell me this is not the response she was looking for, but it's all that I could think of with everything swirling around in my head.

"He asked me why I never had a child of my own."

My throat bobs once, and then I can feel the tears start to prick the corners of my eyes, the quiver of my chin start to lose control. *You'll always be disappointed that you didn't have a child of your own, with your blood, and your brain, and your perfect cheekbones*. I can't believe I said that. I can't believe I was that insensitive, especially about *this*.

I'm vile. I hurt him, the man who's done nothing but heal me.

"Lucy, I want you to know that Henry didn't betray your trust. But our house is old, and sound carries, and well, I'm just a nosy old woman who rarely has guests. I heard you two arguing last night and I didn't tell Henry, but I do feel as though I need to tell you." She pauses and takes my hand in hers. The gesture is so sweet, something I don't deserve.

"You poor girl. Everything you said is wrong. Don't let that Jack character take away your happiness. He wants everything in life to be easy? He'll die young of boredom. Or he'll die young because I've tossed him in the Thames." A burst of laughter escapes me, but Mary's face is stoic. I make a note to never cross this woman.

"I'm so sorry, Mary. What I said must have really hurt you, both of you. I feel horrible." I want to show her how sincere I am, that I wish I could take it back, but she waves her hand in front of me.

"Lucy, listen to me. You didn't hurt anyone; you haven't disappointed anyone. Your mother would be so proud of you. You've had an extra-thick, double-knotted, dipped-in-tar string of bad luck. I know what it feels like, but it doesn't have to be forever. Forget about the man who wasn't strong enough to stand by you. He's in your past, but you can choose your future. You will be an amazing mother, if that's what you want, but . . . don't choose to be unhappy."

My tears are falling freely down my face. I'm trying so hard to keep it together, but my emotions are overwhelming me. It feels like all I've done is cry lately. How do I have anything left?

"And, dear, I don't mean to meddle, but Henry seems to be very much in love with you. If you feel the same way, please do his mum a favor and let him know that. He hasn't received nearly enough love in his life."

This—breaks me. I remember Henry telling me about his "faults," how he wanted a relationship where they wouldn't scare someone away. I thought he was joking, because to me, he's always been flawless. If there's one thing I'm sure of, it's that Henry deserves to be loved. He is the kindest man I've ever known. He cares so deeply about others, and I'm just now realizing how difficult his life has been.

"What did you tell him?" I'm a mess, barely able to enunciate but I have to know the answer.

"What do you mean, dear?"

"When he asked why you never had a child of your own. What did you say?"

"I told him he was my own. And then I told him he was such a piece of work that after him I couldn't even think of having another."

We found lighter topics of discussion on the journey back to Bedford. But when we got off the last train, I thanked her for sharing her story. Then I asked her if she would be interested in adopting me.

"I think Henry may have some objections to that, sweetheart. But you're welcome here any time, no matter what happens with you two."

"Do you ever think about throwing her in the Thames? Henry's birth mom?"

"Oh, I've thought of many worse ways of ending that woman. But no, most of the time when I think of her, and I do think of her often, I remember what joy Henry has given me, and I wonder if maybe things all worked out the way they should. Maybe she has a family of her own and they're all perfectly happy, never dwelling on her past mistakes."

I'm so impressed with Mary's attitude; she's such an amazing mother. And I think—yes, she is absolutely a mother.

Why have I kept doubting that I could be one?

"Although, sometimes, when I'm watching the news and I see some horrid event, a stabbing, shooting, you know. I do secretly hope it's her. I'm only human."

When we get to her street, she tells me she's going to a neighbor's to spend the evening.

"I think you two could use some privacy. Thin walls, you know." She taps her pointer finger to her nose. "I will probably stay the night with Jeanette. She's a bit of a lush, tends to rub off on me when we visit. Good luck, dear."

And now I'm on the front step of his house, trying to figure out what I want to do, to say, when I see him.

Don't choose to be unhappy.

I open the door before a single decision is made.

40

• • •

Henry

I WALKED the entire town this morning. And then I did another lap.

A girls' day. A *girls'* day? Mum wouldn't say anything else, but she seemed determined as all hell. She was claiming Lucy today with or without my acquiescence. I'm glad they seem to get on so well; it's what I was hoping for. I'm just not sure if it even matters anymore.

I'm still trying to figure out what happened last night. It felt like an ending. An ending I refuse to accept. I keep running through our conversation, trying to pinpoint the exact moment I could have changed its course. I should have said . . . more.

Never in my life have I talked willingly about my early childhood, about my own complications with the word *family*. My upbringing was unconventional to say the least. I've seen therapists, have been told how unhealthy it is to keep these things locked away; but truthfully, I feel best when I imagine that my life began here, with the Turners. Is it so wrong to choose my own story? To choose my own happiness?

But Lucy let me in, shared her most painful truth with me.

Why couldn't I do the same? I'm a fucking coward, that's why. Of course I don't deserve her if I can't be as honest with her as she is with me.

I decide right now I am going to tell her every last detail. I cannot just give up without knowing I tried everything I could to keep her. Maybe it won't make a bit of difference, but maybe it *will*. Maybe she'll realize she's wrong about me, about what's most important to me, about what I want from her. Because all I really want is to have her by my side, to find new ways to make her smile every moment that I can.

I make my way back home, back to the piano, the one place I can distract myself from everything pulsating in my head. I think it's time I finally finish the piece I've been working on for the last two months.

I'm ready.

41

• • •

Lucy

WHEN I WALK INSIDE, Henry is sitting on the couch, elbows resting on his knees with his head cradled in his hands. His red-rimmed eyes find mine when his head pops up. It looks like he hasn't slept, and I feel a flood of guilt for all the ways I've caused him pain.

I'm not sure how I didn't notice it yesterday, but there's a quote framed on the wall behind him next to the piano, the same one he has in Malibu by Stevie Wonder: *Music is a world within itself, with a language we all understand.* I don't think I ever realized the significance before, why his music is such a huge part of him. My throat tightens with emotion.

I still don't have the right words, but I walk over to Henry, needing to be close to him again. We're almost eye to eye with him sitting down on the sofa.

Say something, Luce.

"I'm sorry." It is incredibly insufficient, but it's all I can choke out right now. A single tear escapes from my eye.

He looks up at me, brings his hand to cup my face and swipes his thumb across my cheek, catching my tear. He follows it with a feathery kiss to my brow before lacing his arms around my waist and pulling me onto his lap. He presses warm, soft kisses to my temple, my nose, my mouth, my cheek, my forehead, my mouth again. His kisses aren't sensual, they're sweet, tender; they're perfect. He pulls back and rests his forehead against mine. We sit there like that for a few moments, physically connected in so many ways, his hands delicately stroking up and down my back.

I close my eyes and breathe deeply, letting his scent fall over me like a magic shield. "I think I may have been in love with you for a while now. I'm sorry I didn't tell you sooner. That was rude of me."

He jerks his head back to look at me.

I think he might say something, but he doesn't. Maybe he feels more comfortable communicating without words.

Before I met Henry, I had to fill every silent moment with words. It was a habit I never thought I'd break. But now, I feel content in our shared silence. Until I realize there's so much more I need to say.

"I should have been honest with you a while ago—about everything." I see him open his mouth to speak but I have to get this out. "No, just let me say this, okay?" He nods. "I was scared about my past repeating itself, and I'm sorry for not listening to you, for not even trying. I was too in my head to even hear you, but I'm trying to get out." I take a deep breath and feel his hands tighten around my waist. "I know sorry isn't enough, but just . . . I never wanted to hurt you. That was the last thing I wanted. You might be the best thing that's ever happened to me."

I suck in more air, forcing myself to get the words out. Henry's unwavering gaze gives me the confidence I need. "I want to try, okay? I can't promise that my insecurities will go away, or that I won't wonder if you'll change your mind about me, if you'll change the way you feel. But that's okay, because you're allowed to feel however you want, even if it means—"

He kisses me again, and this time it's anything but delicate. He pulls me closer to him so that every inch of our bodies is touching; he moves his lips from my mouth to my jaw, down to my neck and tugs my hair to the side so he can reach my favorite spot.

His words brush my skin, just below my ear. "I'll never leave you Lucy. I'll never resent you, or try to change you. I'll never break your heart." The affirmation makes my insides flutter. "Can you trust me?"

"Yes." I kiss him fervently, trying to prove it to him, willing him to know that I'll never run away again.

After a few moments he slowly pulls back to look at me.

"I, erm . . . I spent most of the day finishing a new song. Something that's been in my head for a while. I think you may have inspired it."

His gaze roams over my face while his fingers find the pendant hanging from my neck. He turns it over, giving it a gentle rub while his eyes follow, focusing on the bit of gold like it's a precious memento of his own. "I was thinking of calling it *Under the Rainbow*."

"What's *under* the rainbow?"

His idle hand reaches up to tuck a piece of hair behind my ear, and then, he smiles at me.

"Well, dreams are over the rainbow—you know, with the bluebirds." He grins as he drops the necklace and leans in to kiss my nose. "But under the rainbow, that's how I feel when I'm with you. Like the storm has just ended and I can finally see the sun. You're *my* fairy tale, Luzu."

I blink at him a few times before I know what to do or say next. He drops his gaze just slightly, like maybe he's embarrassed. His *fairy tale*? God, I'm in love with him. And he wrote a song inspired by *me*? "I'd like to hear it."

"Later." And then he sweeps his arm under my knees and carries me upstairs.

I'm able to appreciate the private plane much more on the way back to LA. My nerves are non-existent; I feel sated and happy and hopeful. We took full advantage of having the house to ourselves that night, and spent three more days in Bedford before Henry had to get back to work.

I told Henry I knew about his adoption. I didn't want there to be any secrets between us, but I didn't share anything else from Mary's story. That was hers alone to tell. But he wanted me to know everything anyway. I comforted Mary while he told us the story from his perspective; she was even more of a blubbering mess than I was.

We had a real conversation about what being a mom meant for me, something Jack never gave me the chance to do. It was nice to speak so openly about everything I'd been through with endometriosis; the pain, the surgeries, the hysterectomy I'm planning on getting. And especially how I've been handling the fact that I'll never have biological children. With Jack, he made me feel like I was failing him as a wife, like I had done something wrong. Even before that fateful day, he treated my chronic illness as an annoyance, something he'd prefer to ignore.

I don't know why I assumed it would be like that with every man. Henry's concern was for me, for my health, for the loss I felt not being able to experience something I had been hoping for my entire life. I knew it was early to talk about these kinds of things. I wouldn't normally discuss family planning with someone at this point in a relationship, but he insisted, and honestly, it made me feel lighter. No matter what happened with us, I wouldn't have the burden of this discussion looming over me.

Right before we left, Henry asked me to officially be his girlfriend. He even got down on one knee. I'm pretty sure this was for Mary's benefit; she was there for the big moment and seemed quite pleased with how it all played out. It made me feel a little silly, and maybe a little giddy. The joy radiating from her made me miss my mom, but it also made me feel so lucky to have her in my life. On our way out the door I told Henry I loved him, and I made sure it was loud enough for her to hear me.

I haven't been able to get Mary's story out of my head. My heart aches for everything she went through, but I also know that she's living an extremely happy and fulfilled life. Her relationship with Henry is so special—seeing them together, their closeness, I understand Henry so much better now. I'm going to start channeling my inner Mary. *Don't choose to be unhappy*. I want to choose happiness. I know that it's not that simple, I can't predict the future; but right now, I'm feeling hopeful. And I'm done thinking about endings, I'm only worrying about now.

And *now*, Henry and I are floating across the Atlantic, watching the final cut of *The Dragon Wars* pilot. It's wild to watch a show with absolutely no music, it's almost eerie. I've only heard bits and pieces of what Henry's prepared for this, but I know it's going to be amazing. He warned me that this is going to keep him and HAAAM pretty busy for the next couple of months, but I don't mind. I have about a million new book ideas I want to start working on.

Henry's hands haven't left my body since we got on the

plane. I also noticed he told the flight crew we were not to be disturbed. It was sweet of Mary to give us the one night to ourselves, but once she was back, knowing how thin the walls were, I enforced a strict PG policy on our nightly activities. I can tell how hungry he is for me and I can't say I'm not enjoying it. He promised we could watch the show, but now that it's over, his kisses have turned sultry and my dress is down to my ankles.

Kissing Henry is something I don't think I'll ever tire of. He told me that music is how he learned to communicate, that before he learned to play the piano he couldn't figure out how to express himself, how to find his words. I feel this with every press of his lips, every touch of his fingertips on my skin, like he's conveying all his thoughts to me through physical contact.

I'm thinking about all the moments we've had together, ones that I will cherish, ones that appear in my dreams, and then one pops into my head that I never understood.

"Why the harp?" Henry has successfully undressed me down to my thong. I don't mean to ruin the moment but I can't get that thought out of my head.

He doesn't move his lips from me and speaks into the skin between my breasts. "I'm sorry, what about the harp?"

I shove him gently to make a sliver of space between us. "That night at the pool, when Jayce wanted me to say what instrument I'd be. You said I'd be a harp, and you said it so matter of factly, like it was an objective thing. Was it a joke? Is there some pun I haven't been able to figure out?"

He laughs quietly and murmurs something under his breath. "You are a harp to me. The most beautiful sound you'll ever hear is made with a harp." I feel swoony. Of course Henry wasn't making a crude joke. He wasn't messing with me, he loves me. "And if I'm going to play Jayce's silly little game, if I had to *play* you, I'd have you in the crook of my neck, with my arms wrapped around you, and I'd pluck you gently, with purpose." He raises his eyebrows at me, giving me a look that says 'Is that a sufficient answer? May I please continue what I was doing?'

Well, that was definitely more eloquent than Graham's response. And then I remember something else—I completely forgot to google it.

"What's flutter tonguing?"

Henry chuckles lustily. "Lie down. I'll show you."

encore

Everything is scary if you look at it. So you just got to live it.

-Mary J. Blige

42

. . .

Henry

NINE MONTHS LATER

BEAUTIFUL BEASTS WAS RELEASED in February and it's already a national bestseller. Lucy is in negotiations with Netflix for the television rights; they want to turn it into a whole series. She's still deciding if she's open to it, but she promised she won't sign a contract without naming me as the head of music and Adamma as an EP. Her book tour has taken her away from me more than I'd prefer but getting to see her success makes every minute apart worthwhile. She said she finally felt like a real writer once she stopped focusing on a happy ending.

I've seen such a change in her ever since we got back from our trip to England, like a weight has been lifted. She seems fearless—she's surfing every day, and not like before, she's *really* surfing. I have to admit, she still struggles with her balance, but it's been incredible to watch her transformation. She, Graham and I even went to Maui together last month to test her skills. Her fear of the ocean has evaporated completely.

I don't know exactly what happened while we were in England, but it must have been something she needed. I have a feeling my mum had something to do with it. They've started FaceTiming weekly, sometimes for hours. They *bake* together. Seeing them grow close has only validated every one of my feelings for Lucy.

And she's not the only one who's changed. Being with Lucy, really *being* with her has given me a whole new life. Graham must have some sort of sixth sense because, believe it or not, Lucy *loves* golfing. We've played several times now. It was quite rocky for me at first but I'm getting better. It turns out he was also right about the strangers aspect of the game. We've been paired up with other twosomes based on our tee time twice now, even though we requested to play alone. I'd like to say I was fine, completely normal, but nothing miraculous occurred, just my incredibly supportive girlfriend. The first time it happened, she told the other men I was the lead singer of a rock band and had to rest my voice, so they shouldn't expect me to speak at all. They were quite confused but all eighteen holes went well for everyone. And the second time we were paired up she just kissed me whenever it seemed as though they wanted to make conversation. I could tell it made them a bit uncomfortable, but they did give us a wide berth when it came to chit-chat. Luckily by the back nine I was so relaxed from the game—and Lucy's kisses—that I was able to enjoy their company; we even had lunch together afterward.

Did she fix me entirely? Of course not. I'll always be a bit broken. But she changes things, makes life outside of my personal habitat bearable. I'm not afraid when she's by my side. No matter where we go, what we do, she's like my own miniature wrecking ball ready to break through any situation I can't handle on my own.

But tonight? Tonight is fucking *terrifying*.

Lucy has somehow convinced me that attending the Academy Awards is a good idea. I do have a nomination for best original song, though I doubt I'll win. But she thinks otherwise, and that since it'd be my fifth potential Oscar, I can't stay home. She promised to write me a speech and swore numerous times that I won't be able to mess it up. Still, the fact that she's refused to show me said speech beforehand is mildly alarming. Something about bad luck, she keeps arguing.

"Look at her dress. She can't even sit in it! See—she's just leaning over the table, she's not actually touching her seat." Lucy covers her mouth to hide her laughter.

"Dami, I'm pretty sure that's the exact silhouette you picked out for your wedding dress. Did you make sure *you* can sit in it?"

"Please. That one's just for the ceremony. I'm still searching for the party dress."

I have no clue what Adamma is talking about but the two of them have been gossiping about dress designers and visible Botox for over thirty minutes. I love how close they are but I'd be lying if I didn't admit to wanting Lucy all to myself tonight. My nerves are crushing me from the inside out.

Graham turns toward me and pats my shoulder. "I can't believe we're here, mate. I know you've already won a few of these, but look around. Think about where we were ten years ago. Remember me banging on the door to that grimy theatre off Broadway? Screaming at them to let you play the piano?" I nod. Not my favorite memory but I'll never forget those days. I'm not sure how my career would have been shaped without

Graham bulldozing the way. When you ghost on meetings with people in the movie or theatre industry they rarely give second chances. "Do you kind of miss it though? We were scrappy. And I fucking loved watching their jaws drop once they heard you—after making us beg for a chance to play. Those are my favorite moments."

I lift an eyebrow. "And now, what? I can't impress anyone anymore?"

"Do you care? You never seemed like you cared about impressing people before. You just wanted to write your own music, and now you get to. No one's going to disagree with you after four Oscars."

"Five." I hear Lucy clear her throat as she joins in the conversation. She threads her arm through mine and balances her chin on my shoulder.

"Should we make a wager?" Jayce chimes in. Oh, not this again. I swear Jayce may have a gambling problem with how often he tries to do this. Well, considering who he brought tonight as his date, I'd say he definitely has a gambling problem . . .

"No way," Preston cuts in. "That Pixar movie is definitely going to win. Henry doesn't have a shot."

"Well, I think he has it in the bag. What are you willing to put up for it, boys?"

Jayce looks intrigued. "Damn Luce, are you a gambler now? I'll take that bet."

I wonder how many of them would bet against me. Lucy won't, that's all that matters.

Lucy starts rubbing her hands together, and I see a familiar twinkle in her eye.

"All right, here's the deal. If Henry loses, which he won't"—she presses a light kiss to my cheek—"I'll write my next book about both of you. You'll each have whatever names, physical descriptions *and* superpowers you choose. And it'll include a very heartfelt dedication." Preston and Jayce are nodding along with smug smiles on their faces and next to me Graham is pouting. They've all been asking her for this lately.

"But if he wins, you're both house bitches for a month. I mean full-on servants, waiting on the rest of us, taking care of our every need. Henry wants a human metronome? You comply. Rowan and I want snacks delivered to us by the pool? I snap my fingers and one of you is there with an assortment of treats. Do we have a deal?"

To my utter surprise, they shake on it. My girlfriend and housemates are honestly betting on my success. As if I needed any more reason to be in a state of terror right now.

Everyone at the table quiets down as they announce the nominees for best original song. When I hear them announce my name for *Under the Rainbow* as the winner, my mouth goes dry. Suddenly I'm not sure I can remember how to breathe. What the hell was I thinking? I can't go up there. Even with HAAAM by my side, I'll be the one they expect to physically accept the award.

"Breathe, Henry." Lucy is hugging me and hands me a piece of paper. "Trust me, you've got this. Actually, no, you're shaking like a scared bunny. But I've got *you*. Just . . . look at it and get up there. I'm so proud of you." She kisses my cheek and sits back down. How is she so confident in this absolute disaster of a situation?

My nerves settle as soon as I look at the paper she handed me:

Smile
Hold up five fingers as high as you can
Hold up the Oscar with your other hand
Now get out of the way so Graham can read the other speech I wrote
I love you!

For the first time ever, I'm quite happy to be speechless.

author's note

Living with a chronic illness is something I've dealt with my entire life. While Lucy's story isn't my own, I hope it feels relevant to anyone suffering with their own invisible disability. It may seem like Lucy's insecurities weren't entirely warranted, and that was the intention. Because sometimes it's hard to get out of your own head, and people aren't going to understand what you're feeling. I've had these kinds of insecurities for most of my life. It didn't matter what my friends, family, boyfriends, or even my husband said. The feeling of being unworthy was entirely my own.

Writing this story has helped me work through a lot of my internal struggles with chronic health issues, and I hope that it might help anyone else who is suffering, to feel seen. If you know someone with a chronic illness, understand that it can be difficult for them to explain what they're going through. Show compassion, be kind, let them know they're not alone.

As an avid reader, I've seen about every topic under the sun covered in books. But far too often I see stories referencing infertility and adoption in negative or extremely unrealistic ways. My hope for this book is to show that a woman who cannot—or chooses to not—get pregnant can still have her happy ending (without a miraculous conception). I also wanted to show that an adoptive backstory can be a happy beginning instead of a destructive one. I know this isn't the reality for everyone. But it exists, and that was important for me to share.

acknowledgments

First and foremost, thank you to my very first beta readers. Embarking on this writing journey was such a spontaneous and terrifying feat. Without your feedback and support, this manuscript would forever be a google doc lost to the cloud. Elizabeth, Amanda, Jenna, Taylor, Allie, Hannah, Alyssa, Jordyn: I appreciate you all more than my words here can ever express.

Thank you to my parents for being so incredibly supportive, even if you both seemed shocked that I could write. And dad, I'm sorry I didn't make Rowan into a crime-fighting canine companion. It was a great note and I'll consider it for a spinoff novella one day.

Erik. Instead of a thank you I'm going to apologize. Mainly for all the times I asked you to say something devastatingly romantic when I needed inspiration. And for all the times I compared you to the fictional men in my head. In my defense, some of their best qualities came from you. So thank you for never saying goodnight without a kiss, and for always getting me Tiramisu in a time of need.

Caroline, thank you for being the editor of my dreams. I cannot praise you enough for all the ways you helped to elevate this story.

Britt, I don't know if I should thank you more for helping to polish up this book or for your voice memos that had me crying at six in the morning. I'll go with both. Thank you so much for your help and support. I can't wait to meet in real life and go island hopping!

Sam, you absolutely created the perfect cover for my story. Thank you for your talent, and incredible patience and poise while dealing with all my changes!

I'd be remiss if I didn't thank Hans Zimmer and all the other amazing and talented songwriters who make movies come alive through their scores. Your music inspired this entire story and continues to ignite creativity I didn't know I was capable of. While my childhood dream of scoring movies never came to be, writing about this fictional song-writing team has been equally fulfilling.

Lastly, and most importantly, thank *you*! For taking a chance on an unknown author and sharing this story with me that means so much to my soul. Books are magic, and I hope you felt a little from this one.

about the author

LINDSEY LANZA is a bookstagrammer turned author originally from Columbus, Ohio. She is a tech start-up enthusiast by day, a voracious reader by early mornings, nights and weekends, and now writes love stories when she gets a spare moment. She currently lives in New England with her husband, Erik and Sheepadoodle, Wally.

www.lindseylanza.com

instagram.com/readwithli

Printed by Libri Plureos GmbH in Hamburg,
Germany